"Everyone calls me Mick."

"I thought your name was Michael," Emily said. "I mean, that's what the sign on your window says," she added. "Michael Dante Investigations. Besides, you don't seem like a Mick."

His dark eyebrows rose at that. "What do you mean?"

Emily shrugged. "Well, Mick seems like someone rough and indifferent. Michael sounds like someone more... perceptive." She paused. "Michael fits you much better. May I call you that?"

"If it makes you comfortable. But I think you've got me pegged all wrong."

He tried not to show it, but what Emily had said made him feel both warm and stupid. Warm because he loved the way she said Michael, and the fact that she alone called him that made it all the more intimate. But he knew it was stupid to let her get to him.

He did not want to get involved with Emily Thorne. Sure, she could be a nice little diversion for a while— if she were someone different. Someone a little rougher around the edges. But she was kind and caring and completely inappropriate. She was just too good.

Getting close to Emily could only lead to trouble and thoroughly disrupt his life. Mick liked things the way they were. He wanted to avoid anything that could end the tranquillity he'd sought so long and finally found.

Dear Reader,

Welcome to the Silhouette **Special Edition** experience! With your search for consistently satisfying reading in mind, every month the authors and editors of Silhouette **Special Edition** aim to offer you a stimulating blend of deep emotions and high romance.

The name Silhouette **Special Edition** and the distinctive arch on the cover represent a commitment—a commitment to bring you six sensitive, substantial novels each month. In the pages of a Silhouette **Special Edition**, compelling true-to-life characters face riveting emotional issues—and come out winners. All the authors in the series strive for depth, vividness and warmth in writing about living and loving in today's world.

The result, we hope, is romance you can believe in. Deeply emotional, richly romantic, infinitely rewarding—that's the Silhouette **Special Edition** experience. Come share it with us—six times a month!

From all the authors and editors of Silhouette **Special Edition**,

Best wishes,

Leslie Kazanjian, Senior Editor

P.S. As promised in January, this month brings you Curtiss Ann Matlock's long-awaited first *contemporary* Cordell male, in *Intimate Circle* (#589). And come June, watch what happens to Dallas Cordell's macho brother as... *Love Finds Yancey Cordell* (#601).

ELIZABETH BEVARLY
Close Range

Silhouette Special Edition

Published by Silhouette Books New York

America's Publisher of Contemporary Romance

With love for Mom and Dad,
two people who have been
more supportive, more patient and more giving
than any ten people could ever be.
You guys are the best.
Thanks.

SILHOUETTE BOOKS
300 East 42nd St., New York, N.Y. 10017

ISBN: 0-373-09590-2

First Silhouette Books printing April 1990

Books by Elizabeth Bevarly

Silhouette Special Edition

Destinations South #557
Close Range #590

ELIZABETH BEVARLY,

an honors graduate of the University of Louisville, works as a sales associate for a chain of retail clothing stores. At heart, however, she's an avid voyager who once helped navigate a friend's thirty-five-foot sailboat across the Bermuda Triangle. "I really love to travel," says this self avowed beach bum. "To me, it's the best education a person can give herself." Her dream is to one day have her own sailboat, a beautifully renovated older model forty-two-footer, and to enjoy the freedom and tranquillity seafaring can bring.

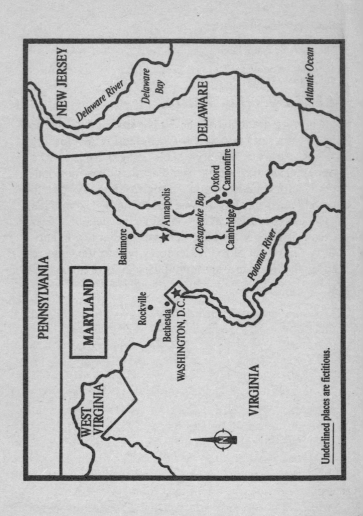

Underlined places are fictitious.

Prologue

The newsroom of *The Capitol Standard* was dim and quiet, virtually empty at such a late hour when a solitary, huddled figure skittered in nervously, glancing around quickly. In a far corner, illuminated only by the green glow of a computer screen and the naked bulb of a desk lamp, a single reporter tapped irregularly at his word processor, oblivious to the woman's entry, his two index fingers hammering away as he transcribed his notes.

Cautiously the woman neared him, her eyes assessing him doubtfully, her brain surging frantically with indecision. If anyone in the family caught her, if they knew what she was up to, they'd kill her on sight, plain and simple. Destri would see to that himself, the little sadist. She knew of more than one man who had been disposed of for less betrayal than the one she was about to commit.

Mason Thorne was so absorbed in his latest investigation for the paper that he never noticed the woman who approached him until she was directly in front of his desk and uttered his name in a low, heavily accented voice. His head snapped up in alarm, and a panicked gasp escaped in a rush past his lips.

"Jeez, you scared the hell out of me," he told the woman as his hands fell from the keyboard of his word processor. He covered his heart with one to still its runaway pounding and ran the fingers of the other through his straw-colored hair.

"Are you Mason Thorne?" the woman repeated. Her voice alone indicated to Mason that she was from out of town. Way out of town. Like maybe from some secluded mountain hollow of the Appalachians or Blue Ridge. But even if she hadn't spoken, he would have suspected something similar. She looked like the typical backwoods impoverished woman. Small, skinny and pale, her hair a limp mass the color and texture of dry wheat, the woman wore an ancient dress of faded, flowered cotton, dingy white socks and heavy farm boots. She was far from attractive, but her eyes were huge and dark brown, bright with emotion. In one hand she carried a battered purse, in the other a stained and ragged envelope. She trembled visibly, though the air conditioner in the newsroom was off, and Mason thought it uncomfortably warm.

"Yeah, I'm Mason Thorne," he said, deciding on closer inspection that she was really little more than a girl, probably still a teenager. Yet something had aged her considerably before her time, narrowed her eyes with fear, tightened her lips with anxiety. "What can I do for you?"

"You the one investigatin' the Connery Corporation?"

Normally Mason's beat for the paper was Central America, but a recent tip from an especially reliable informant had revealed to him that a widely respected and nationally known U.S. corporation was involved in some highly illegal drug traffic that originated in several small Latin American countries. With the groundwork for the story already laid, and with a relationship already established among trusted informants within the company, Mason had talked his editor, Paul Kelly, into letting him pursue the story domestically as well. But very few people knew that. Certainly not some country girl who obviously had little to do with the corporate world.

He looked at her suspiciously. "What makes you think I'm investigating the Connery Corporation?" he inquired carefully.

"My name is Lou Lofton," she began by way of an explanation. "It's really Halouise, but everybody calls me Lou. I'm from Hack's Crossin', West Virginia. You prob'ly never heard of it, but it ain't that far away. I come inta town with my cousin, Maynard, to deliver some thangs for a 4-H show. Least that's what Maynard says they was. I ain't sure, though. I never knowed Maynard to be part of 4-H."

"Uh, it's nice to meet you, Miss Lofton, but I'm kind of busy, here. Just what was it you wanted?" Mason didn't even try to hide the fact that he considered her presence an annoying intrusion. He had enough to occupy him now without the ramblings of some hayseed slowing his progress.

Lou gazed at him uncertainly before saying, "I got some information that might help you find what you're lookin' for."

"How do you know what I'm looking for?" Mason leaned back in his chair with feigned nonchalance and smiled at her mildly.

"I seen a newspaper back home that my Uncle Fairmont was readin' and cussin' about. Mr. Destri left it behind after one of his visits. There was a article you wrote about the Connery Corporation and some illegal thangs they was doin'. I can read," she added defensively, in case he didn't believe her. "And write, too. I ain't stupid."

Mason seemed to ignore her last statements and focused instead on what she'd said about his story. "I never wrote that they were doing anything illegal," he assured her. "That would be libel. They could sue me for a lot of money. I only suggested they might have their fingers in things beyond standard corporate activities."

"They do," Lou whispered low. "Some bad thangs. Real bad."

Mason's attention centered fully on the girl standing before his desk. He indicated a chair to her left and invited her to sit down.

She shook her head slowly. "I cain't stay. Maynard dropped me off and told me to go sightseein' while he took care of his business. I gotta meet him soon."

"What do you mean by bad?" Mason asked her.

Lou had nearly wadded up the envelope she still gripped in her damp palm, and she smoothed it out flat on Mason's desk before releasing it. "I wrote down everything I can think of about Uncle Fairmont's doings with the Connery Corporation. You read it. I'll call you in a few days, and you can ask me any questions you want. There ain't a lot in that envelope, Mr. Thorne, but maybe it'll help set you off in the right direction. There's a lot goin' on I ain't sure about, but I seen some thangs that even Uncle Fairmont don't know about, either."

Mason reached across his desk and gingerly picked up the wrinkled envelope, passing it through his fingers from one hand to the other. "And just where do you fit into all this, Miss Halouise Lofton?" he asked her quietly, his blue eyes fixing hers intently.

"I don't work for my uncle the way most Loftons do," she responded evenly. "Like the whole town of Hack's

Crossin' does. But I know enough to keep my mouth shut about what's goin' on there.'' She paused for a moment, then her eyes became darker with anger. ''Leastways, I used to. But I cain't stay quiet no more.''

''What's going on in Hack's Crossing, Lou? And what does the Connery Corporation have to do with it?''

''You just read what I wrote down there, you hear? And you put a stop to it, Mr. Thorne, before anyone else gets killed.''

Chapter One

There she was, right on time, Mick thought, unconsciously releasing a sigh. It was 8:45, he guessed, because it was Thursday, and he knew the bookstore where she worked closed at 8:30 on Thursdays. Checking his watch in the dim glow of the beat-up antique lamp on his desk, he verified his estimation. Then as he did at this time every Thursday evening, he switched off the lamp and sat alone in the darkness, waiting while the woman who lived across the street from his office ascended the stairs to her apartment above the Republic and Maryland Insurance Agency. He watched with casual interest as she went from room to room turning on lights, removed her sweater, fed her cat and finally went to the stove to start a kettle of water for her evening cup of tea. Cleveland Street was only two lanes wide, so not much distance separated the two buildings. It was easy for Mick to loosen his tie, lean back in his chair and prop his denim-clad legs up on his desk to make himself comfortable while he observed the activities of the woman across the way.

Mick Dante's Thursday night ritual of spying on his neighbor had become just that about four months ago when he had been working late one night on a case and saw her come home from work. That was when he realized to his complete delight that after the sun went down and her lights came on, he could view her life at home, just as he had been watching her daily activities in the neighborhood. But his fascination with the daily activities of the young, auburn-haired woman had begun long before that, only a few days after he had moved to the small Chesapeake town of Cannonfire, Maryland.

It had begun well over a year ago, a bright, warm, sunny day, when he had been unpacking books and supplies for his new office, and she had breezed out of her apartment across the street like a breath of fresh air. Mick had dropped a thick volume of criminal procedure on his foot, then swearing a blue streak had hobbled to the window to watch her pass by. The wind had lifted her full, flowery skirt above her knees, revealing perfect, slender legs, and the sun had danced in hair the color of fallen autumn leaves. His heart had hummed wildly that day, and he remembered thinking many warm and dangerous thoughts.

Since that morning, Mick had looked for her every day and was seldom disappointed. He had her comings and goings clocked almost perfectly: she left for work at 8:15 and, other than Thursday nights, came home either empty-handed at 6:45 or with two bags of groceries at 7:15. On more than one occasion, he had taken advantage of a slow day at work and leisurely followed her from a distance to discover more about her. He knew that her first name was Emily and that she worked in a bookstore a few blocks up the street, and that at every establishment on Cleveland

Street she entered, she knew the proprietor by name and was greeted warmly. In nice weather, she sometimes ate lunch at Modesto's Café, outside at a sidewalk table, and when it grew colder she opted for the bar at the Jubilee Coffeehouse, where she and Agnes Pennypacker, the old woman who owned the place, laughed about Shakespearean comedy. More often, though, she packed her own lunch in a small willow basket and ate it on the lawn of Cannonfire's tiny town square or in the public library reading room, depending on the weather.

She was always reading something, usually Emerson or Hawthorne, and she loved the poetry of William Blake and Lord Byron. Sometimes, though, when she thought she was safely unobserved, she indulged in paperback novels with elaborate cover artwork of two people embracing, a pounding sea or rampaging army in the background threatening their ardor. These books she read with considerably more interest than the others, her changing facial expressions reflecting the drama and passion unfolding within their pages. Mick thought her a joy to watch at times such as those, and he could no more keep his thoughts away from her than he could stop his heart from beating.

He knew she lived alone except for her cat, but once in a while, she went out with one of a small group of men she knew in Cannonfire. These men did not bother Mick, for he knew she wasn't serious about them and only dated them for their company. She had said so to Agnes Pennypacker just the other day. There was, however, one man who came to visit her from time to time. A man who did worry Mick. A young man. A good-looking man. A man who spent occasional weekends with her and most holidays with her. A man she hugged and kissed, a man with whom she had dinner, with whom she linked arms and with whom she laughed a great deal. A man who made her smile. A man who made Mick's gut wrench.

But that man was not with her tonight. And Mick felt no remorse or guilt as he watched her intently from his hidden roost. He had watched many people in this way on many occasions and had been paid very well for it. He'd even done it at the government's request for ten years. But his time with the FBI was pushed to the back of his mind now. For nearly a year and a half he'd been in business for himself. And if being a private investigator meant giving up a steady paycheck, it had at least provided him with other, less tangible benefits.

Not the least of which was his auburn-haired neighbor, who at the moment was pulling a pale blue satin ribbon from her hair, running her hands through the mass of copper curls in an attempt to tame it. Mick smiled. He loved her hair. He loved to watch her brush it at night, and he loved to watch the sun and wind caress it. It used to spill in a tangle to the center of her back, and the day she'd cut it short, up to her chin, he'd wanted to run out of his office into the street and throttle her. But a year had passed since then, and the russet tresses had grown out nicely. Tonight her hair danced around her shoulders as if it had resented her attempt to confine it all day. Unconsciously Mick ran his fingers through his own black locks, wishing it could be her curls instead. In mute frustration, he reached into his shirt pocket for a cigarette and lit it, inhaling deeply, drawing the bitter smoke into his lungs. He was killing himself with those damn things, he thought, but couldn't find a good reason to quit. If he died, he died, and the world would go on. Ah well, it had always been that way; why had he thought leaving the Bureau would change that? Joining the Bureau certainly hadn't.

Mick Dante had grown up in a middle-class Chicago neighborhood. His dad had worked on a factory line and was retired now. They didn't speak much. Hadn't for over twenty years. Not since Mick's mother had died when he was fourteen. Hell, he knew her illness wasn't the old man's fault, but he couldn't help resenting his father for not treating her better during her last years. The two elder Dantes had fought bitterly for as long as Mick could remember, over everything from paychecks to ceiling paint. He supposed at one time the pair must have been in love, but he certainly hadn't witnessed much of it in the years he had lived with them. They were both to blame for their spiteful behavior, he supposed, but when it was learned his mother had only a short time left, she'd tried to make amends, and his father would have none of it. After her death, there was very little to bind the two Dante men together. They quickly drifted apart, both wrapped up in their own lives. And once Mick had left for college, there had seemed no reason to stay in touch at all.

His mother's death and father's withdrawal affected Mick in other, subtler ways as well. All his life he'd found it uncomfortable to maintain close friendships, save the one he shared with his ex-partner, and he seldom became involved with women beyond a superficial, physical bonding. It was because he was restless, he'd convinced himself—because he was restless and because he liked being a loner. He treasured his solitude and would sacrifice it for nothing or nobody. As a result, Mick Dante had found himself a solitary man for most of his life.

After college, it had been easy for the FBI to recruit him. He had no family, no close friends. He was uncertain about what to do with his degree and prelaw studies and was not altogether sure that law school was the route he wanted to go. At twenty-two he'd been willingly drafted into the

Bureau. He'd liked it for a while, the gathering of evidence and pursuit of criminals, the travel, the adventure, the danger. But he'd seen some pretty ugly things during that time, and the ugliness just seemed to get starker and nastier with each passing year.

But that was all over now. Now he had a business of his own that kept him going strong, even if it wasn't making him rich. He had deliberately chosen a sleepy little town like Cannonfire because it was so rife with decency. There was little to investigate here, aside from the occasional straying spouse, or the financial status of said spouse should he or she be caught in something dirty and wind up in divorce court. After some of the experiences Mick had survived in his ten years with the FBI, the less dangerous and adventurous the jobs now, the better. He didn't want to wind up with a bullet in his shoulder again. Maybe he wasn't living the life of Reilly, but he was living a life. He enjoyed his work and felt at home on his sailboat berthed at the Cannonfire Marina. His was a quiet life, a predictable life, a solitary life. It was a life that suited Mick just fine.

The soft rap of knuckles on his office door stole his glance from the apartment across the street where the object of his attentions was beginning to casually unbutton her blouse. Irritably Mick pushed his chair back from his desk and rose to unlock and answer his door. A fair-haired, mild-faced man stood outside wearing a travel-rumpled suit and a knowing grin, clutching a plain brown paper bag to his heart.

"I knew I'd find you here, Mick." The man smiled good-naturedly. "What's she up to tonight? Have I missed anything good?"

"Dammit, Sam, what are you doing here?" Mick asked, exasperation evident in his tone. "Things get boring in the Pacific?"

His ex-partner lived in the Nation's capital but was a fairly frequent visitor to Mick's office and sailboat in Cannonfire. However, he hadn't seen Sam much since the other man had taken on his most recent case, one involving a contracting scam and a union boss who had faked his own death, only to turn up in the Mariana Islands.

"Good to see you, too, old buddy, and the Pacific is just the same as it was when you were there in '83." Sam placed his palm on the office door and gently pushed it open wide, then sauntered past Mick and went straight toward the window that faced the apartment across the street. He'd known about Mick's fascination with the woman who lived there almost from the time it had begun.

"Looks like the show is over for the night, Mick. She closed the blinds on us."

Mick swore softly and nudged the office door closed with his shoulder. Glaring at the other man, he informed him, "She was starting to get undressed when you interrupted."

"Gee, that's the farthest you've ever gotten with her. How long before you think the two of you will go all the way?"

"That's enough, Sam. She's not that kind of girl," he said, only half joking.

"I guess I should be relieved that you've stopped short of using binoculars when you spy on her, but honestly, Mick, how much longer are you going to be a Peeping Tom, eavesdropping on her life? Why don't you just go into the bookstore where she works and introduce yourself?"

"I'm not interested in her," Mick asserted defensively, returning to his desk and switching on the lamp. "I just like to pass the time when business is a little slow. Now unless you've come for a reason, I have a lot of work to do."

Sam followed, situating himself on the edge of Mick's desk. "Yeah, I could see that by the way you were sitting here in total darkness. The way you sit here in total darkness every Thursday night because you know you'll be able to look in her window and make sure she's not doing anything she shouldn't be with that guy who makes you so crazy when he's in town. Jeez, Mick you act like you're in love with her, and you've never even spoken to her.''

Mick screwed up his face at his friend and pulled a file out of his desk drawer to affect an appearance of having something to do. "I'm not in love with her," he stated softly. "I've never been in love in my life, and you know it. She's just a casual diversion."

"That's just the point," Sam said. "We've been friends for a long time, Dante, and I've never seen you stay interested in a woman for more than a month, two at the most. This has been going on for over a year now." He paused for emphasis. "For over a year you've been watching her. You know everything there is to know about a person except her last name."

"I don't know everything about her," Mick denied wearily, thinking back on all the conversations he'd heard her share with Agnes Pennypacker.

"What's her favorite color?" Sam shot at him.

"Deep rose," he replied automatically.

"Favorite food?"

"Eggs Benedict for breakfast. Pasta primavera for dinner. But she likes seafood, Mexican, Chinese and Italian, too."

"Favorite music?"

"Sergey Prokofiev and Hoagy Carmichael."

"Favorite writer?"

"Nathaniel Hawthorne. And Jude Deveraux," he added as an afterthought.

"Any other pertinent statistics you'd like to add?" Sam prodded with a whimsical note.

"She loves to attend the local ballet, especially when they're performing *Romeo and Juliet*. She plays the piano and wants very badly to visit Great Britain and France, all right?" Mick responded, annoyed with himself for knowing so much about her. Then with a sigh, he pulled open his upper left-hand desk drawer and removed a pair of battered binoculars, holding them up sheepishly for Sam's inspection. "And incidentally..."

His ex-partner laughed outright. "Some casual diversion."

Mick tossed the binoculars back into his drawer and pretended to be wrapped up in the case that lay open on the desk before him, but he couldn't help thinking over what his friend had said. He wanted to disagree with Sam, but knew deep down that his accusations were valid. Despite the fact that he had never spoken to the woman, had never even gotten within five feet of her, there was something about his neighbor that appealed to him, something beyond her obvious physical allure. He felt the two of them had something in common, something nameless but nonetheless very real. A longing of some kind, perhaps, for something different, something more. She seemed to live a quiet life, just as he did, but he could sense in her a dissatisfaction, a restlessness of spirit similar to his own.

"Look, Sam, it doesn't concern you, so just drop it, okay?"

Sam shook his head at his friend and shrugged. "All right, Mick. For now. But I'm telling you, you ought to just go into the bookstore and tell her that you're madly—"

"There must be some reason you drove all the way down here from D.C. tonight," Mick interrupted before Sam could begin another discourse on how to talk to women. "So spill it or beat it."

"Boy, the way you do turn on the charm." Sam grinned. "Okay. I'll get right to the point. Congratulate me."

"Why?"

"Because I am about to enter what has heretofore been a mystery of life to us both."

"Sam." Mick's tone was less than patient, more than perturbed.

"I'm getting married."

"Say what?"

"And I want you to be the best man."

"I reiterate: Say what?"

"Mercy, you idiot!" Sam shouted, jumping up from his perch on Mick's desk.

"Why are you asking for mercy?" Mick wanted to know.

"No," Sam moaned, grasping great handfuls of sandy-colored hair in a frustrated gesture. "Mercy Malone. Don't you remember?"

"Mercy Malone," Mick repeated thoughtfully, searching his memory for the source of the vaguely familiar name.

"Phoenix, Arizona?" Sam added encouragingly. "Tate Memorial Hospital?"

Mick's eyes widened with the memory. "The little nurse who took care of you after Carmine Venturi's thugs got hold of you?" he asked incredulously. "The brunette with the long..."

"Long legs," Sam sighed reverently. "And she's not so little. She's five-ten. You think everyone is little compared with your great hulking mass, Tarzan."

"Six-five is not a hulking mass," Mick sniffed indignantly. "I happen to be in prime condition."

"Yeah, yeah. Well, anyway, try to keep it that way until after February fourteenth."

"Valentine's Day?" Mick asked with an obvious smirk.

"Mercy's idea." Sam smiled a little goofily. "I thought it was kind of romantic."

"Romantic, Sam?" Mick inquired with growing surprise. "Romantic? What kind of word is that coming from a federal agent?"

"An appropriate one. She's quite a woman. A very romantic one. She could teach you a lesson or two about romance, fella. Not that I'd let her get within fifty feet of you before the wedding, mind you. Women do have a tendency to get a little too familiar with you, if you know what I mean."

"Now, Sam, you know I'd never poach."

"Yeah, right," Sam huffed. "Just like you didn't poach when I was going out with Carla Stanford."

"Hey, Carla Stanford came after me."

"Sure." Sam smiled, knowing he had his ex-partner on the hot seat and enjoying it immensely.

"She only wanted your money anyway. You should thank me for saving your neck, not to mention your inheritance and family jewels."

"Let's not bring my family or my jewels into this, all right?" Sam grinned at his friend, and if Mick had had a fanciful bone in his body, he would have told Sam he looked radiant. Instead he just grinned back. What Sam looked was happy. Really happy. Mick was beginning to remember Mercy Malone fairly well, and he wasn't all that surprised that Sam had kept in touch with her for these three years.

"Guess this sort of explains all those trips out West, doesn't it?" Mick asked. "I just thought you had a thing about the desert climate."

Sam laughed. "Nope. True love, Micky my boy. True love. Something similar to what you harbor for yon leggy redhead across the street, though a good bit less one-sided. If you know what I mean."

"I'm not in love with her," Mick insisted.

"Right," Sam agreed with a deadpan expression that clearly suggested he didn't believe his friend for a second.

"I'm not."

"I said okay, okay?" Sam presented the brown paper bag he still held in his hand and, with an exaggerated flourish, opened it and pulled out a bottle of champagne. "Now toast my good fortune, all right?"

Mick took the bottle from Sam's hand, examining it intently before raising his eyebrows. "Six bucks?" he asked. "You really are celebrating."

Sam snatched the bottle back and vigorously began to rub at the price tag with his thumbnail. "I, uh, I thought I'd taken that off," he said with an embarrassed chuckle.

"Same old Sam." Mick laughed, a deep rumble that bubbled up freely from his brawny chest. "I hope Mercy appreciates what she's getting."

Sam's laughter joined Mick's as his friend reached into the bottom right-hand drawer of his desk and pushed aside a bottle of bourbon to retrieve two mismatched dime-store drinking glasses. He wiped them out with his necktie and presented them to Sam, who promptly filled them to the brim with tepid sparkling wine.

"Here's to you, Sam," Mick saluted his friend and raised his glass. "To you and Mercy. Be happy."

Sam nodded nobly in gracious recognition, and the two men lifted their glasses to their lips. "And here's to you, Mick," he contributed. "I should say the same to you and the redhead, but I won't because you're not in love with her as you continually remind me. But here's to you, and you alone. Try to be happy."

Mick looked at Sam with a veiled expression, and then his eyes wandered past his friend to the apartment across the street. Her lights were still on. He could see into her kitchen.

But there was no sign of her, so he assumed she must be in the living room or her bedroom. He thought of the time a few months ago when he'd seen her rush home from work, running up the stairs to her apartment only to throw herself into the arms of the man waiting there for her. He thought of the times he'd watched her go to her bed alone, her white cotton gown making her look innocent and untried. He took a deep swallow, emptying his glass of the cheap champagne, and decided what he really wanted was a shot of good whiskey instead.

Wordlessly he reached back into his drawer and removed the bottle left there. As he continued to watch the curtained window across the street, Mick splashed a few fingers of the amber liquid into his glass and tossed it down his throat, grimacing at the burning heat it brought with it.

Sam watched the action and sighed wearily. "Good luck, Mick," he whispered before carefully sipping his champagne.

Chapter Two

In her living room, Emily Thorne sat in quiet concern, cradling her telephone receiver between her shoulder and ear. Once again she had tried to reach Mason by phone, and once again she had been forced to leave a message on his machine.

"Oh, Mason," she pleaded impotently with her brother, "where are you? Why won't you answer your phone?"

Her brother had been missing for three weeks, but it was impossible for her to find anyone else who would admit it. At first, she hadn't been overly concerned by his lack of communication, because she understood that being occasionally incommunicado was one of the hazards that went along with being an investigative reporter. Mason's job with the number-one newspaper in the nation had taken him to some pretty scary places, areas as remote and dangerous as they could get. He'd covered terrorist activities in distant Latin American villages with names she couldn't begin to pronounce, and drug wars in the densest jungles of Central America. But even during those times, he had generally managed to get word to her that he was all right. Emily had told herself repeatedly in the past weeks that this time, Mason was somewhere so remote, or else undercover so deep, that even he was unable to get a message to his sister.

When Emily began to make inquiries about Mason's whereabouts, strange things had started to happen. Her calls to the newspaper asking about her brother's agenda had been referred to people she'd never heard of in departments other than Mason's. Some of them had explained away his silence with reference to "unsteady political atmosphere" or the "impossible tropical climate" of his destination before abruptly cutting her off. Yet Mason had told her he was going to some Podunk town called Roadside, Mississippi. Upset about his disappearance, she'd called Roadside Information for the numbers of all the hotels in town. There was only one. Rudy's.

When Emily had telephoned the motor inn, Rudy himself had denied ever registering any guest named Mason Thorne at any time, that unless her brother was interested in trapping some beaver or shooting some doves, he probably wouldn't have any interest in a place like Roadside, lovely and picturesque as most visitors found it. No, the only strangers he'd seen lately were a busload of retirees from Destin, Florida, on a gambling junket to Las Vegas who had stopped in Roadside to gas up, and they definitely did not include the young, well-dressed, socially conscious fellow that she described. But Rudy took her number anyway and promised to pass along a message should this Mr. Mason Thorne turn up at his door.

Not long after that, the phone calls had started. Nothing too odd, really, just an inordinate amount of wrong numbers and people taking the strangest surveys. They asked her about everything from kitchen cleaner to banking practices. She hung up as quickly and politely as possible, excused the calls by deciding her name must have shown up on some new list somewhere, and continued to worry about Mason.

Every time she had a day off, Emily took the train into Washington, D.C., and let herself into Mason's Capitol Hill apartment. His refrigerator was emptied of perishables, as if he had planned an extended trip, and his landlady, Lilah, was collecting his mail and placing it on the dining room table as she always did for him when he went away for long periods. She would wait patiently on her brother's couch all day in the hopes that Mason might come home for something, but he never made an appearance, nor did he or anyone else ever make a call. The only messages on his machine were the frantic ones she had left for him.

Emily's job managing Paradise Found Books prohibited her from taking several days off in a row, so she couldn't make an extensive inquiry about Mason in D.C., but she felt she had to do something. There was no way she could sit idly by when she knew there was something very wrong about her brother's disappearance. He was missing without a clue, for God's sake! she screamed at herself. He didn't just fall off the earth, so he must be someplace. But where? Somebody must know something.

She drained the last of her tea from the frail china cup and walked into the kitchen to pour another. The late September night was warm, and her lace kitchen curtains fluttered slightly in the evening breeze. Emily took her teacup to the window and stared disconsolately down toward Cleveland Street. Cannonfire was a beautiful little town nestled on Chesapeake Bay. She loved it here. Cleveland Street, where she lived, was a side street in the historical section of the community, a road first laid in the 1700s. The buildings that lined the surrounding streets on both sides for nearly four blocks were virtually all registered historical landmarks and constituted a good part of Cannonfire's business district. Beyond them, Cannonfire had grown north and south along the shoreline into residential areas, neighborhoods populated with rambling Victorian homes interspersed with newer, more architecturally progressive abodes. The effect on the whole was an impressive mixture of the historical and the contemporary, the present enhanced by the past.

Emily liked that best about the town. The daughter of college professors who taught history and archaeology, she cherished the past more than most people. She liked the world very much the way it was, but in some ways she was a bit old-fashioned and longed for experiences that could no longer be had in the modern world. The books she loved were all written over a hundred years ago, and the ones she read from contemporary writers all took place in the past. Mason thought she was "unbelievably tacky" to spend so much time reading what he considered "sleazy gothic trash," but those books held for her something of what she felt was missing from her own life—adventure, romance, a passion for living that she just didn't see in many people, herself included. Usually books were enough. But sometimes the desire for more opened up an emptiness in her heart. It wasn't a vast void that prevented Emily from enjoying life, but it was enough to bring on a melancholy feeling from time to time.

She missed Mason. Usually when she was feeling a little sad, she could call him, and without fail he would cheer her up. But Mason was out of reach right now. Somehow she knew that he was in trouble, and she simply couldn't stand by worrying, doing nothing. As she looked out her kitchen window onto Cleveland Street, her eyes settled on the building across the way. Inside one of the upstairs offices, a lamp glowed warm amber. Two men sat at a desk laughing, the sandy-haired one facing her seeming to enjoy the joke considerably more than the dark figure with his back to her. The scene made Emily smile. On one of the windows, in large gold letters outlined in black, she read the words she had seen so frequently, but to which she had never paid much attention. Michael Dante Investigations, they said. She assumed the two men must be private investigators for the firm, working late on some tough case, trying to piece together clues that would ultimately lead them to what they wanted to know.

Suddenly a little light went on in the back of Emily's head. Private investigators. That's it, she thought. She could hire someone at Michael Dante Investigations to locate Mason, since she had neither the opportunity nor the know-how to do it herself. During her lunch break tomorrow afternoon, she would go to see Mr. Michael Dante himself. She knew she should probably make an appointment with the man, but there just wasn't time for that. Every day that Mason remained out of touch caused Emily's fears to grow a little larger. She wouldn't stop worrying until he was found and could offer her a decent explanation for his disappearance. Michael Dante could do something to discover her brother's whereabouts. And the sooner she saw the man, the better.

Her heart a little lighter for the decision, Emily filled her teacup again and returned to the living room. Sophie, the orange tabby she claimed for a roommate wove in and out of her legs until she picked her up and cuddled the furry creature under her chin. The regular thrumming of Sophie's purr made Emily relax further. Soon she would have an explanation for her brother's absence. Soon she would know what had happened to Mason and how to get him out of trouble. Michael Dante would help her do that. Even though she had yet to meet the man, she knew he would be able to take care of everything.

Mick was finishing the paperwork on a closed case the following afternoon when his secretary, Eleanor, knocked lightly on his office door.

"Yes, Ellie?" he mumbled with some distraction, not bothering to look up from his work.

He heard the door open. "Mick, there's a young woman here to see you. She doesn't have an appointment, but she wants to hire you."

At this, Mick looked up and frowned. Normally he required a prospective client to call and make an appointment. "What kind of job?"

"Missing person."

"How does she seem?"

Mick generally wanted to know the nature of his clients if he hadn't spoken with them previously to set up the appointment. It was his way of avoiding surprises and maintaining a cool exterior when dealing with strangers. Above all else, Mick wanted to at least seem in control, even if circumstances sometimes prohibited it. He needed to establish immediately for his clients that he was the one in charge, the one who would call the shots, regardless of the nature of the case he was accepting.

Eleanor adjusted her eyeglasses and shrugged. "A little nervous. I think you should talk to her. She seems pretty scared about something."

Mick closed the file folder before him and leaned back in his chair, rubbing his eyes. "All right. Our caseload is pretty light right now, and missing persons isn't all that tough. Send her in."

Eleanor smiled, then turned to look over her shoulder as she began to open the door wider. "Miss Thorne?" he heard her say coaxingly, as if speaking to a frightened child. "Mr. Dante will see you now."

"Thank you," a quiet voice replied.

In the next few moments, Mick Dante's world of peace and predictability exploded in his face. His first thought concerning the woman who entered his office was that for once she had left her hair unbound, as if she'd known how often and how badly his fingers had itched to tangle themselves within it. His next realization was that her eyes were as green and as vivid as expertly cut emeralds and that he had never truly known their color until this moment. She wore a voluminous, shin-skimming dress of white cotton, sleeveless and bound around the hips with a dark green scarf. Her high cheekbones were flushed a very enticing, very soft pink, and her full lips parted in what could have been surprise, trepidation or desire. Mick took a deep breath as the woman who had occupied his thoughts, his dreams and his fantasies for nearly fifteen months approached him, extended her hand and spoke.

"Mr. Dante?" Her voice was a gentle caress. "My name is Emily Thorne."

So Emily had a last name, too. Emily Thorne. It fit her nicely. It was earthy and feminine, unobtrusive and soft.

"I hope I haven't inconvenienced you by coming without an appointment," she continued hesitantly. "I only live across the street and noticed your sign some time ago. I never imagined I'd need a private investigator, and I'd give anything not to have the necessity now. Not that it isn't nice to meet you or anything."

She paused, flustered, knowing she was saying more than he wanted to hear. Quite frankly, Michael Dante, Private Investigator, wasn't turning out to be what she had expected. She had rather assumed the man in charge would be frumpy and middle-aged, dressed in a somewhat outdated suit and utterly nondescript. She certainly hadn't anticipated someone so...big. And handsome. And thoroughly, overwhelmingly, unbelievably attractive. Instead of an outdated suit, Michael Dante was dressed in slightly faded, form-fitting Levi's, a charcoal shirt the exact color of his eyes, and an absolutely hideous necktie spattered with what looked like black and teal-blue poinsettias. He was captivating in a rugged, sort of sexually magnetic way, if that was what turned you on. Her friend, Stella, who worked with her at the bookstore, would probably like him, Emily thought, but he certainly wasn't the type she normally dated. Not by a long shot. He seemed like one of the many heroes in one of the many paperback romances she read—roguish and steely and just fine to read about. But where real life was concerned, Emily preferred the company of a quiet, gentle man. Someone with whom she could share a peaceful moment or tender embrace. This man would probably crush her if he held her. And then he would probably break her heart in two.

"I'm sorry," she went on quickly, feeling her heart rate accelerate at the thought of being crushed by this man. "I, uh, don't mean to ramble. I'm not normally so, um, jumpy." When Emily realized Michael Dante had yet to respond to her introduction, she grew worried that she had interrupted him in the middle of some important work. "Have I caught you at a bad time? I can come back later, but I really need to talk to someone."

Mick hoped she didn't think he was as big a fool as he felt at that moment and finally took her still extended hand in his. It was small, fragile and warm, and it was swallowed by his big, callused fingers. Yet, despite their differences, her hand felt as if it belonged in his. He held it longer than was necessary, caressing her fingers lightly as he released them, staring intently into her overly bright eyes. Oh, yes. Emily

Thorne had caught him all right. And it was at a very bad time. He could easily lose himself in her eyes and probably already had. They were clear and inviting, big and expressive. She was definitely worried by something. And if he could help her in any way, he would sell his soul to do it.

"Miss Thorne," he began, hoping his voice betrayed none of his anxiety. "Please excuse my rudeness. I was just finishing up another case, and my mind hasn't quite left it yet."

Emily's knees buckled a little at the sound of his voice, and a hot flame ignited in her stomach before spreading to her every fiber. His voice reminded her of good cognac, dark and smooth, warm and intoxicating. It was the voice of a man who was confident in himself, a man who had strength in his body and his mind. That was what she needed right now. Someone who could think clearly and help her find Mason.

"Ellie said you seem to have misplaced someone," he continued, gesturing toward a chair, trying to make her feel more at ease. She ventured a small smile and sank gratefully into the seat he indicated. Mick came out from behind his desk and leaned casually against the front of it, closing the distance between them.

He was so close Emily thought she could feel the warmth of his big body and smell the smoky fragrance of his aftershave. "How can I help you?" he asked softly.

"It's my brother, Mason."

"Your brother?"

Emily nodded. "I haven't heard from him for three weeks."

"Is that unusual?"

"Well, I don't normally see him all that often, but once in a while he spends the weekend with me, and he calls every Sunday, without fail, to make sure I'm all right." She grinned sheepishly. "He can't accept the fact that I'm a grown woman. He still has to check up on me from time to time.''

"I see." Mick's heart soared. The man who came to visit her was her brother, not her lover. Not some jerk who made love to her, held her warm, lush body next to his all night, only to callously leave her when Monday morning rolled around. There was no one special man in her life, he realized suddenly, no threat to him, no rival. Immediately his mood lightened, and he looked at Emily with renewed interest. Mick had to sympathize with her brother. She was definitely a grown woman; his raging hormones and galloping pulse rate could vouch for that. But there was also something in her that made him want to protect her, too. Not a weakness or lack of intelligence, but a vulnerability that he feared someone without a conscience would try to extort or take advantage of. She seemed a person whose feelings could be hurt easily because she trusted too readily. From the times he had observed her and overheard her conversations, he sensed that she had been rather sheltered for much of her life and probably hadn't seen a lot of the world. Suddenly and inexplicably, he wanted to take her by the hand and show her all the things in life she had been missing. He would start with thoroughly and passionately kissing her. Then he would lift her into his arms and carry her to the tattered sofa where she would be introduced to the limitless pleasures of making love. Instead he tried to calm himself down and continue their conversation in a normal manner.

"And have you tried getting in touch with your brother?" he asked, allowing none of the warm fantasies he was entertaining to show on his face.

"Every day," Emily assured him. "His answering machine is on, and I leave all kinds of messages, but he hasn't returned any of my calls. That just isn't like him. I've gone to his apartment in D.C., but there's no sign that he's been there recently. His mail is really piling up.''

''What does he do for a living?''

''He's an investigative reporter for *The Capitol Standard*.''

Mick's expression changed dramatically at that statement.

''What? What are you thinking?'' Emily demanded.

''Maybe he's on assignment somewhere and can't get in touch with you,'' Mick suggested.

''I've thought of that, but it isn't likely,'' Emily told him. ''He's been on assignment in places like El Salvador and Nicaragua during massive political unrest before, but he's always managed to let me know that he's safe. If nothing else, he sends word to someone at the paper who will ultimately contact me.''

''Maybe this time he's deep undercover and can't get word to you without endangering himself.''

''I've thought of that, too. But there's more to this than just his lack of communication,'' she added.

''Like what?''

''Well, a lot of weird things have been happening in the past few weeks.''

''What kind of weird things?''

''There are just a lot of things that don't add up. The last time I spoke to Mason, he called me from a little town called Roadside, Mississippi where he was investigating some story whose details he didn't describe. He was in a crummy motel, told me the place was boring and awful and that he'd be home by the end of the week. We even made plans for that Sunday. That was three weeks ago, Mr. Dante,'' she told him urgently. ''After that, I didn't hear a word. I tried calling the only hotel in Roadside, but they told me that he had never been there, that they'd never heard of him. Whenever I call the paper, they say Mason is on assignment out of town, but give me all kinds of conflicting stories about tropical climates and political upheaval. I even tried calling the police, but they said as long as the paper says he's on assignment and there's no evidence of foul play, there's nothing they can do to help.''

Mick studied Emily carefully. There was something more that was bothering her, something she was neglecting to mention. He could sense it in her edginess, the fact that she seemed to want to say more.

''Is there something else that's concerning you, Miss Thorne?'' he asked her quietly.

Emily looked at Mick, unable to tear her gaze from his smoky quartz eyes. What was it about him that made her feel as if he could peer straight to the very depth of her soul, could sense every nuance, every aspect of her character?

Breathlessly she continued. ''I...I don't know if this has anything to do with Mason's disappearance, but I've been getting a lot of odd phone calls lately.''

''Such as?''

''Wrong numbers, surveys, salesmen, people who don't say anything when I answer. I know that's not unusual occasionally, and my number isn't an unlisted one, but I never used to get calls like that.''

''Do you think they're related to all this?''

Emily shrugged helplessly, a silent plea brightening her green eyes. ''I just don't know, Mr. Dante. I can't tell you how worried I am.'''

She didn't have to, Mick acknowledged. He could detect the fear and apprehension in her expression and in the way she continually shifted around in the chair. If it was true that her brother was on a routine assignment in Mississippi, then there probably should be no reason why he hadn't gotten in touch with her. Unless, of course, there was something seriously wrong. And by the look on Emily's lovely face she, at least, was convinced that there was. Mick thought for a moment. His caseload was light, and D.C. was only two hours away. Not to mention he could use the extra income from the case. The boat needed some repairs done before the weather turned too cold to make them. But most important, Emily Thorne had asked for his help. She needed him. And to Mick Dante, that was the only reason in the world.

"I'll take your case," he told her decisively.

"Thank you, Mr. Dante," she said earnestly. "You don't know how much this means to me."

They discussed his fee, and Emily supplied him with as much information about her brother as she could. The only thing she was unable to tell Mick was what kind of story Mason had been working on most recently.

"He never, under any circumstances, discusses his stories with me," she said.

"Why not?"

"A variety of reasons," she explained. "For one thing, he doesn't want to risk having me slip and say something to someone who shouldn't hear it. Some of the things he's worked on have been potential threats to national security if reported incorrectly. And, quite frankly, he's investigated some pretty dangerous people, too. He doesn't want me to have any information about them that could cause me trouble. More than once, I've asked him to get into something a little safer, but he simply won't have it."

"Likes a life of danger, does he?" Mick asked dryly, more than a little uncomfortable that the description of Mason's life fit his own past so well.

"I suppose so," Emily sighed. "I guess it's understandable, really."

"Why do you say that?"

"Mason and I were brought up in pretty august and regimented surroundings. Our parents were both college professors, and we lived on campus at a variety of prestigious universities. Dad taught history, Mother taught archaeology. Both of them were very academic and relentless in their studies. They insisted that Mason and I do the same. But I guess the brilliance gene skips a generation, because neither Mason nor I had any inclination toward education. We both got degrees, but neither of us pursued a career in our discipline."

"What's your degree in?" Mick wanted to know.

"History," Emily replied. "Why?"

"Just curious."

"Mason's degree was in Literature, but he chose to go into journalism instead. I think more than anything he needed to rebel, to reject the role my parents tried to force us into. They went out of their way to let us know that we were both big disappointments to them. I was able to just let it go, but Mason had this obsession with really sticking it to them, to show them that he refused to be molded into the intellectual genius they were determined to prove they had bred." Her face fell for a moment, but brightened again almost immediately. "He started working for this unbelievably sleazy tabloid in New York right after he graduated." She laughed. "Boy did that make my parents angry. Mainly because he used his real name. I was still in high school when it happened, and they swore they'd disown him and we'd never be allowed to see one another again. They didn't want him polluting my mind. I still had a chance to become an intellectual monster as far as they were concerned."

"Then what happened?" Mick tried to appear casual, but was ecstatic that she was offering him snatches of her past without his even having to ask. He was curious as hell to know everything about her, but the last thing he wanted to do was seem interested. Getting involved with a client was a definite taboo. Getting involved with Emily Thorne was an even bigger taboo. And despite his recent discovery that she wasn't seeing anyone, he didn't want to encourage anything between them. He was curious. Period. Sam was completely wrong about anything else.

"They made good on their threat," Emily said, saddened by the memory. "Mason and I had to meet secretly whenever he was in town, and we could only keep in touch through letters. And usually mine from him were confiscated unless I managed to get to the mailbox first. When I graduated from college four years ago, I moved down here to be closer to him. My dorm mate's father lives in Cannonfire and owns Paradise Found Books up the street. He offered me the job of managing it, because he was retiring. It seemed like a nice, quiet job that would allow me to be independent of my parents as well. I don't quite have the ambition that Mason has. I just want to live peacefully and enjoy life's basic pleasures. That aspect of campus life agreed with me, anyway. I guess deep down I'm still kind of boring."

Mick vehemently disagreed with that but kept his mouth shut on the subject. Instead he asked, "Where are your parents now? Could Mason have tried to contact them?"

Emily shook her head expressively. "Absolutely not. They live in Princeton, New Jersey, now. I rarely speak with them. Mason completely refuses to even ask about them. None of us was ever very close, except for Mason and me. They cloistered the two of us the whole time we were growing up. We had very few of the normal childhood experiences because we were always involved in special classes to accelerate learning or teach creativity, or doing homework, or taking piano and violin lessons, or what have you. I suppose I resent them to a degree for denying me the simple enjoyment of playtime. That's probably why he and I *are* so close. I was his only friend, and he was mine."

"And despite the efforts of your parents, the two of you have remained very close," Mick concluded.

"You've got to help me find him, Mr. Dante," Emily pleaded, her eyes haunted and fearful. "He's the only family, the only friend, I've ever really known. He's all I've got."

Her voice, filled with love for her brother and a dread that something terrible may have happened to him, caused Mick's heart to hammer hard in his chest. He understood that there was more to her apprehension than her obvious concern for Mason's welfare. Emily was terrified of being left alone. She had disassociated herself from her unloving parents, and from what he knew of her, she had no really close friends, despite her many acquaintances on Cleveland Street. If something happened to her brother, she felt she would have no one.

He sighed and bent forward from his position against the desk and looked searchingly into her eyes. He wanted to say something reassuring, but instead, his hand rose involuntarily to brush a russet curl behind her ear. On the journey back, his fingers paused and he gently cupped her cheek in his rough palm. Her skin was soft and warm and felt like the petals of a rose. She smelled of springtime and wildflowers, and her lips looked, oh, so inviting. Mick tenderly stroked her bottom lip with his thumb and saw her eyes widen in surprise, her pupils grow deep with anticipation.

"Don't worry, Emily," he murmured so low she thought she had tumbled into a dream. "I'll find Mason for you. And you won't be alone. Not if I have anything to say about it."

When he realized what he was doing, Mick quickly withdrew his hand and straightened, trying to regain some composure. Emily took a deep but shaky breath, uncertain of what exactly had passed between them.

"Thank you, Mr. Dante," she managed to say, but she was breathless, and they both noticed it.

In an effort to cool off and put a little distance between himself and Emily, Mick moved back to his original position behind his desk and sat down.

"Emily," he began, again using her first name although she had not issued him the invitation to do so. Oddly it didn't irritate her the way it normally did when men became so familiar after such a short time. It seemed quite natural, really. What was strange was that she had originally felt uncomfortable when he had called her "Miss Thorne."

Mick continued when she looked up. "Do you mind if I call you Emily?" he asked belatedly, then went on without waiting for her reply. "I think we're going to be speaking quite frequently, and perhaps a little personally, so it seems fitting. I wouldn't mind if you called me Mick." Wouldn't mind? That was the understatement of the year. He'd walk barefoot over glowing embers to have her get personal with him.

"I thought your name was Michael," she said, surprise evident in her voice. "I mean, that's what the sign on your window says," she added unnecessarily. "Michael Dante Investigations."

"Everyone calls me Mick," he explained.

"You don't seem like a Mick."

His dark brows rose at that. "What do you mean?"

Emily shrugged. "Well, Mick seems like someone rough and indifferent. Michael sounds like someone more... perceptive." She paused for a moment. "Someone considerate. Michael fits you much better."

"No one ever called me Michael except for my mother," he tossed off coolly.

"May I call you Michael?"

"If it makes you more comfortable, but I think you've got me pegged all wrong." He tried to sound indifferent, but what Emily had said to him made him feel warm and stupid. Warm because he loved the way she said Michael, and the fact that she alone called him that made it all the more intimate. But he knew it was stupid to let her get to him so badly so quickly. This whole episode could turn into one big problem. He did not want to get involved with Emily Thorne. She could be a nice little diversion for a while if she were someone different. Someone a little rougher around the edges. But she was kind and caring and completely inappropriate. She was just too good. Getting close to Emily could only lead to trouble and thoroughly disrupt his life. Mick liked things the way they were. He wanted to avoid anything that could create waves and end the tranquillity he'd sought for so long and finally found.

"Maybe," Emily conceded after a moment, bringing Mick's attention back to the young woman seated in his office. "But maybe not."

"Do you have a photograph of your brother?" he asked, ignoring the implication of her statement and the little explosion that went off in his midsection.

"Oh, I didn't even think of that. I have several over at my apartment. I could run over and get you one," she offered, "but I'm on my lunch hour, and I'm already late getting back. Could I drop it by your office this evening?"

"Why don't I just meet you at your apartment, and you can give it to me," Mick suggested. "It will save you a trip, and I'll be on my way out anyway."

"Okay. If you think that's best. I live right across the street, over the Republic and Maryland Insurance

Company," she told him again, her gaze wandering over to the window behind Mick. "In fact, you can see my apartment from this office. How about that?"

Mick hoped he managed to keep his expression bland and smiled indifferently. "Well, what do you know?"

They arranged a time to meet, then quickly shook hands and murmured hasty goodbyes. When Emily got back to Paradise Found, Stella Beauregard, her assistant manger, was looking meaningfully at her watch.

"Takin' extended lunch breaks now, are we?" the statuesque brunette drawled playfully at her friend.

"Sorry, Stella," Emily apologized. "I had an important errand to run. You can leave early today if you want."

"Oh sugar, I was only kiddin'." Stella smiled. "Honestly, sometimes you're just too serious for your own good. I don't mind that you were late. You should do it more often. It would greatly assuage my fears that you're perfect."

Emily smiled back at Stella. She liked the other woman a great deal. The two of them had many things in common, a love of books, an overly romantic nature and a weakness for manicotti and M & M's, though not necessarily on the same plate. Stella was from Charleston, South Carolina, and just by opening her mouth to say hello, which usually came out something like, "Hey, y'all," she could enchant anyone. Where Emily was prone to live in the past and get a little too caught up in the stories she read, Stella had her feet planted firmly in the present. And Emily's serious nature and tendency to dwell on the negative nearly always caved in to Stella's whimsy and sense of humor.

"Thanks, Stella."

"Don't mention it. Heard anything from that very attractive brother of yours recently?" she asked offhand.

Emily had expressed her concern to Stella a week ago when Mason had missed two consecutive Sundays of telephoning her. She hung up her purse on a coat hook behind the counter and looked at Stella worriedly.

"Nothing," she stated numbly.

"Oh, Emily, don't be upset," Stella tried to sound optimistic. "There's bound to be a very good explanation for what's keepin' that boy so quiet. Just wait. You'll see."

"I can't wait much longer. It's driving me crazy. Today I even hired a private investigator to look for Mason."

"An investigator? You mean like Magnum, P.I.?"

"More than you know," Emily muttered to herself.

"I'm sorry?" Stella asked, needing clarification. "I didn't quite catch that."

"Nothing," Emily said quickly. "That's where I was on my lunch hour. Meeting with the investigator."

"Does he think he can find Mason?"

"He said he'd try."

Emily didn't elaborate. Instead she went about the duties that awaited her attention. There was a shipment to check in and orders to complete, and since tomorrow was the first of October, the monthly paperwork for September had to be completed and mailed off to Mr. Lindsey. She hoped hard work would distract her from her worries.

Chapter Three

Emily was a little late getting home from work that evening because of the monthly paperwork that she should have been doing during her lengthy lunch break. Michael was already there waiting for her, seated comfortably on the bottom step that led up to her apartment. Emily's pace slowed as she took him in, noting with feminine appreciation how handsome he was, bathed in the warm sepia tones of the setting sun. He had loosened his tie and unbuttoned the first two buttons on his shirt, and in the balmy Indian summer evening had slung his sport coat over the wooden banister to his left. His long legs were stretched out before him, his booted ankles crossed easily, and he leaned back on his elbows, which were propped up on the step behind him. A smoldering cigarette dangled neglected from his fingertips, curls of wispy white smoke spiraling upward.

He really was very attractive, Emily thought. There was a rakish, almost dangerous, quality about him that set him apart from most men she knew. Michael had a carelessness about him, indicated by his unfashionably long and casually cut hair, and the fact that he evidently felt no need to dress in conventional business attire. She waited until she was nearly beside him before she stopped to quietly greet him.

"Hello, Michael," she said softly.

At the sound of her voice, Mick looked up, annoyed that his heart trip-hammered double time. He had been thinking about her all day, trying to convince himself that she had completely lost all of her fascination now that he had spoken with her and knew a little bit about her. But it was no use. The more he thought about her, the more he learned about her, the more he wanted to know. And the fact that she now stood before him looking so quietly desirable did very little to still the stirrings of his libido. Slowly he raised himself to his full height and looked down at her, then he dropped the remainder of his cigarette and stubbed it out on the sidewalk.

"I didn't hear you coming," he told her.

She really was very beautiful, he thought. The setting sun made her hair sparkle in burnt hues, and her eyes glistened like fathomless green seas when he gazed into them. If he wasn't careful, he might just go overboard and drown in those depths.

"I didn't mean to startle you," she said.

"I was just thinking."

"About what?"

Mick looked again at her face, so open and inviting, and smiled a cheerless smile. "I was thinking about what to take with me to Washington tomorrow."

"You'll be going so soon?" Emily asked as she began to ascend the stairs. She fumbled in her dress pocket for her keys as she climbed. "Come on up," she invited unnecessarily, as Mick had already started to follow her. "I guess you'll be needing that picture of Mason sooner than I thought."

"I don't have any cases that are urgent right now," Mick told her in lieu of an explanation. "Tomorrow is Saturday, so I may be able to get some answers from somebody on the newspaper staff while there's a minimal crew working and anyone encouraging misinformation about your brother's schedule might be home for the weekend. Besides, I have a good friend in D.C. I wouldn't mind dropping in on. I have a story to tell him that I think he's going to find pretty amusing." He didn't bother to add that the sooner he tied up this case and was able to go back to watching her from a distance where she posed considerably less threat, the better.

Emily unlocked her front door and paused before entering her apartment as a new thought struck her. "I could give you the key to Mason's apartment if you want," she offered. "Or better still, I could even go with you to Washington."

"Emily," Mick began, but she quickly cut him off.

"Stella can watch the shop for one day; she won't mind. I've done it for her before. Or Susan, our part-timer, could come in for me."

"Emily, I don't think it's a good idea for you to get directly involved with the case," he told her.

"But I could answer any questions you might have. I could show you where all of Mason's haunts are."

Mick had to admit she had a point. The more he discovered about Mason Thorne, the more he would want to know. Certainly more questions would arise during his investigation, questions that Emily would be able to answer.

"I could help you, Michael," she told him. "You could use me."

He couldn't avoid the suggestive smile that formed on his face at her choice of words. Emily blushed becomingly and stammered a clarification.

"I mean, you could use my help."

"All right," Mick conceded. "But I'm still going to need that photo."

"Yes, of course," she mumbled, still a little flustered. "Come on in."

Mick paused at the threshold of Emily's home, almost unwilling to enter it. How many nights had he sat across the street staring into this apartment, never expecting to see it, or its occupant, at such close range? It was almost like a sacred place to him, and it seemed sacrilegious to defile it with his humble presence.

"Michael?" Emily asked curiously, noting his reluctance. "Is something wrong?"

"No, nothing," he assured her as he forced his feet to move into the living room. Immediately his eyes began to wander, hungrily devouring every inch of his surroundings. This is what he looked into every Thursday night, he reminded himself. He was finally getting a chance to see her life up close, and he wanted to savor it while he could. Soon he would find her brother for her, and then she would no longer have any need of him. He would become yet another of her many acquaintances on Cleveland Street, and he would have to suffer in silence when she happened to see him and greet him in the same way she would Agnes Pennypacker or McGroarty the butcher or Vincent the baker. Michael the flatfoot, that's what he'd be. Just another member of the Cleveland Street Social Circle.

Her living room immediately made him feel uncomfortable. The furniture was small and feminine, a sofa and overstuffed chair and ottoman covered with huge scarlet cabbage roses, and chaise longue of pink damask. An ivory

rug with pastel flowers covered much of the room, dotted
here and there with fragile-looking marble-topped tables
housing tumbling plants and porcelain and crystal knick-
knacks. Paintings of fruit baskets and English gardens
adorned the milky walls, and in the fireplace, where Mick
would have had a raging fire blazing away, she had arranged
a huge bouquet of flowers. He was afraid that if he moved
in any direction or touched any object, he would crush
something beautiful or soil it irreparably. So he stood firm
in the middle of Emily's apartment and waited.

Emily, meanwhile, had gone straight to the kitchen after
inviting Michael to come inside. Out of habit, she poured
cat food into Sophie's dish and refilled her water bowl, then
put the kettle on the back burner to start a pot of tea.
Eventually she realized that Michael had not accompanied
her past the front door and went back out to check on him.
He looked completely out of place in her home, dwarfing
everything in her living room, making it look like a child's
dollhouse. And worse, he seemed to be unpleasantly aware
of the fact.

"Would you like a cup of tea?" she asked before consid-
ering the incongruity of a man like Michael Dante drinking
tea from her English china. "Or coffee?" she added hopefully.

"Thanks," Mick managed, "but if you'll just get the
picture of your brother for me, I'll be on my way."

"Yes, of course, I'm sorry," Emily rattled off nervously.
"I'm sure you must be very busy."

She turned to leave the room, but not before Mick noted
the wounded look that appeared in her eyes. He remembered his initial impression of her that she could be easily
hurt by some heartless sap. He hadn't considered then that
he might be the sap so easily capable of such an act, yet he

seemed to have a talent for saying just the wrong thing to make her feel bad.

When Emily returned to the living room, she offered Mick a fairly good selection of photographs, and he sifted through them carefully, inspecting each one independently of the others. The man he'd so often seen her with in Cannonfire was definitely her brother, though the two of them bore little resemblance to each other. Instead of Emily's auburn curls, Mason's hair was a thick thatch of sandy flax, and his face was ruggedly lined where Emily's was softly curved. They were a good-looking pair, though, Mick thought. He had to give her parents credit for that, if nothing else.

There was one photograph of Mason that was an especially good one, clear and full-faced. But Mick chose a different one instead. He chose the one of Mason and his sister on Emily's twenty-sixth birthday, telling himself it was because it was the most recent of the photographs, being only three months old, not because it contained a smiling Emily, radiant, festive and happy.

"Mind if I take this one?" Mick asked, handing the others back to Emily.

"No, of course not," she told him, glancing quickly at the remainder of the photos, entertaining flash-card memories of Mason. Wordlessly she looked up at Mick for some kind of reassurance, but he tucked the picture into his shirt pocket and silently returned her gaze.

"Do you think you can find him?" she finally asked.

"I'll do my best."

"I know you will."

His stomach tightened at her declaration of trust. "I'll be here tomorrow morning at eight," he said quietly.

"Thank you, Michael."

He felt himself wanting to touch her again, to bury his hands in her hair, to take her tempting mouth with his, then swore at himself for having such desires. As he was about to tell her goodbye, her telephone rang abruptly, a shrill annoyance disturbing the hushed moment that had enveloped them. Emily forced herself to look away from Michael's stormy eyes and picked up the phone with some distraction.

"Hello?" she said tentatively into the receiver, her eyes involuntarily wandering back to meet Michael's. When silence met her greeting, but the caller maintained the connection at the other end of the line, Emily's stomach began to swirl in a worried knot. "Hello?" she repeated, turning her back on Mick, not wanting him to see her concern at yet another questionable and disturbing phone call. "Is anyone there?" she asked further.

Someone was there, she knew, because whoever it was didn't hang up, even when he clearly knew he had reached a wrong number. The same someone who seemed to be telephoning at regular intervals for no apparent reason but to unsettle her. And he was beginning to succeed.

"Please try to dial more carefully next time," she muttered to the unseen caller with a nervousness in her voice that she was unable to conceal. "This is beginning to get rather tedious."

With that, she gently settled the receiver back into its cradle and stood with her arms crossed uneasily over her abdomen, her back still turned on the man watching her with a worried frown.

"Emily?" Mick asked with obvious concern. When he received no response, he ventured a few slow steps toward her. "Is everything all right?"

Emily pivoted quickly, the smile she had forced onto her face completely at odds with the anxiety darkening her green eyes.

"Everything's fine, Michael," she told him shakily. "Just a wrong number."

"Same person as the others?"

"I don't know," she confessed. "Usually whoever it is doesn't say anything. He waits for me to say something, then he just sits there, doesn't speak, doesn't hang up. Just tries to scare me."

"Is it working?" Mick asked softly.

"Yes," she stated honestly.

Mick's better judgment told him he should leave now and be on his merry way, but his conscience, not to mention his heart, forbade him to leave Emily alone in her current state. He hated seeing her frightened and sought to lighten her spirits in any way he could.

"Have you eaten dinner?" he finally asked her hesitantly.

"No, I was just going to fix a salad or something," she told him.

"There's a little seafood place down by the marina," he heard himself say, all the while mentally kicking himself for what he was about to do, knowing he would regret it later. "Why don't we go down there and grab a bite, and you can fill me in more on your brother and these phone calls that have been plaguing you."

Who was he trying to kid? Mick chastised himself. He just wanted to be alone with Emily, and they probably both knew it.

"Thanks," she smiled a little more easily. "That's nice of you. Seafood sounds wonderful."

It *was* nice of him, Emily thought. He could tell she'd been shaken by the phone call and wanted to keep her mind off her troubles. Her eyes roved hungrily over the handsome man standing so near her, his slate eyes filled with quiet concern. And that's all the invitation had been, she reminded herself. A noble gesture on Michael's part to try to ease her worries about Mason. She had hired him to help her find her brother. They had a working relationship. She'd be better off remembering that, not entertaining romantic fantasies that centered on Michael Dante.

Hastily she gathered her purse and preceded Mick through her front door, down the steps and toward his car parked on the street below. Mick watched her with mixed feelings. He was giddily happy to be spending an evening with her, yet he was troubled by a sense of forboding such as he had never before experienced. He just couldn't help but feel that he was about to let himself in for a lot more than a quiet dinner with a beautiful woman. Emily Thorne's case might just prove to be one that Mick would never be able to close.

Nickleby's Wharf, the restaurant where Mick and Emily found themselves later, was a quiet haven for the boaters and landlubbers of Cannonfire alike. Nestled at the end of a large pier near the marina, Nickleby's afforded a spectacular view of Chesapeake Bay and the Cannonfire Marina, enhanced by the restaurant's nautical ambience and warm, candle-lit dining room. Despite the fact that it was a Friday evening, the restaurant crowd was small and subdued, almost as if it were an intimate gathering of friends. The hostess greeted Mick amicably by name and instantly led the two diners to a table by the window in a secluded corner of the dining room. A waitress was there almost immediately, and the couple ordered drinks while they scanned their menus.

"Do you come here often?" Emily asked Mick when he nodded in recognition to a couple seated at the bar a short distance away.

"Once or twice a week," he told her. "I'm not much of a cook, I'm afraid. And this is only a short walk from the boat."

"The boat?" Emily suddenly realized that although Mick knew a great deal about her, she knew next to nothing about him.

"My sailboat," he clarified. "*Hestia*. She's berthed at the marina. That's where I live."

"Your boat's name is *Hestia*?" Emily asked with interest as their waitress returned with a glass of chardonnay and a bourbon and water.

"Thanks, Sandy," he said to their server. "We're going to need a few more minutes before we order."

"Sure thing, Mick. Just let me know when you guys are ready."

Mick nodded, then turned back to Emily and said, "Yes, *Hestia*. Why?"

"It just seems kind of an unusual name for you to give to a boat."

"How's that?"

"Hestia was the Greek goddess of the hearth and home life," she remarked, taking a sip of her wine. "You don't appear to be particularly domestic." On the contrary, she thought. He seemed like a predatory animal, one who made the darkest, most mysterious part of the jungle his home.

"I just thought it was a beautiful name," Mick acknowledged. "I didn't consider any implications behind it."

"Oh."

They turned their attention once again to their menus, and after they made their decisions, Mick signaled to Sandy and gave her their orders.

"You have a lot of friends here," Emily commented after yet another man had greeted Mick.

"I know a lot of people here," he corrected her, indicating that there was a difference. He wanted to say that she was the one who had a lot of friends, all up and down Cleveland Street, but kept himself quiet, unwilling to reveal how much he knew about her.

"Can we see your boat from here?" she asked suddenly, looking out the window toward the marina.

"No, she's on the other side that faces away from the town."

"I see."

Michael Dante certainly gave the impression that he wanted to be left alone by society, Emily thought, but she was having trouble believing that was actually the case. He tried to act as if he was a loner in every sense of the word, but there was something about him that suggested otherwise. The name he'd given his boat for example. And the way she caught him looking at her from time to time. He didn't seem like a loner, she decided. What he seemed was...lonely. She could almost feel it. But for some reason, he was unwilling to reach out, unwilling to accept a friendly overture from her or anyone as anything but a gesture of common courtesy. He claimed to only know the people of Nickleby's Wharf, not to be their friends, despite the obvious warmth with which they addressed him.

"Did you grow up in the Chesapeake area?" Emily asked in an effort to draw him out and learn more about him.

"No, Chicago," he answered simply, offering her nothing further.

"Do your parents still live there?"

"My father does. My mother died when I was fourteen."

"Oh, I'm sorry," she told him genuinely.

"It was a long time ago," he said, looking away from the obvious sorrow clouding her eyes. "Look, do you mind if we talk about something else?"

"Sure," she mumbled, disheartened once again that she had done something to put him off. "What do you want to talk about?"

You, he wanted to say.

"Your brother, Mason. Tell me more about him."

Emily sighed. The case. The reason she had hired him. She might as well get used to the fact that Michael Dante just wasn't interested in her. Or at least he didn't want to be. Basically it amounted to the same thing. But why was she complaining? She didn't want to get involved any more than he did. She should be relieved that his only concern was to find Mason. That was her only concern, too, wasn't it?

They spoke for some time on the topic of Mason and what little Emily knew about his job and life-style in Washington. She'd only been there to visit him on a few occasions, because he generally made it a habit to drop in on her in Cannonfire. She knew something of his friends and acquaintances and the places he liked to frequent, but not everything. She began to feel somewhat uneasy when she realized how very little she did know about her brother's way of life. If Mason had been trying to protect her from something, he had definitely succeeded.

When their dinner arrived, Emily and Mick sat in comfortable silence, enjoying their meal and each other's company. It had been a long time since Emily had shared a table with someone besides Mason. She liked the feelings she experienced while she was with Michael. He made even the most mundane activities seem very special. Normally she went home from work and put something in the microwave for dinner or threw together a salad or sandwich, then watched the news on television while she ate. With Michael, eating became a sensual pleasure, the food more delicious, the wine more intoxicating. She wished she could spend every evening this way.

"What made you decide to become a private investigator?" Emily asked as they enjoyed coffee after dinner.

"I had bills to pay," Mick told her evasively. He didn't want to talk about himself. He wanted to learn more about her.

"But how did you get involved in that line of work?" she persisted. "Was it something you wanted to do as a little boy?"

"Hardly," he muttered. "I used to work for the FBI, and after I resigned, this just seemed the most likely line of work to enter."

"You were with the FBI?" She smiled. "That must have been interesting. Was it very exciting?"

Mick liked her smile. And the fact that he seemed to fascinate her so thoroughly made his heart hum dangerously and his chest tighten with warmth.

"Actually it doesn't involve nearly as much action as people think," he confessed. "A lot of paperwork and dead ends."

"Why'd you quit?"

"I was getting too old," he stated flatly.

"Oh, please." Emily laughed, noting again with pleasure what tremendous physical shape he was in.

"Honestly," Mick assured her. "I couldn't keep up with some of the kids they were bringing in. They all seemed so young. So innocent." He took a sip of his coffee, and Emily's stomach seemed to burn as she became entranced with the way his strong throat swallowed and his full lips thinned slightly above the rim of his mug. He had looked directly into her eyes as he voiced the word *innocent*, and

Emily felt herself color, unable to look away. She wasn't innocent. Not exactly.

"I don't know," Mick continued, his eyes shadowed as he remembered some of his experiences. "I guess I just saw more of the world and the nature of mankind in that ten-year period than I wanted to see."

"What do you mean?" she asked softly, still hypnotized by his ever-changing eyes.

Mick gazed at the woman who sat across from him, marveling at her freshness of spirit, her simple way of life and uncluttered conscience. "Never mind, Emily," he said quietly. "It isn't important anymore. How about you? How long have you worked at the bookstore?"

She shrugged slightly, trying to hide her distress that he had dismissed her curiosity and broken the spell that had surrounded them so easily. "I've been managing Paradise Found for about four years, I guess."

"Any plans for the future?" he went on casually, trying to effect an air of disinterest, as if he simply wanted to keep the conversation going. It seemed to work, because Emily was looking more disappointed and saddened as she continued.

"Not really," she replied. "Nothing concrete anyway. I might go back to school someday for my master's. And I've always wanted to try my hand at—" She paused abruptly, alarmed at herself and what she had been about to reveal. She'd never told anyone about her desire to write, not even Mason.

"Try your hand at what?" he prodded.

"Nothing," she told him.

"What?" he urged.

"Nothing, really. It was just an idea I got once during college, that's all."

"What is it you want to try, Emily?" Mick asked her again.

She hesitated for a moment. "Someday, I'd like to write a sweeping historical saga." She hurried on defensively before he could laugh at her. "I've been reading books since I was a child, and every day at work I'm surrounded by them. I took some creative writing classes in college and loved them." She stopped suddenly, waiting for Michael to shoot down her dream.

"What did your teachers think?" he asked.

"They all told me I was very talented."

"Then what are you waiting for?"

Emily exhaled a relieved breath. "Inspiration, I guess," she admitted. "I've written some short stories and descriptive narratives, but I can't seem to develop anything cohesive."

"Inspiration will come, Emily," he said with certainty. "Just give it a chance. Don't worry."

It wasn't the first time he'd told her not to worry, and strangely, Emily hadn't since she'd met him. Once Michael Dante had entered her life, she'd almost immediately been bathed in a feeling of deliverance, as if she were no longer facing life's obstacles alone. It was marvelous to think she had someone to lean on, someone with whom she could share her fears and daily encounters, even if for only a short time. She only wished that Michael felt that way, too, and that it could be more than temporary.

Unfortunately he seemed to be perfectly comfortable with himself alone, thoroughly unwilling to open his life up to anyone. But Emily sensed something more to Michael Dante. He was alone and embittered by something and determined to punish himself for some unknown reason she couldn't fathom. He was a riddle. But he was a riddle she definitely wanted to solve.

As they left Nickleby's Wharf and crossed the parking lot to Mick's aged Mustang convertible, a cool breeze swept off the bay, riffling through Emily's auburn curls, bringing a brisk shiver to her bare arms. Instinctively she brought her hands up to cup her elbows, and Mick noted the gesture uncomfortably. When they reached the car, he took his jacket from the back seat where he'd tossed it and draped it around her shoulders, pulling on the lapels of the blazer until they overlapped at her neck and smiling at the picture she made.

The garment virtually swallowed her, so great was the difference in their sizes, but it smelled like Michael, and Emily pulled it snugly around her, wishing it was he filling her with warmth instead of his jacket.

Slowly Mick's hand traveled to her shoulders, smoothing the fabric of his blazer where there was no need to smooth it. He softly grasped her upper arms and gazed intently into her eyes, then gently pulled her toward him. For a moment she thought he would kiss her, and perhaps for a moment he had intended to, but he only clasped her to his heart tenderly, briefly, in an attempt to chase away her chill. As quickly as the embrace had begun, it was over, and Emily found herself back where she had started with a small distance between them, still wrapped in Michael's coat, feeling almost, but not quite, as if he still held her.

"Warming up any?" he asked her softly.

"Yes, thank you," she replied automatically, wondering if he felt as muddled and feverish as she.

Mick felt that and more. As he opened the door for Emily and helped her into the car, he caught another hint of her flowery perfume, and his knees began to feel like water. It was with considerable effort that he walked around the front of the car, opened his own door and settled himself into the driver's seat.

Holding Emily had been . . . nice. More than nice. It had been wonderful. Incredible. She'd melted into him as though she were a part of him, and for the most fleeting of moments, he thought she had been. Emily Thorne felt good to hold, he decided. She was small and delicate, but he sensed a strength in her that was unbendable. He knew it was difficult for her to deal with the circumstances of her brother's disappearance, but she was searching for answers and wouldn't quit until she found them. In addition to everything else, Emily was a fighter. Mick liked that.

When they returned to Emily's apartment, he escorted her up the stairs and waited a moment inside until she had gone into the kitchen and made certain everything was all right. When she came back into the living room to say good night, she saw Michael standing awkwardly beside her sofa, looking for all the world as if he couldn't wait to leave.

"Thank you for dinner, Michael," she told him as she drew nearer, extending his jacket in her right hand. "And thanks for your jacket. It was sweet of you."

Sweet, he echoed hollowly to himself as he took the garment she still held out to him. He didn't think anyone had ever called him sweet before. He shifted the blazer onto his shoulder, then once again, his hand seemed to act of its own free will as it rose and stroked her hair. He briefly bunched a handful of the silky strands in his fist before forcing himself to release it.

"I'll see you tomorrow morning at eight," he told her as he began to back toward the front door. "Try not to be concerned, Emily," he encouraged her again, stepping outside to look in at her through the screen door. Outside looking in felt like a much more appropriate place for him to be. "Everything will be fine."

With that pledge, he was gone, and Emily was left alone with her thoughts. For the first time in weeks, they weren't centered on Mason. Instead all she could think about was the man who had just left her apartment. The man who had touched her hair and looked into her eyes as if she were his last hope in a bitter world.

Chapter Four

The following morning was clear and beautiful, without a hint of autumn in the air. Indian summer had settled over the Chesapeake Bay, despite the arrival of October, and Emily dressed accordingly in a short-sleeved cotton dress splashed with tiny blue and yellow blossoms. She tied her unruly hair back with a pale yellow ribbon, and didn't understand the reason for Michael's frown when she met him at her front door.

Mick wasn't happy when he saw that she once again confined her curls from tumbling freely around her shoulders. But at least maybe this way he'd be able to keep his hands to himself. Maybe.

"Good morning," he greeted her in that deep, velvety voice she found so comforting. As his eyes skimmed over the rest of her, settling on her small waist and the enticing swell of her hips and breasts below and above, his frown grew into a warm smile, and his smoky eyes fairly glowed like scorching embers.

"Good morning," Emily replied a little breathlessly, pleased that his frown was gone, but somewhat unsettled by the expression that had replaced it. "You're right on time," she rushed on in an attempt to steady her erratic pulse rate. "Would you like some coffee?"

"I think it would be better if we just got under way," he told her. "It's only a two-hour drive, and traffic should be fairly light, but you can never tell how the Beltway is going to be."

"Okay," she agreed, still a little flustered. He was wearing jeans again, very faded ones that lovingly hugged his lean thighs and trim hips. His white shirt was open at the throat, and dark coils of hair peeked out at her teasingly, encouraging her fantasies about what lay farther below. Emily drew in a shaky breath. They would be seated together in a small car for over two hours. Then they would spend the day together in Washington. She gazed again at the smoldering expression on Michael's face. It was going to be an interesting day.

"I, um, I'll just get my purse," Emily said quickly as Mick began to descend the stairs. "And make sure Sophie has plenty of food," she added, watching the steady sway of his strong arms, the rhythmic rocking of his broad shoulders. "And throw some water on this fire raging through my body," she went on in a whisper, licking her lips against the dryness that constricted her throat. Oh, boy, was it going to be an interesting day.

The drive from Cannonfire to Washington, D.C., was a beautifully scenic one, but Emily paid little attention. Her scrutiny was fixed on the man in the car beside her, the man who shifted gears with fluid grace, whose black hair was fondled affectionately by the October breeze, who looked very sexy in aviator sunglasses. He had left the top down on his sleek, black Mustang, and the morning sun beat down on them with guileless warmth. It was a gorgeous day for a drive, but Emily could only appreciate the fact that she was with Michael for a whole day.

It was a feeling that brought with it both joy and fear, an alien feeling, but one she definitely welcomed. Emily had never been in love before. Not really. Not the way people were supposed to fall in love. While she had lived with her parents, her studies had been the only thing she had been allowed to pursue. Consequently friendships and social activities had bypassed her, had become things she saw other people enjoy but could never have for herself. Since college, she'd had little luck with men. What few relationships she'd found herself in had always seemed to result with her feeling empty, distant and unfulfilled, wanting to end the liaisons amicably, but end them nonetheless. She understood that there was love in the world, for other people if not for herself, because she'd read of it in books and seen it in films. But love and passion had forsaken Emily Thorne. The gods had inexplicably deemed it unnecessary to allow her the enjoyment and satisfaction that most mortals knew, and she had dealt with it philosophically, deciding she must have been intended for some other purpose here on earth.

At least that's how she'd felt until she had met Michael Dante. But from the moment she had walked into his office, had looked upon his rugged face and sculptured body, had seen the loneliness in his eyes and felt the longing in his heart, she had known a wanting such as nothing she had ever experienced. It was a new and glorious feeling, but one accompanied with some confusion. She had developed many torrid ideas where Michael was concerned, but she did not understand why they should be so intense, so demanding, when her feelings toward other men had been so tepid and weak. Nor did she know how she should approach this potent new desire. He disturbed and delighted her, and Emily wasn't sure which bothered her more. What she did know was that her immediate future was a disconcerting one.

The city of Washington, D.C., reminded Emily of a huge ivory-and-emerald necklace. In the heart of the city lay the green, green mall, lined with trees and tourists, populated by memorials and museums. It was one of her favorite places on Earth, a city she had called home for two years when her parents had taught at one of the universities there. As they drove toward Mason's Capitol Hill apartment, Emily remembered many moments as an adolescent spent wandering in the National Gallery, through the impressionist room and visiting exhibits, loving the quiet beauty that filled every painting. She had come to the mall nearly every day to do her homework or to watch the people and had been sad to leave when her parents accepted positions at Notre Dame University.

"What are you thinking about?" Mick asked her when he saw the faraway and melancholy expression on her face.

Emily looked at him quickly, embarrassed that he had caught her in such a personal moment. "I was just thinking about when I used to live here," she told him.

"When was that?"

"A long time ago," she said. "When I was about thirteen. We only lived here for a couple of years, but I loved it."

"Your parents taught here?"

She nodded. "At Georgetown."

"Did you move around a lot while you were growing up?" he asked.

"Every two or three years, I guess. My parents didn't want to limit themselves to one university," she explained.

"They wanted to expand their horizons, and mine and Mason's as well. They only stayed at Brown University for four years because I was working on my degree."

"I guess all that moving wasn't real conducive to maintaining long friendships," Mick grumbled thoughtfully.

"I wasn't kidding when I told you Mason was the closest friend I ever had," she assured him. "It wasn't just the moving, though. Mother and Dad always made us come home immediately after school to study. We weren't allowed to go out unless it was to a museum or some kind of cultural function. It was their way of making sure we got a complete education."

"A complete education includes more than lessons," Mick mumbled. "It means learning how to enjoy life, too."

"I agree with you," Emily said. "Unfortunately my parents considered most social pursuits pointless. If it didn't enrich the intellect, it was meaningless as far as they were concerned."

Mick had never even met Emily's parents but nonetheless harbored resentment toward the two people. How could they inhibit someone like Emily, restrain her spirits and emotions? He could almost envision her as a girl, impatient to be outside running through fields, skinning her knees, touching life, breathing in the pleasure of simple existence, only to be yanked into the house to ponder algebraic theories or scientific logarithms. It didn't seem fair. She had been cheated out of so much as a child.

"Take the next right," Emily instructed abruptly, bringing Mick out of his reverie. "The third house on the right is where Mason's apartment is."

The street was quiet, lined with big trees and well-kept, recently renovated brick town houses. The one that Emily indicated had a wrought-iron railing encasing the porch and stairs and window boxes full of bright red geraniums in the first-floor windows.

"Mason lives on the third floor," Emily informed Mick as they approached the house. "His landlady, Lilah, lives on the first floor, and an artist named Cinnabar Gamboge lives on the second floor."

"Cinnabar Gamboge?" Mick asked doubtfully, his mouth in a comic smirk.

Emily chuckled. "Her real name is Phyllis Murphy, but she uses Cinnabar Gamboge professionally. She's really not a very good artist," she intimated parenthetically, "but since her husband died and left her a small fortune, she paints and sculpts to keep herself occupied."

"How old is she?"

"Eighty-seven, I think. But she probably lies about her age."

"Eighty-seven?"

"And she acts like she's seventeen."

"Sounds like my kind of woman."

Emily smiled indifferently and wondered exactly what kind of woman did suit Michael Dante. Probably one a lot more hip to the dating game than she was, she mused. Certainly not one with a losing record who knew very little about pleasing a man.

She used her key to open the front door of the town house, then they climbed the stairs to the top floor apartment and unlocked that door, too. Inside the apartment, it was silent and still, looking undisturbed and uncluttered. The furniture was old and functional, with a remarkable absence of decorative touches. The apartment was clearly a man's abode. There was a couch and chair of a cream and light brown pattern, a small television and stereo, bookcases lined with books and notebooks, an old, freestanding brass lamp, and a steamer trunk for a coffee table. And there was a desk. A huge, walnut desk stacked with note-books, newspapers, magazines, maps, legal pads, envel-opes and any number of other things. It was without question the center of Mason Thorne's enterprises, the very heart of his investigative endeavors.

Beyond the living room to the left was a small dining area and kitchen, several stacks of letters and other mail nearly obscuring the small dining table. To the right of the living room was Mason's bedroom, consisting of one bed, one nightstand, one dresser and another chair.

"Mason's not what you would call an excessive person," Emily stated blandly, indicating the sparse furnishings.

"You're right about one thing, though," Mick said pen-sively. "He hasn't been home for some time."

Mick wandered through Mason's apartment, sifting quickly through his mail before turning his attention to the walnut desk.

"I could be a while going through all this," he told Em-ily almost apologetically.

Emily knew she was being dismissed and tried not to let it hurt her feelings. "I could go down and talk to Lilah and Cinnabar to see if they've heard anything from Mason," she volunteered.

"Good idea," Mick agreed as he picked up one of Mason's notebooks and began to flip through it.

"I'll be back in a little while," she said as she backed to-ward the front door.

"Fine," he mumbled distractedly, already caught up in something Mason had written.

"Fine," Emily repeated softly, feeling like a child who had been excluded from some secret club.

She went to the ground floor first to see Lilah Cameron, a woman in her fifties who had grown up in Washington and loved to tell political anecdotes. She had met Emily twice before and insisted the younger woman come in for a cup of tea. Emily wasn't in much of a mood to be entertained, but Lilah was personable and chatty and quickly cheered her guest to a point of relaxation, even sociability. The two women wound up spending a very interesting morning together.

Cinnabar Gamboge was equally pleased to see Emily, and showed her every new piece she had completed in recent weeks. She also described in vast detail her works-in-progress, particularly a plaster-of-paris buffalo currently in a crucial stage of creation. Unfortunately she, too, was unable to report news of Mason. Neither woman had heard a word from their neighbor for several weeks.

"Although, there was one evening," Cinnabar remembered at one point, "when I thought I heard your brother upstairs moving around."

"Mason was home?" Emily asked excitedly. "When?"

The old woman ran a thin, spotted hand through white hair she had streaked with a red lightning bolt and thought for a moment. Then she looked at Emily with clear blue eyes and said, "It was about two weeks ago, about a week after he left. I remember thinking that he must be home again, because a week had passed and he had said he would be home in a week."

So Mason *had* been there! But what had happened to him since then?

"Did you see him?" Emily asked the older woman. "Or talk to him?"

"No, dear, I'm sorry, I didn't. It was late evening when I heard him upstairs, and I was working on the buffalo and didn't want to quit while the muse was visiting me. I figured he'd come down in the morning to have coffee with me like he usually does, but he didn't show, and I didn't hear anything more upstairs after that."

Emily's face fell at the announcement, her hopes that Mason had been home at one point dashed. If Cinnabar hadn't actually seen him or spoken to him, there was no proof he'd actually been there. For all she knew, he was still in Mississippi or anywhere between here and there. It would appear that coming to Washington was getting them nowhere.

"Thanks, Cinnabar," she said to the other woman.

"Sorry I couldn't be more help, kiddo," the artist told her.

"That's okay."

"I'm sure your brother will turn up, Emily. And he'll have a perfectly reasonable explanation for all of this."

"I hope you're right."

"I'm sure I am."

Emily looked at Cinnabar, at the smile that crinkled the old woman's blue eyes and deepened the crags in her face. She couldn't help but feel assured and smiled in return. Then her eyes strayed to the clock and she was shocked at the length of time that had passed. Surely Michael had made some progress with the pile of information on Mason's desk. He would probably be hungry, too, she thought, since it was well past lunchtime, and she was feeling a little empty herself. After saying goodbye to Cinnabar she walked the short distance up the street to a deli she knew Mason frequented and bought sandwiches, potato salad and iced tea. As an afterthought, she bought two bottles of beer, in case Michael would want that instead.

When she got back to Mason's apartment she found Michael seated at the desk, most of what had been heaped there before now lying in several stacks on the floor. He was reading one of Mason's notebooks, one hand rubbing the forehead bent intently over the pages, the other hand holding a pen, scribbling notes in the margin of the page. He looked very serious and completely absorbed in what was contained in Mason's notes. Particles of dust, disturbed by the shifting of Mason's belongings, danced around him, sparkling in the late-afternoon sun that streamed in through the window beside him. He hadn't even heard her come in.

"Michael?" she called quietly, her throat dry and her lungs nearly empty of air. Why did her heart start beating rapid-fire every time she saw him?

Upon hearing her voice, Mick immediately turned to look at Emily. He glanced down at his watch, then back at her, amazed that so much time had passed and at how much he had missed her while she was gone.

"I thought you might be hungry," she said. "I went to a deli up the street and got some sandwiches."

"Sounds good," he told her, his voice a little rusty from disuse. "I am pretty hungry."

Mick pushed back his chair and rose slowly to stretch, all six-plus feet of him, seeming to expand and harden as he did so. He lifted a sinewy arm to the back of his neck, the corded muscles in his forearm flexing enticingly as he rubbed the stiffness out of a sore spot. Leisurely he strode toward her across the living room, his boots quietly scuffing the hardwood floor in the otherwise silent room. Emily's mouth went dry, her eyes widened in alarm, and she hurriedly stumbled past him in a wide arc toward the kitchen.

"I wasn't sure what you liked," she rushed on nervously, "so I got a little of everything."

Mick was at a loss as to why she suddenly seemed so frightened. Had she learned something from one of the women downstairs? What was going on?

"Emily?" he ventured cautiously as he followed her into Mason's tiny kitchen.

To Emily, the already-small room shrunk into a suffocating narrowness with Michael's entrance. What was wrong with her? Why did she suddenly feel so threatened by this man?

"There's chicken salad," she announced blithely as she began pulling small parcels from the two paper bags. "And pastrami, corned beef and turkey."

"Emily," Mick repeated.

"And potato salad and chips," she concluded unevenly. "I wasn't sure if you'd want iced tea or beer, so I got both."

When she'd stopped talking but kept her back turned and continued rattling paper bags and plastic cartons, Mick closed the short distance between them and placed his hands on her shoulders. Gently he turned her around to face him and cupped his hand under her chin, tipping her head back slightly to gaze down into her overly bright eyes. She was scared of something, and he'd be damned if he knew what it was.

"What's wrong?" he demanded quietly. "What's happened?"

"Nothing," she managed hoarsely. Then when she realized how stupidly she was behaving, she cleared her throat and tried to inject a little more certainty into her voice. "Nothing is wrong," she reiterated.

Mick continued to gaze at her, feeling himself falling once again into the green seas of her eyes, wanting to know if her lips were as soft as they appeared. She was so beautiful. And he wanted her so badly.

With that realization, Mick experienced his own kind of fear, one that nearly crippled him. He had to stop thinking about Emily this way. It would only bring them both heartache when their time together came to an end. Emily Thorne was a nice kid. She deserved a nice life with a nice guy. Not some quick affair with a battered up old relic plagued by haunting memories and a cloudy conscience. It could be incredible for a while, of that he was sure. But it would eventually come to an end, as it always did, and it would leave them both feeling bruised and barren.

The hand cupping Emily's chin rose and softly touched her cheek, then quickly dropped back to Mick's side. He exhaled a breath he hadn't been aware of holding, then reached past her for one of the bottles of beer that sat on the counter.

"You say you got corned beef?" he asked halfheartedly, unscrewing the bottle cap and tossing it back with a clatter onto the countertop.

"With mustard," Emily told him, relieved that a tense moment had passed.

"That'll be a good start." He took the paper-wrapped sandwich she offered him and walked to the dining room table, pushing aside a stack of envelopes to make room for their late lunch. Emily chose for herself the turkey sandwich then joined him, sitting on the opposite side of the table.

"What did you find out from Lilah and Cinnabar?" he asked her.

"Neither one has heard a word from Mason, but Cinnabar says she heard him moving around up here one night about a week after he'd left."

"How does she know it was Mason?"

Emily shrugged. "I guess she just assumed. Why? Do you think someone else might have been up here?"

Mick took a thoughtful swallow of beer, then said, "Maybe. None of his mail has been opened. Even things postmarked just after his disappearance that would have been here a week after he left. If he was home then, why wouldn't he have opened them?"

"You think someone could have broken in?" she wondered fearfully.

"There was no sign of forced entry on the door," Mick told her. "I haven't checked all the windows, but nothing seems to be out of place."

"True," Emily agreed hesitantly.

"Still, we can't rule anything out yet."

"What about the newspaper?" she remembered. "Did you call them?"

Mick nodded. "They weren't very cooperative. They said Mason was on assignment and couldn't be reached."

"Did they mention the unpredictable climate or massive political upheaval?" she asked him sarcastically.

"No, actually," he told her mildly. "It was the geographic isolation and intrepid landscape this time."

"They haven't used that one for a while," Emily commented with derision. "Makes it sound like he's lost on Tierra del Fuego or fallen into Mount St. Helens."

"It does reinforce the fact that something is definitely going on. And the newspaper knows it. They can't even decide on a joint excuse for his absence."

"Did you discover anything from Mason's notes?" she asked hopefully.

"Not really. Generally everything on Mason's desk is research from stories I assume have already been published. Certainly there's nothing there that's earth-shattering or politically threatening." He paused for a moment, deep in thought. "There's got to be more to this than we've been able to uncover," he said with sudden vehemence. "A man doesn't just drop off the face of the earth for no reason." He pushed his chair away from the table and went back into the kitchen. At the door he halted and looked back at Emily. "Could Mason have gotten into something he shouldn't have and been forced to go underground?"

"Go underground?" she asked, clearly puzzled.

"Made himself disappear because of some trouble he found himself in?" Mick clarified.

Emily thought very seriously before responding. "No, I honestly don't think so. If that were the case, I think he would have let me know somehow so that I wouldn't worry. He and I are so close, Michael. Mason would never leave me hanging this way, not for this length of time. He'd do something to let me know he was all right. If he was able to."

Mick watched her with some concern. She was worried again, and he was responsible. Dammit, why couldn't he figure this thing out? There had to be *something*, some clue that would at least hint at Mason's whereabouts.

"There must be some other explanation then," he muttered. "If only we could come up with one good idea. Then maybe other pieces might start to fall into place."

Emily watched Mick go into the kitchen and pull another sandwich from the bag on the counter. She knew that he was as frustrated as she, but try as she might, she could come up with nothing that might help them in their search. When Mick rejoined her at the table, he tried a different tack.

"You mentioned you knew some of the places Mason frequents," he reminded her. "Bars? Nightclubs?"

"There's a jazz club in Georgetown called Havern's Tavern," Emily told him. "Willie Havern is a friend of Mason's from college. He might know something, I guess."

"It's worth a try," Mick said, draining the last of his beer and biting into the pastrami sandwich. After he swallowed, he smiled at Emily. "Feel like going to hear a little cool jazz tonight?"

Emily smiled back. "Cool, nothing," she told him. "Willie and the Wailers play some of the hottest sessions this side of New Orleans. And the food at Havern's is fabulous."

"It's a date, then."

Our second, Emily realized silently, wondering where this whole escapade would lead them. Hopefully to Mason, she tried to tell herself confidently, ignoring the other hope that took hold of her heart, the one that wished for something more with Michael. Right now she would focus her attentions on finding her brother. Only then would she allow herself to anticipate something more. Only then could she explore these new feelings pushing their way into her heart.

"A date," she repeated softly and sipped her iced tea. One that, with any luck at all, would ultimately lead to more than just a clue to her brother's whereabouts.

Havern's Tavern was by no means the swankest or most talked-about night spot in Washington, D.C., but at some point in the evening, Mick decided that it was probably the hippest. Hidden halfway down an alley off a side street of a side street, its entrance obscured by a fire escape and a Dumpster, Havern's was packed with a young, well-dressed, jazz-loving clientele. They were a crowd who spoke low and sipped their drinks languidly in deference to the bluesy, smoky music radiating from a four-piece band that blew cool notes from a tiny stage squatting in the corner of the dark room. The bar was humid and close, but not unpleasantly so. It revived Mick's awareness that he was alive, real, as if the music flowed straight into his soul. His heart thumped in time with the rhythm of percussion, his blood meandered in his veins to the ceaseless wailing of the saxophone. As he followed Emily through the dim room, past the lines of rocking, swaying people, Mick felt the day's tensions ease from his body, replaced by a desire to sit at a table in the shadows, sip a cool, frothy beer, and kiss Emily between songs when the dusky light fell even lower.

Instead they found themselves at a small, meagerly lit table near the bar, a position that inhibited any intimate behavior on Mick's part, but which provided quick service for that much-needed beer. When the waitress arrived with their orders, Emily asked if Willie would be performing tonight and was answered with a brilliant smile from their server.

"Oh, you bet," the young woman told them. "The Wailers's first set isn't until ten, but Willie's been edgy as an alley cat all night."

"Could you do me a favor?" Emily asked her.

"Sure thing."

"Could you find Willie and tell him Emily Thorne, Mason's sister, is here and would like to say hello?"

"You're Mason's sister?" The woman's smile brightened further.

"You know him?" Emily's voice was laced with something akin to relief. Talking about Mason, meeting someone else who knew him, seemed to reinforce her confidence that he was all right.

"'Course I know Mason," their server continued. "Everybody here knows Mason. My name is Rose. I'll tell Willie you're asking after him."

"Thanks," Emily told her, lifting her glass of wine to her lips.

"Your brother seems to be very popular," Mick commented after a moment.

"He's something of a ladies' man," Emily admitted. "He can charm more than the socks off a woman. Even Cinnabar has a crush on him."

Mick thought about that for a moment, then took a substantial swallow of his beer. Emily's frank implication of Mason's sexual prowess surprised him. Not just the fact that she spoke of it, but even that she knew about it. Certainly she was a grown woman of an age where sexual activity was no great mystery of life. But there was a beguiling absence in her character of the usual suggestiveness or innuendo he normally received from women he met or dated. The only hints of her interest in him came from subtle changes in her facial expressions, changes that he found both fascinating and irresistible. Emily Thorne was a woman with strong desires. Desires that had so far been left unappeased by other men. How long before her hunger grew to the point where she would no longer be able to tolerate simply gazing at what would satisfy her appetite? How long before she would reach out to touch, to taste?

Mick watched her sip her wine slowly, entranced by the moisture left behind on her tempting mouth. Her lips parted softly, then the tip of her tongue appeared briefly to lick the dampness away. Mick felt his body stir, felt the longing rise within him to touch her again. When the band began to play once more, something slow and sensuous and sweet, he suddenly heard his voice break the silence between them, though he couldn't remember having chosen to speak.

"Dance with me," he murmured to Emily, leaning close so that his words had only a short distance to travel. He didn't know why he asked her to dance. Hell, he didn't even *like* to dance. But it was a way to be close to Emily, to hold her, to feel her, without seeming as desperate as he felt.

A flash of panic coursed through Emily at the simple request. She had never danced with a man like Michael. A man who made her blood simmer and her heart jump just by walking into a room. But she wanted to dance with him. Wanted more than a dance. Much more. For now, though, just to be near him, to touch him, would satisfy her wants. For now, a dance would do.

"Okay," she managed, her voice barely above a husky whisper.

He took her hand in his and guided her carefully through the crowds of people who seemed to sense him coming and moved easily out of his way. On the tiny, linoleum-covered dance floor, he enveloped Emily in his big arms, wrapping them tightly around her shoulders to effectively trap her close to his heart in an unescapable embrace. Emily felt almost overwhelmed by the absolute possession of her he seemed to want to display, but instead of being offended by it, she was inexplicably reassured. She laid her head softly upon his chest, listening to the gentle *thump-thump-thump* of his heart beneath her ear and smiled at the simple joy the sound brought to her own heart. As Mick's hand left her shoulder to slide up to her nape and tangle freely in her hair, she closed her eyes and tried to concentrate on steadying her breathing and slowing the quickened pace of her blood. But when she felt Michael lower his head to place a chaste kiss on her temple, she opened her eyes again and lifted them to meet his. A dark storm raged within their gray depths, a whirlwind of emotion and conflict clouding any hint of what he might be truly feeling. His feet stilled their languid paces then, and the subtle sway of their bodies that had passed for dancing ceased as he lowered his head once more and tenderly brushed his lips against hers in a soft caress. Emily's eyes fluttered shut and she sighed involuntarily, a breath of longing that became a quiet moan.

"Oh, Michael," she groaned almost painfully. "Please kiss me."

Mick was ready to obey with the most heated and heart-stopping kiss in his arsenal when a man's voice called out toward the dance floor from some distance away.

"Emily! Where'd you go, baby?"

Her eyes snapped open immediately, and she felt confused and irritated, as if startled awake from an utterly peaceful dream by a raucous fire alarm.

Mick swore softly at himself for having lost control and for allowing himself to be swept away by the woman he still held in his arms. Then in a burst of realization, the last word of the faceless man's inquiry sunk in, and Mick grew angry that someone was calling his Emily "baby."

"Baby?" he muttered petulantly.

"It's Willie," Emily explained breathlessly. "He calls everybody 'baby.' Sort of a trademark with him. Like his sunglasses."

"Sunglasses?"

"And his hats."

"Hats?"

"He always wears hats and sunglasses. You'll see."

This time it was Mick who followed Emily back to their table, admiring her feline grace as she wound through the people who'd seemed to triple in number during their short interlude on the dance floor.

"Willie!" she called to a reed-thin, well-dressed man who stood near their table with his back to them. At her summons, the man turned around, and Mick smiled at the epitome of a jazz musician who grinned broadly at Emily and swept her up in a hug. Willie wore a thin-lapelled suit of some shimmery, wine-colored fabric, a gray shirt with tiny wine and black diamonds on it, and just about the skinniest black necktie Mick had ever seen. Willie's sable-skinned face was accented by a black goatee, black wayfarer sunglasses and a black beret tipped cockily to one side. On his left pinky, a small ruby ring winked in the dim light of the bar.

"Emily, baby." Willie laughed and gave her a final hug. "Long time, no see. How you been, kid?"

"Fine, Willie. How about yourself?"

"Can't complain."

"I'd like you to meet a friend of mine," she continued as Mick took his place beside her. "Willie Havern, this is Michael Dante. Michael, this is Willie."

"Call me Mick." He took the hand Willie extended and shook it firmly. "Nice to meet you. This is quite a club you have here."

"Thank you," Willie acknowledged with a nod. "Glad you both came by." To Emily he asked, "How's Mason? I haven't seen him for a while. When Rose told me you were here, I thought he might be with you."

Emily's face fell at the statement. "I haven't seen him, either, Willie. We were kind of hoping you had."

Willie's gaze shifted from Emily to Mick and back to Emily.

"What is it, baby?" he asked Emily quietly. "Has something happened to Mason?"

Emily sank slowly into her chair, and the two men followed suit. For a moment she only sat silently, absently turning her wineglass at the base, and stared unseeingly into its transparent depths. Then her eyes fell to the scarred tabletop and she sighed.

"Mason's missing," she told Willie numbly. "And I'm beginning to think we'll never find him."

"Missing?" Willie grimaced. "How can a man as big and noisy and downright obnoxious as your brother be missing?"

Emily smiled sadly at his attempt to lighten her mood. "He's just disappeared. No one's seen him nor heard from him for three weeks."

"What about the newspaper?"

"They say he's on assignment."

"Well?"

Emily's eyes became fearful. "They're lying, Willie. I know they are. Something has happened to Mason, and they won't say what. It's driving me crazy."

Willie looked to Mick, who held the musician's gaze and said nothing, silently concurring with Emily's allegations.

"Have you called the police?" Willie wanted to know, turning back to Emily.

"They can't help as long as the paper is sticking to its story."

"How about the feds?"

Emily looked up. "The feds?"

"Yeah, baby. You know, the FBI."

"Won't they just tell me the same thing the police did?"

"Yes," Mick finally spoke up. "They will." But it gave him an idea. When he called Sam in the morning, he could ask him to look into Mason's disappearance as a favor. After all, he owed Mick. Mick was the one who'd found Sam broken and beaten up in the desert three years ago and had driven like a banshee to get him to Tate Memorial Hospital in Phoenix. If it hadn't been for Mick, Sam never would have heard the words "Mercy Malone."

"And just where do you come into all this, Mr. Dante?" Willie asked Mick with just a hint of menace in his voice.

So Willie felt it, too, Mick thought with wry humor. This protectiveness, this sense of needing to keep Emily safe. He was concerned for her welfare, too, and Mick couldn't fault the man for his somewhat threatening behavior. If the situation were reversed, if Mick was the one who questioned Willie's intentions in the matter, who wondered just what the guy was up to, he'd probably have the other man by the throat about now. Instead he took a deep swallow of his beer and met Willie's warning with a benign expression.

"I'm helping Emily look for her brother," he stated simply.

Willie's face relaxed a little, but he still looked to Emily for confirmation.

"I hired Michael," she assured him. "He's a private investigator."

The other man nodded agreeably, but Mick still sensed that he remained a little suspicious. Mick could respect that. But he knew it was completely unnecessary. From now on, he would be the one who kept an eye on Emily, who made certain she was well protected. Whether she knew it or not, whether she liked it or not. It wasn't a desire for male dominance that made him feel that way, nor was it a primitive, animalistic sense of territorial rights. It was, quite simply, a fact of life, a law of nature. Mick Dante would watch out for Emily Thorne, would see that she was safe and be there for her when she needed him. And things would be that way forever. That's all there was to it.

"Look, Mr. Havern . . ." Mick began.

"Willie."

Mick smiled indifferently and mumbled, "Thanks." Willie tilted his head forward in acknowledgement.

"Willie," Mick started again, "whatever has happened to Mason, I believe it has something to do with his most recent assignment for the newspaper, simply because they're being so evasive about this whole thing."

"Sounds logical," Willie concurred.

"But we're having trouble figuring out what his last assignment was. We're getting mixed signals from the paper, and we have absolutely no leads. Now, how long ago did you last see Mason?"

"I haven't seen him for a couple of months, I guess," Willie said thoughtfully. Then a sudden memory lit his face. "No, wait a minute. He came in on Gizelle's birthday to have a drink."

"Gizelle?" Mick asked.

"My lady."

"Ah."

"It was at the end of August," Willie went on. "The twenty-ninth."

"Did he mention anything about going out of town?" Emily asked hopefully.

"Yeah, but he just said he was heading down south. I asked him if he was going as far as New Orleans, because I have friends there, and he said he might be able to make a quick trip into the Big Easy."

"He told me he was going to Mississippi," Emily said.

"Well, if he was going to the right part of Mississippi, he was only a frog's groan away from New Orleans," Willie told her. "I offered to give him some numbers of people to call there, but he never got back to me, so I figured maybe he didn't go."

"He went," Emily asserted. "I know he did. He called me from there."

Mick's brain lurched into gear at her statement. "Emily, does Mason have a long-distance credit card?"

"I'm sure he does. He makes so many long-distance calls from so many places that it's a necessity."

"His phone bill was in with the mail on his dining-room table," Mick muttered, to himself more than anyone. "I was so preoccupied with going through his notes, I barely glanced through it all."

Boy, Emily really had him rattled, Mick mused. He was forgetting to use the most basic of his investigative skills. If he wasn't more careful, he was going to blow the whole investigation. He looked at her and hoped she wasn't regretting her decision to hire him.

"It isn't a lot," he told her with soft reassurance, "but it's a start. At least it will verify where he's been, who he's called."

"There is one other thing," Willie told them.

"What's that?" Mick asked.

"Mason was with a woman when he came in on Gizelle's birthday."

"He's always with a woman," Emily stated with a careless shrug. "That's no big surprise."

"This one was different," Willie remarked mysteriously.

"Different?" Mick asked.

"She was like no woman I've ever seen Mason date. And I've seen the man date quite a few."

"What do you mean?" Emily's eyes narrowed doubtfully.

"It's hard to explain," Willie continued. "She was just, I don't know, like no one I would ever imagine Mason asking out. She was real young for one thing. She probably wasn't legal for the club, but she was with Mason, and she didn't drink, so I didn't ask."

"How young?" Mick wanted to know.

"Late teens, probably. And she wasn't particularly good-looking, either. I thought that was kind of unusual."

"Looks aren't everything, Willie," Emily sniffed indignantly.

"I know that, baby, but have you ever known your brother to go out with a woman who wasn't drop-dead gorgeous?"

"No..."

"Well, then."

"What else, Willie?" Mick prodded.

"She was very quiet, didn't seem well educated, wasn't especially well dressed, and she didn't like the band. No taste, I guess," he added with a quiet mutter. "She also didn't have much of a sense of humor. What she did have was a strong backwoods accent. She also seemed kind of uncomfortable in a crowd."

"Uncomfortable?" Mick asked.

"Kept looking over her shoulder. Didn't want to hang around. We were all just blown away by the fact that Mason Thorne was out on a date with such a shy, quiet, unspirited woman. They were just too different from each other, and she was definitely a far cry from the women he normally dates."

"Do you remember her name?"

"Something weird," Willie said, shaking his head slowly in an attempt to remember clearly. "Something totally un-feminine. I recall thinking, 'Jeez, poor kid. No looks, no brains, no personality and a dumb name to top it all off.'"

"Willie!" Emily chided.

"Sorry, baby, but I calls 'em like I sees 'em."

Emily frowned at her brother's friend.

"I do remember her saying she was from West Virginia, though," Willie concluded triumphantly.

Mick was going to ask him something else, but they were interrupted by another member of Willie's band, a young, wiry, dark-haired youth who looked far too young to be playing in bars.

"Willie-man," the other musician said, clapping Willie on the shoulder. "You're going to have to say good-night to your friends now, 'cause we gotta be onstage in twenty minutes."

"Stovepipe, baby." Willie grinned at the other man. Like Willie, he wore a skinny necktie and sunglasses with his suit, but had the added accessory of two drumsticks poking out of his jacket pocket. "Meet some friends of mine. Emily Thorne," Willie indicated Emily, who extended her hand to Stovepipe.

"You Mason's sister?" Stovepipe purred.

"Guilty," Emily confessed with a laugh.

"*Very* nice to meet you," he murmured as he lifted Emily's open palm to his lips and raised Mick's hackles in the process.

"And her man, Mick Dante," Willie continued, sweeping his open hand playfully toward Mick, who rose to his full height and glared down at Stovepipe. He knew he should discourage any kind of introduction that suggested he was "Emily's man," but at the moment, he kind of liked the sound of it.

"Yipe," Stovepipe mumbled, quickly releasing Emily's hand. "Mr. Dante," he went on in greeting. "Sir. Pleasure to meet you."

"Yeah, right," Mick grumbled, his back up at the younger man's formal address. He wasn't *that* old, dammit.

"Stovepipe," Emily said thoughtfully, her face displaying a faraway expression. "That's an unusual nickname. How did you get it?"

"Mason always calls me that," the young musician explained. "I think it's because I'm so skinny and I always wear dark gray or black."

"I see." Something had started to open in the back of Emily's brain when she had heard Willie say "Stovepipe," some memory that had begun to surface. Mick watched her expression with growing curiosity, but said nothing. If she was remembering something important, he didn't want to interrupt her recollection.

"Stovepipe," she repeated thickly. Memories began to tumble freely from the hazy window that had opened in her mind. "Stovepipe," she said again, more loudly this time as the image became clearer.

"Yes?" Stovepipe responded.

Emily stared at him blankly for a moment as if she didn't know who the boy was or what she was doing in a Georgetown jazz club. Stovepipe continued to stare at her questioningly, and finally Emily snapped back to reality.

"No, not you." She laughed as one might laugh after unlocking the secrets to the universe—with uncertain delight. "I mean, stove pipe! Why didn't I think of it before?" She grasped Mick's hand firmly in her own. "Michael, we have to get back to Mason's apartment immediately."

"What is it, Emily?"

"I'll explain on the way. Come on!"

She rose from her chair so quickly that she almost toppled it over, yanking on Mick's hand so urgently that he nearly spilled his beer. As an afterthought, she remembered the two musicians.

"It was nice meeting you, Stovepipe," she called over her shoulder as she turned to make their exit. "And thanks for the info, Willie. If you remember Mason's date's name, give me a call. I'll be at Mason's."

With that she pulled Mick toward the door of Havern's Tavern, out into the alley, past the Dumpster and the fire escape, to the side street where Mick's car awaited them.

Chapter Five

I can't believe I didn't remember this right away," Emily remarked excitedly as she and Mick unlocked Mason's front door. "When we were kids, my parents absolutely forbade us to read anything they considered frivolous or intellectually damaging. With me it was teen heartthrob magazines. My hiding place for them was under the Oriental carpet in Dad's office."

"Didn't he ever find them?" Mick asked her.

She shook her head. "He wasn't the world's most observant man. And Mason always hid his comic books in the kitchen exhaust flue. It was perfect, because my mother hated to cook. She never went near the stove."

Emily hurried into the kitchen, flipping on the light switch as she passed it, and before the fluorescent bulb had even sputtered to full power, was at the stove inspecting the fan above it.

"We'll need a screwdriver," she announced. "Phillips head."

Mick had followed her hasty flight to the kitchen and now leaned casually in the doorway, looking a little skeptical.

"Are you sure about this?" he asked uncertainly. "I mean, this seems a little unlikely. That a grown man would resort to—"

"Michael," Emily interrupted, "trust me. I know my brother." She went to a drawer beside the sink and began to search furiously for a screwdriver. "Come on, Mason," she grumbled, "I know you've got one in here somewhere."

With a sudden, quick tug, she pulled the drawer completely out and turned it upside down, emptying its contents onto the kitchen floor.

"Emily!" Mick cried, kneeling when she did to sort through the collection of odds and ends. "Relax, will you? We'll find it."

"Why do men have to be such pack rats?" she asked no one in particular as her fingers came into contact with fuses, rubber bands, batteries, assorted keys, a flashlight and some paper clips, among other things. "I'll bet he never even uses half this stuff."

"Is this what you're looking for?" Mick held up a screwdriver as if it were a trophy.

"Is it a Phillips?"

"Of course."

"That's it," she responded, reaching for the instrument in question.

"I'll do it," he told her as he rose and moved toward the stove. "You clean up that mess you made," he added, indicating the pile of junk she had scattered to every corner of the kitchen floor.

"You're beginning to sound more like Mason every minute," Emily mumbled under her breath. "You're bossy and you think you know everything."

Mick smiled at the playful banter they were enjoying. It surprised him that he could be in a kitchen with a woman having a wonderful time.

"I'm beginning to think I'll like your brother when I meet him," he told Emily as he began to unwind the last screw.

"The two of you should get along famously," she agreed lightly, then sobered when a new thought pushed its way into her mind. "I only hope you do get to meet him, Michael."

Mick frowned at her anxious expression, wishing he could say something to ease her mind. When he finally loosened the screen that covered the oven fan, he carefully removed it and placed it on the countertop, then held his breath as he slowly reached inside. Emily came up behind him, her attention focused fully on the muscular arm that entered the fan's exhaust system.

"I don't believe it," Mick spoke quietly in the silence that had surrounded them. "There's something in here."

Carefully he grasped a handful of papers and cautiously began to remove them from the flue. Emily watched with wide eyes as Michael's hand freed what had been caught in the pipe, then slumped her shoulders with defeat when she beheld the two Batman comic books that unfurled as he cradled them so warily in his hands.

"Damn you, Mason," she moaned. "You'll never change, you jerk."

Mick frowned at the comic books and tossed them onto the counter beside the screen, then shoved his hand back into the exhaust flue, reaching farther up this time.

"Wait, Emily, there's something else in here," he told her firmly.

"Yeah, probably the Silver Surfer," she remarked dryly. "He liked those, too."

Mick made a face, then carefully pulled a rolled-up file folder from the flue.

"I think maybe this held a little more interest for your brother than comic books," he muttered thoughtfully. "Now let's see what we've got, shall we?"

He carried the file folder almost reverently into the living room, pausing only briefly at the dining-room table to retrieve Mason's phone bill from the pile of mail. Then he and Emily sat down on the sofa and opened the folder to spread its ample contents across the steamer trunk that passed for a coffee table. Inside were several pages of handwritten notes, copies of some memos and letters bearing the Connery Corporation letterhead, booklets of commercial information on the company, and well-worn maps of the United States, Mississippi and West Virginia.

"Well, if nothing else, your brother is certainly thorough in his investigations," Mick muttered. "It could take days to get through all this stuff."

"I could have told you that Mason takes his work *very* seriously," Emily assured him. "He never does anything halfway, and he's responsible to a fault when it comes to getting his story."

"Well, at least it brings us much closer," he proclaimed as a flicker of interest ignited his eyes. "This file will probably hold quite a few of the answers we've been looking for."

"And then some," she mumbled.

They spent the rest of Saturday evening inspecting Mason's notes of what was evidently his most recent story for *The Capitol Standard*. What had begun as an investigation into some questionable activities of a nationally known and widely respected industrial community known as the Connery Corporation, or more familiarly ConCorp, had apparently led to Mason's discovery that the company was little more than a front for organized crime whose kingpin was none other than Everett Connery himself.

"This is incredible," Mick said at one point as he flipped through several pages of notepaper covered with Mason's scrawling handwriting. "If what your brother thinks is true, it would appear that the Connery Corporation has gotten itself into something highly profitable, but very illegal."

"What kind of something?" Emily asked him, dropping the pamphlet she had been scanning onto her lap. She rubbed her eyes wearily. "I'm getting nothing from what I've read so far. Just a long discourse on how ConCorp chooses its trade routes."

"Ignore it. That's just PR. Everett Connery is going to have a lot more than trade routes to explain after this story gets out."

"What are you talking about, Michael?"

"Organized crime," he told her emphatically.

"Organized crime? What would a company like Con-Corp have to do with organized crime? That's like calling the Pillsbury Doughboy a gangster."

"One of the oldest reasons in the book," Mick said. "Greed. Pure and simple. They're into everything from illegal gaming to extortion and bribery. They've even got a drug-smuggling operation going."

"But that's ridiculous," Emily countered. "The company probably makes more money now than they know what to do with. Besides, they'd have to be insane to think they could get away with it. They're far too exposed to public scrutiny."

"Not insane, brilliant," he contradicted. "According to your brother's notes, they've established some very successful smoke screens and completely untraceable outlets for all of their operations to prevent a finger ever being directed at them.''

"But Everett Connery is one of the most successful and respected businessmen around. He's all over the papers, nearly every day, and he owns practically half of the country. Why would he risk all that by getting involved with criminal activities?''

"Emily, it's not clear here how long this has been going on, but Mason seems to think that the crimes are occurring in nearly every area of the corporation, with old Everett's consent. He may have originally financed his entire empire this way years ago. He rose pretty fast in the business world, from pretty meager beginnings."

Mick's eyes were radiant with the light of discovery. He could hardly believe some of the things revealed in Mason's investigation. If all the allegations Emily's brother made were true, a huge, immensely powerful corporate dynasty and a vast number of seemingly innocent businessmen could be no more than the world's largest crime syndicate. And if Mason ever provided evidence to substantiate the charges, he would probably find his name on every hit list in the country. Whenever a single, honest working man went up against a totally corrupt corporate giant, he could pretty well kiss his life-style and loved ones goodbye. What Mason had stumbled onto could put a lot of greedy, amoral people in prison for a long, long time and completely strip them of their wealth and status. And, well, greedy, amoral people generally didn't take too kindly to that sort of thing.

Emily was quiet for a long time, lost in thought. "It seems like Everett Connery would have been caught long before now if that were the case," she finally said.

"Not if he was very careful," Mick told her. "And from the looks of what Mason has discovered, caution is first and foremost in the man's mind. Especially where the smuggling operation is concerned. And that seems to be where Mason was focusing his investigation when he disappeared."

"What do you mean?"

"I mean that Mason was going down to Roadside because that was the origin of one of ConCorp's smuggling routes for narcotics." He opened up the map of Mississippi and spread it across the piles of clutter on the steamer trunk, then picked up a pencil and absently threaded it through his fingers as he explained the essence of Mason's notes to Emily.

"If everything he's recorded here is true, the Connery Corporation and a large number of its subsidiaries and executives, Everett Connery among them, could be charged with smuggling, conspiracy, racketeering, extortion, bribery, illegal trade practices, even murder."

Emily's eyes grew wide with fear. "Murder?"

"Your brother could be in a lot more trouble than you know."

"Oh, God." She swallowed with some difficulty and drew a trembling breath. "Just what all did Mason discover?" she asked worriedly.

Mick raised his brows and sighed. "Well, Mason had been investigating ConCorp for a variety of crimes until last August when he turned his attention to the smuggling operation. His notes indicate that someone named Lou came to the newspaper and told him about her family business in West Virginia."

"West Virginia?" Emily sat up in full attention and let the ConCorp brochure on her lap drop to the floor. She remembered Willie's statement about Mason and the woman from West Virginia, the woman with a "weird" and "totally unfeminine" name. "Do you think that's who was with Mason when he saw Willie at Havern's?"

"I'm sure of it."

"What else is in Mason's notes?" Her look of concern forced Mick to continue, even though he knew she would be far more worried by the time he finished.

"You're not going to like it," he warned her.

"Tell me."

"Mason's trying to prove that Everett Connery is a crime boss in every sense of the word, and that in addition to a wealth of conventional crime, the man is promoting a huge smuggling operation. Your brother has uncovered an entire network of obscure communities across the country that are acting as drop-off points and distribution centers of illegal narcotics. And because ConCorp has corporate offices and subsidiary companies in just about every state, certainly every major city, not to mention a fleet of trucks and commercial vessels at their disposal, they can run a very effective operation without raising much suspicion. At least, they could until Mason came along."

"What do you mean by 'obscure communities'?" Emily asked.

"ConCorp has located several very rural, backwoods towns, and through the promise of money and a few choice terror tactics, has convinced their inhabitants to participate in the smuggling. I'm sure Roadside is just such a community. And we know Mason was there because his call to you from there appeared on his phone bill. Look, it isn't even on the Mississippi map. Mason drew it in himself." Mick indicated a smudge of ink near the borders of Mississippi, Louisiana and Arkansas. "Unfortunately Lou's town in West Virginia is identified in his notes only as *HC*, and I'm betting it won't be found on any map, either. That puts our investigation at something of a dead end, since Mason hasn't made any calls from West Virginia."

There was another question floating with surprising calm through Emily's mind, one she was almost afraid to ask. She closed her eyes and said softly, "Earlier, you mentioned the word *murder*."

He had been waiting for her to bring that up. "Yes."

"Just what exactly were you referring to?" When she opened her eyes, she saw that Michael's expression had adopted a harder, almost brutal quality.

"Mason's notes indicate that there's a ConCorp executive, Steven Destri, who's essentially in charge of the smuggling operation, the man whose job is to make sure things run smoothly at any cost. He seems to achieve this through some pretty nasty means."

"Like what?"

"Some of the families in these communities were no doubt lured into the operation by the promise of a good deal of money. I'd imagine quite a few of them were unbelievably poor to begin with."

"But?"

"But the ones who were morally or ethically opposed to getting involved were...persuaded...through other means."

"You mean they were threatened," Emily said.

"Yes."

"With murder."

"Yes."

"But, Michael, threatening is one thing. Carrying out those threats is altogether—"

"They weren't idle threats, Emily," he interrupted. "There's evidence that Steven Destri arranged the deaths not only of people found to be disloyal to the operation, but that he also was the triggerman at the murder of two federal agents."

"Oh, Michael!" Emily's hands flew to cover her open mouth in horror, and she felt her blood turn icy. "If they're capable of that, then they're capable of . . . I mean Mason was only a reporter. They wouldn't think twice about . . ." She couldn't say it. She wouldn't allow herself to even think it. Mason was alive. She was as certain of that as she was her own life. But she was also aware that time was passing quickly. Mason had been missing for weeks. How much longer did they have to find him before ConCorp caught up with him, if they hadn't already?

"There's some hope, Emily," Mick tried to reassure her.

"What hope could there possibly be?" she muttered.

"Mason already has hard evidence in his possession that could incriminate Everett Connery and Steven Destri and several others on a number of felony charges."

"What kind of evidence?"

"He doesn't say. His notes only specify that it's substantial and in safekeeping. I don't know where."

"Why should that be reassuring?"

"Emily, if Mason is in trouble, the very fact that this evidence exists could ensure his safety."

"In what way?"

Mick took her hand gently as he spoke. "The threat of discovery could dissuade anyone at ConCorp who might consider disposing of Mason."

"Disposing of him," she repeated quietly. Her eyes glittered as fearful tears gathered. Mick was stunned at the feeling of helplessness that overcame him as he watched fat tears tumble silently down her pale cheeks. He wanted to fold his arms around her, envelop her in a cocoon of protective intentions and kiss away her sorrow. Yet he remained still and uncertain, and reluctantly released her hand.

"Oh, Michael," she finally mumbled. "What are we going to do?"

"It's too late to do anything tonight," he told her softly, finally allowing his hand to travel to her face and gently brush the dampness from her silky skin. Her emerald eyes lifted to his stormy ones in unspoken thanks for his concern, and she smiled a little shakily. He returned her smile and continued. "Tomorrow morning, there's someone I want to see, a friend of mine who might be able to help us."

"How?"

"Look, it's too long a story to go into tonight. After I see him we can go back to Cannonfire to regroup. How early do you have to be at work?"

"The bookstore is closed on Sunday," she told him, "so it doesn't really matter what time I get back."

"Good. Then right now I think a little sleep is in order. I'll take the couch," he offered. "Where does Mason keep his extra sheets?"

Emily was more than a little uneasy to be sleeping under the same roof with Michael, and the flash of alarm that passed through her eyes alerted him to her feelings. He still scared her a little, he thought with some discomfort. He supposed that was a good thing, though, seeing as how he wanted to keep her at a distance. But for some reason, the idea that she found him intimidating bothered him. He wanted to show her that he could be tender, could love her gently, then he wanted to kick himself for entertaining such desires. He remembered his avowal to Sam and repeated it to himself. He wasn't in love with her. Yet as Emily rose and made her way into Mason's bedroom for extra sheets and a pillow, in his mind's eye he saw himself follow her and close the door behind them.

"Oh, Emily," he whispered almost silently, "the fires we could set together, the stars that we could reach."

"Did you say something, Michael?" She returned from Mason's room with bedclothes and a spare pair of men's pajamas that looked as though they'd never been worn.

"Nothing," he muttered. He took the linens she handed him, but immediately gave back the pajamas. "I won't need these," he told her, but offered no further explanation.

"Fine." Emily felt the color creep into her cheeks as she thought about Michael lying cool and naked so near to where she would lie wanting him. She clasped the pajamas to her heart and pivoted to retreat to the safety of Mason's room. "I'll see you in the morning," she called over her shoulder, hoping she sounded nonchalant.

"Emily." Mick's summons was a softly uttered plea. She turned again toward him, her face a silent question mark. "Don't think about Mason or Mississippi or ConCorp or anything bad. Think good thoughts. Have pleasant dreams."

She licked her lips. Oh, she'd have thoughts and dreams all right. But they wouldn't be so much good and pleasant as they would be wanton and delirious.

"Yes, I will," she promised in low tones then withdrew to Mason's bedroom.

Crouched in the corner of a dank and moldy-smelling boxcar several miles outside the small group of dingy buildings known as the community of Hack's Crossing, West Virginia, Mason Thorne worked methodically at loosening the coarse ropes wound securely around his wrists and ankles. His head still throbbed from the amateurish but well-placed punches of Courtney Lofton, and he suspected at least one rib was cracked as a result of Delbert Lofton's heavy-booted kicks, but all in all, the situation wasn't completely hopeless. At least they'd removed his gag and blindfold. Not that he had anything to say or that there was anything to see in the stinking darkness that currently surrounded him. Only the buzz and bite of several hundred insects assured him that he was still alive and lucid. But there was certainly no guarantee that he would remain so once Destri arrived in town to ask him some questions and send him to his reward.

The Corbin family in Roadside had discovered he wasn't Joe Snyder, land surveyor for ConCorp, despite his certainty that his connections and informers at the company would be able to confirm his identity. He'd been careless, he realized, because Zack Corbin had seen him snooping in Augie Corbin's General Store after hours and had alerted the others. Somehow they'd discovered that he was Mason Thorne, an investigative reporter from Washington, D.C., and in an effort to buy time while they tried to reach Steven Destri, had dumped him onto a rusty, fetid barge along with their most recent shipment and sent him up the river route until he'd finally landed in Hack's Crossing where he now awaited Destri's arrival.

Destri, Mason thought with distaste. Now there was a slimy character lower than the sleaziest scum. From his research, he knew Steven Destri was officially a ConCorp vice president, one of Everett Connery's right-hand men. In fact, he was effectively the ringleader of the eastern half of Connery's smuggling operation, a hatchet man who threw his weight around and had few misgivings about crimes such as kidnapping and murder. The man had no conscience and was utterly driven by the sole desire for money and power. And he had everyone edgy with fear all along the smuggling route, from the Corbins of Roadside to the Loftons of Hack's Crossing.

A sudden loud scraping against the boxcar's big door alerted Mason to the fact that he was about to receive another beating, and he steeled himself to face it silently. So far, he hadn't uttered so much as a syllable since he'd left Roadside, and he certainly wasn't about to become vocal about anything at this point. With a rusty, grating squeal, a section of the boxcar began to slide open. Outside it was as dark and silent as the train's interior, except for the white light and steady hiss of a gas lantern. Then a frightened, quiet voice parted the black night.

"Mason?"

"Lou? Is that you?" Mason gasped, his voice dry and rough from days of disuse. "Thank God you're here! I can't tell you how—"

"Shh!" Lou cut him off sharply. "Be quiet! I'm not s'posed to be here!" She set the lantern inside the boxcar and climbed up after it, then approached Mason slowly, the lantern held aloft, until he too was enclosed in the harsh white circle of light. When she saw the bruises on his face and dried blood on his T-shirt, she cried out softly and dropped to her knees, setting the lantern on the floor with a clatter.

"Oh, Mason," she whispered. "I'm so sorry. I just found out this mornin' you was here. I been tryin' all day to sneak up here, but they got somebody watchin' you all the time. Ol' Georgie's out there now, fast asleep from too much whiskey. Oh, my, what have they done to you?" She lifted a hand to push back his hair, and he jerked back his head as her fingers found a tender spot.

He muttered, "Ow," but couldn't help smiling at her. In the weeks that had passed since Mason had met Lou, she'd been through some changes. She had cleaned herself up and brushed her hair, even wore a lavender ribbon in it to match her hand-me-down lavender dotted-swiss dress. And he'd noticed immediately that she'd said "I'm not" instead of "I ain't." She leaned forward again, gingerly brushing her small knuckles over Mason's cheek. Her brown eyes held his, so full of fear and pain that Mason wanted to reach out to her and tell her that he was all right. Gently he covered the fingers that touched his face with his bound hands and held them away.

"I'm okay, Lou," he assured her quietly. "It looks a lot worse than it actually is."

"Did Courtney and Delbert do this to you?"

"Yeah. They relations of yours?"

Lou sniffed contemptuously. "My brothers."

"Those two goons are your brothers?"

"I ain't ... I'm not proud of the fact," she mumbled. "They take after my father. If Mama was still alive, thangs'd be different."

Mason nodded in understanding, then his mind kicked into gear. "What's going on out there? Can you get me out of here?"

Lou shook her head. "Even if I untied you, there's no way you'd get down the mountain alive. They'd get the dogs after you, or you'd meet up with somethin' unpleasant in the woods."

"Unpleasant?"

"There's some scary animals, and there's lots of traps to discourage unwanted visitors. I guarantee you'll stumble onto one or the other. And if I know the Loftons, you'll wish it was the scary animals."

"Terrific." He thought for a moment, then asked, "Could you get to a phone? Call the paper or the FBI?"

Again Lou shook her head. "My cousin Esme Lofton runs the switchboard. She listens in on everybody's conversations, and she'd tell on me sure as wet dirt's mud. Her daddy's my Uncle Fairmont, the one that runs the business, and he don't take too kindly to traitors."

"How did you contact me before?" Mason asked.

"Well, like I said, that time I come in for the weekend, I told the fam'ly I was visitin' my Aunt Wisteria and Uncle Roscoe Lofton in Tooley. Then when I needed to call you, I went to Tooley again and used a pay phone in town. Wisteria and Roscoe, they aren't in the business, but they don't know I called you. They'd tell, too, if they knowed. They's scared."

"Can't you go back to Tooley?"

"Not without lookin' suspicious."

"Why not?"

"'Cause Wisteria and Roscoe is at a reunion of her fam'ly in Kentucky at the moment. Everybody here knows that."

"Oh."

"Listen, Mason, I heard Courtney tell Uncle Fairmont that Mr. Destri won't be in Hack's Crossin' till next week 'cause he's tied up with somethin' else. You're safe till then." Lou looked again at the bruises on Mason's face, the blood on his shirt, and her eyes glistened with unshed tears. "Least, you'll stay alive till then," she amended. "I'm real sorry I got you into this."

Mason shrugged. "I got myself into this, Lou," he told her. "I didn't have to start this investigation, you know. None of this is your fault, so don't feel like it is. Everything will work out. We've got until next week to formulate a plan."

Lou smiled briefly and swiped at her eyes with her hands. "I gotta go afore somebody catches me," she said quickly. "I just wanted you to know I'm tryin' to work somethin' out to help you. I'm on the case."

"I have faith in you, Halouise," Mason told her, returning her smile. "Now get on home, and for God's sake, be careful. Don't take any risks that might put you in jeopardy. We're partners now, Lou. And partners always take care of each other."

Lou rose and carried the lantern to the boxcar's door, pausing before she left to look back at Mason. "You'd better be careful," she cautioned him with another smile. "I think you're beginnin' to like me a little bit, Mason."

With that she leaped gracefully from the boxcar, rattling the door closed behind her. Mason shook his head slowly from side to side and began to chuckle as he was once again plunged into darkness. By God, he hated to admit it, but he *was* beginning to like Lou. A lot.

Chapter Six

Emily was having trouble sleeping. The knowledge that Michael slept soundly in the next room, his naked, warm, muscular chest rising and falling in steady rhythm as he inhaled deeply and exhaled in quiet sighs was just too troubling to consider. Yet inevitably her thoughts turned to him, her curiosity about him constant and unassuaged, and she tossed fitfully, unable to think about anything else. Michael Dante was, without question, the most disturbing man she had ever met. And why he should affect her so intensely, so heatedly, when she had known him for such a short time was certainly one of life's great mysteries.

With a defeated sigh, she kicked her covers to the foot of Mason's bed and turned to look at his alarm clock. The glowing green numbers informed her that it was nearly three o'clock, that any fool who wasn't currently bewitched, bothered and befuddled by some sculptured piece of Greek-god artwork like Michael Dante would be blissfully lost in slumberland about now. Instead she lay alone, frustrated, unsatisfied and completely miserable. That settled it, she thought. There was only one thing left for her to do. Get up and leave the security of Mason's bedroom to go out toward where Michael lay sleeping and do what any red-blooded American woman in her position would do: finish what was left of her chicken-salad sandwich. If she was very lucky, perhaps there would be some potato salad remaining, too.

Quietly she rose, pushing up the sleeves on Mason's chambray work shirt which she'd slipped on before turning in, and padded silently into the living room toward the kitchen. She paused near the couch, watching Mick as he lay sleeping in the blue-tinged moonlight much as she had visualized him, except that he had allowed the sheet to slide much lower than her imagination would have permitted. He had a magnificent chest, she thought. Lightly muscled in all the right places, with a spattering of night-colored hair that swirled in dark spirals across the solid expanse. At the center of his chest, those sable coils joined and spun downward across his flat, sinewy abdomen, then lower still toward unknown depths veiled now by the dangerously dipping sheet.

For the briefest of moments, Emily considered raising a small section of the sheet, just enough to make Michael stir in his sleep, perhaps to wake him up to the point of semi-consciousness where she might be able to convince him that she had an appetite only he could satisfy. But quickly, and with an embarrassed flush, she changed her mind, chastising herself for even entertaining such uncharacteristic thoughts. Chicken salad, she reminded herself. Chicken salad on whole wheat. That's what would satisfy her appetite tonight.

Hurriedly she continued her journey to the kitchen, first filling a glass with ice water and drinking it down in the hope that perhaps the cooler temperature might also bring down the fever she felt raging through her body. Then Emily turned her attention to the refrigerator, which she opened and stared into vacantly while her thoughts once again circled back to Michael. Or rather, to Michael's chest.

Mick stumbled half asleep into the kitchen. He'd awakened from an incredibly erotic dream, which was centered of course around Emily, only to hear the object of his wanton desires rattling around in the kitchen, and had wondered what she was up to.

Even in the chalky white light that escaped from the refrigerator, Emily was a vision. She had put on one of her big brother's shirts to sleep in, and the faded chambray spilled softly over her luscious body, ending at midthigh to expose long, smooth legs the color of cream and texture of satin. A hot tempest blew wildly in Mick's midsection, spinning wider and harder the longer he beheld her standing there. She gazed absently at the sparse contents of Mason's refrigerator, slightly bent at the waist with one hand settled on a curvy hip, her bare left foot resting on her right. Rusty curls tumbled over her forehead and around her shoulders, and Mick noticed with a difficult swallow that the second button on Mason's shirt was missing, and he currently had a very clear, very fever-inducing view of the silky skin between Emily's breasts.

Suddenly all he wanted to do was run a long finger slowly over that skin, then feel her heartbeat quicken beneath his fingertips as his hand ventured farther below the fabric of her shirt. He shifted his weight from one foot to the other, hoping to alleviate the increasing tightness in his jeans, but only succeeded in making it worse. With a soft groan, he muttered a quiet oath, and Emily turned toward him quickly, a sudden gasp parting her sweet lips.

"Michael," she exhaled in relief. "You startled me."

"I startled you?" he retorted, stepping into the circle of white light from the refrigerator. "You startled the hell out of me when I woke up and heard you in here."

"I'm sorry," Emily tried to say, but wasn't sure she had managed to speak. The sight of Michael, his brawny, bare chest and the roped muscles of his arms bunched indomitably as he rested his hands on trim hips, made her blood pound so furiously in her ears that she could hear nothing but the sound of her own heart going wild. He had put on his blue jeans, but hadn't made it to the top button, which winked at her in the fluorescent light as if laughing at her discomfort. The rich scattering of hair across his chest cascaded temptingly down his strong torso toward that button, disappearing playfully into that unknown abyss, which had so teased Emily before and which she wanted more than anything to explore now. Michael was more than a beautiful face and broad shoulders, she realized with a start. Much, much more.

Mick didn't like the way Emily was looking at him. Well, he *liked* the way she was looking at him, her eyes glowing green embers, her full lips slightly pursed as if demanding a kiss, her cheeks flushed with the heightened awareness of sexual tension. What he didn't like was the way seeing her like that made him want to behave. It was all he could do not to push the refrigerator door closed and urge her to the floor where he could claim her body with his in slow, steady, deeply satisfying strides.

Instead he forced himself to ask, "What are you doing out of bed?"

"I got hungry," she told him artlessly.

"Hungry," he repeated quietly.

Emily felt a little warm and weak-kneed at the way he said it. As if hunger were a condition that only could be satisfied in the most primitive, most physically exhausting way.

"I, um, I was going to have the rest of my sandwich," she explained. "Or maybe some potato salad. But that's okay. I'm not really hungry anymore." It was a lie and they both knew it. Now she was simply hungry for something different.

"That's funny," Mick told her roughly, noting once again the milky smoothness of the skin at the base of her throat. "Because suddenly, I'm starving."

He knew he should turn around and go back to his bed on the couch, but what happened next seemed as natural an action as waking up to the light of the morning sun.

With quiet deliberation and a fiery intensity in his gray eyes, Mick easily closed the distance between himself and Emily with measured, unhurried steps. Her eyes never left his as his big hand closed over hers and removed it from the handle of the refrigerator door. Slowly it closed, the arc of light it had provided growing smaller and darker as the door swung back in on itself. It took only a moment for their eyes to adjust to the newly settled darkness, a moment Mick used to lace her fingers with his own, allowing his other hand to rise and tangle freely in her silky tresses, a moment in which Emily could only feel him touching her, his knowing fingers stirring parts of her body she never knew could respond.

"Oh, Michael," she sighed when he buried his hand in her hair. Her own hand rose to his chest, pressing into the muscles she discovered there, fascinated by the strength and softness beneath her fingertips.

A deep rumble of desire escaped from Michael's chest as her fingers splayed open and she raked her hand across his skin, down his abdomen then back up again to cover his runaway heart. Emily was startled by the intensity of his hungry groan and took a step backward, unnerved with embarrassment. Michael released her hand only to wind one strong arm around her waist and pull her tightly against his long length. Then he brought the callused palm of his free hand gently against her warm cheek.

Emily found herself imprisoned in the welcome circle of his embrace, her fists closed halfheartedly against his chest, her eyes held captive by his own. For a long moment she gazed up into his handsome face, worried that she might do or say something wrong.

When Mick saw the apprehension that clouded her green eyes, he smiled with encouragement, and with his thumb he slowly traced her lips until they parted slightly and her warm breath kissed his skin like a vibrant breeze. Then, still cradling her cheek with his hand, he brought his mouth down to hers, quietly, gently brushing his lips back and forth across hers.

Emily thought she would die from the pleasure of it all. Just when she thought she had reached the summit of sensual experience, Michael's tongue flickered out lightly across her lips, following the path his thumb had explored before penetrating the velvet darkness of her mouth in a kiss that grew hungry and insistent, a kiss that demanded a response.

And Emily did respond. She returned Mick's kiss with a hunger equal to his own, imitating the moves he made, following the instructions he urged her to follow.

"Open your mouth wider, Emily," he told her at one point. "I want to taste every part of you." His hand strayed from her cheek to her nape, and he held her head in place while he continued to plunder the dark recesses of her mouth, to taste and ravage the tender skin of her creamy throat.

When Emily gasped and emitted a wild little cry, Mick stopped, his breathing raspy, his heartbeat unsteady. He looked into her eyes and saw an unbridled passion he knew that he had freed. He knew, too, that he was going to regret the action he was about to take, the actions he'd already taken, but Emily's eyes beckoned, her full lips pleaded silently. And who was he to say no to a lady?

With a ravenous growl, Mick lowered his head again and slanted his mouth across Emily's in the kind of kiss he had longed to give her at Havern's. His hands journeyed across her back, up and down her spine until his fingers were familiar with every vertebra. As one arm roped again around her waist, he let his other hand roam casually around to her ribs, strumming them sensuously as his lips assaulted hers.

Emily's heart raced with excitement. No man's touch had ever set her on fire the way Michael's was able to do. She returned his kisses with equal fervor, her hands exploring every inch of him that she could reach. She marveled that a man's skin could be so soft, yet the muscles of Michael's back and upper arms were like finely textured satin. Her eager fingers matted in the hair on his chest, and when his hand encircled her wrist, encouraged her to continue her exploration in a more southerly direction, she willingly and with fascination allowed him to lead her fingers down across his flat belly, then even lower, where he gently cupped her palm over the tight ridge that had formed beneath the soft denim of his jeans. Her desire was increased at her understanding of his reaction to her, and she stroked him tenderly as he groaned and kissed her more deeply.

Mick felt as if he was spiraling down into a bottomless whirlpool when Emily touched him, and began to go a little crazy because of it. His hand left her rib cage to press into her hip. Then he ground his palm down her thigh until he found the hem of her shirt. With sure, confident fingers,

Mick raised the soft chambray, then let his hand skim lightly over her fanny and back before moving deftly to cover her breast. Emily sighed as he gently squeezed her soft, pliant flesh, then moaned when he discovered the stiffened peak.

As his thumb and index finger pinched lightly at the erect bud, Mick's hand on Emily's back dropped again to splay possessively across her derriere, and he crowded her body into his. In silent understanding, Emily released him and brought her own hands around to cover his firm buttocks. Then she went a little delirious at the mind-scrambling heat that coursed through her when he backed her urgently toward the counter and began to grind his pelvis into the soft cradle of her thighs.

"Emily," he gasped, looking anxiously into her dark green eyes. His breathing was raspy and uneven. One hand continued to massage her breast, while the other ardently caressed her fanny. He paused for a moment at the waistband of her panties only to penetrate that barrier by swiftly dipping inside the supple cotton. Her skin was warm, silky and so very tempting. "Do you know how long I've wanted to hold you this way?" he asked her. "To kiss and touch you this way, and . . . ?"

Emily's breathing was as erratic as his, her hands equally curious as they roved freely over Mick's back and shoulders. In her frenzied state, the implication of his words escaped her. "And?" she whispered.

"And make love to you," he confessed quietly.

Yes! her heart screamed. Take me! But Emily's mind, her silly, rational, deep-thinking mind prevented her from forming the words.

"Michael, I . . ." she began, uncertain about what she wanted to say. She was thrilled by his seductive admission, but frightened that her own feelings were so volatile and unrecognizable. She felt almost like a stranger to herself.

She'd had no idea she was capable of this kind of response to a man. She wanted Michael to know that she had never experienced the things he made her feel, wanted to ignore her misgivings and surrender herself to him wildly and with utter abandon.

But at the same time she reminded herself that she'd only known the man for a short time, had only been out with him on real dates twice, and only because he was working for her. She tried again.

"Michael, I'm not . . ."

"I know," he said, still caressing her warm skin.

"Know what?"

"You're not that kind of girl." He smiled sardonically, then removed his hand from her pants and lowered the other one from her breast to her hip. But he kept her pinned against the kitchen counter, unwilling to release her just yet.

Emily wanted to deny his assertion, to say yes, she was that kind of girl, had been for years, and travel farther into this frenzied world of sensual delight, but Michael stopped her with another kiss, this one less heated but as full of promise as the others. He lowered his head to place one final, lengthy kiss on the heated skin between her breasts revealed by the open shirt. Emily closed her eyes and enjoyed the sensation, feeling her knees buckle and her body turn to warm honey.

"Michael, I want . . ."

"To go back to bed," he supplied for her, straightening to his full height to steady them both before he gently released her.

"Yes," she murmured with a smile, this time placing her own hand against the roughened skin of his square jaw.

"Alone," he added, covering her hand with his. For a moment he simply basked in the gentleness of her touch.

Then he removed her hand from his cheek, kissed her delicate palm, and then let it drop back to her side.

She shook her head silently, not feeling nearly as brave or adventurous as she wanted to appear.

Mick searched her face, wondering if she was saying what he thought she was saying, or if she realized what the final outcome would be. Lord, he wanted to take her up on her offer. But she was just too good, too trusting. She *didn't* really understand what she was asking him to do, didn't realize that it could never amount to more than a brief affair. It just wasn't in him to give her any more than that. As much as he might want to.

"Yes, Emily," he finally told her. "Alone."

"But . . ." She knew he was right, of course. It was crazy to even consider making love to a man she had just met. But to Emily, it seemed she had known Michael all her life. Still, the fact remained that she ultimately knew very little about him. And the circumstances under which they had been brought together were unusual at best. Maybe the reason she responded so immediately to Michael was simply that her feelings were raw from worrying about her brother. And if that were the case, then when Mason was found and her reasons for being with Michael were no longer an issue, who was to say either one of them would want to continue a relationship of any kind?

She would, she knew. Maybe she was more highly strung than usual, but Emily realized, too, that Michael Dante was no ordinary man. After Mason's whereabouts were discerned and the case was closed, she'd still want to see a lot of Michael. The question now was would he want to keep seeing her?

Suddenly her actions seemed incredibly forward and tawdry. She was in her brother's darkened kitchen in the middle of the night with a half-naked man whose pants weren't even completely buttoned, and she had been...doing things...with him that she'd rarely done with men she knew far better. She felt color creep into her cheeks at the realization and was thankful for the absence of light.

"Oh, God, Michael," she mumbled. "I really didn't mean to...I hope you don't think...I mean, I'm not usually so..." Her mind raced with confused excuses. "I'm sorry," she finally muttered and tried to push past him in an effort to escape total embarrassment and his certain disapproval of her suggestive behavior.

She got as far as the middle of the small kitchen before Mick's long arm reached out, and his hand easily clamped over her retreating wrist. He spun around to face her and then tugged gently on her arm to bring her back to the circle of his embrace. Reluctantly Emily let him hold her, but bent her elbows to rest her forearms against his chest as a symbolic barrier between them.

"Emily," Mick said quietly, his eyes seeking hers in the darkness. "Do I really scare you so badly?"

Her heart thumped a little more quickly at the genuine uncertainty and solicitude that was so evident in his voice. For a moment all she could do was gaze at him somberly, then slowly she nodded her head.

"Yes," she whispered helplessly. "Yes, you do."

Mick sighed, then gently cupped her face in his big hands. "You scare me, too, Emily," he told her. "A lot."

He dropped a final chaste kiss on her forehead, then let his hands fall to his sides. "You still want that sandwich?" he asked her halfheartedly.

She smiled a little guiltily that at the bottom of all the tumultuous feelings she had just experienced, she was still hungry. "Yes," she confessed with a chuckle.

Mick smiled back at her. "I'll make you a deal. You can have the sandwich if I can have the potato salad."

"Can I have the last pickle spear, too?"

"Oh, all right."

As quickly as the sexual tension had risen, it seemed to fade to a safe level. What was left of their lunch disappeared with their hunger for food, and Emily and Mick returned to their beds with one appetite satisfied anyway.

When she awoke the following morning, Emily found Mason's coffeepot full of a fragrant brew, a box of a dozen doughnuts minus four and a note from Mick that read simply, "Gone to see that friend of mine. Be back shortly. Michael." Emily grinned at the signature, smug and happy that he thought of himself as "Michael" not "Mick" where she was concerned.

She poured herself a cup of coffee and was delighted to discover that he had also purchased a small carton of milk, which had not been opened. He was very considerate, she thought as she carefully selected a jelly-filled, powdered doughnut from the collection. She liked that in a man. Sensuous images of the previous night's tryst in the kitchen paraded through her memory, and Emily grew warm. There were quite a few things she liked about that particular man.

She couldn't help wondering how things might be between them if they had met under more normal circumstances. Would she have responded to him as strongly, as immediately as she did if she hadn't been so anxious about Mason's situation? Was he perhaps responding in kind to her heightened emotions, behaving intensely simply because she herself was so intense? Did he honestly care for her? Or was his just a physical attraction? And how could she possibly find the answers to these questions? Time will tell, a voice somewhere inside assured her. Just give it some time.

And speaking of time, she thought, she had no idea when Michael had written the note. "Be back shortly" could translate to "Be back any minute." This time plucking a chocolate-frosted doughnut from the box, Emily hurriedly returned to Mason's room to collect her clothes, then retreated to the bathroom for a shower.

Across the Potomac River in a Roslyn high rise, Mick Dante rapped lightly on Sam Jackson's front door for the fourth time. It was opened some minutes later by an unshaven, bleary-eyed Sam who was busy trying to tie a knot in a plaid flannel robe that had seen better days.

"Jeez, you still have that awful robe?" Mick made a face at his friend. "I hope you've started planning your trousseau. You can never begin too early with that sort of thing you know."

"Just who I need to see after an all-night stakeout," Sam grumbled. He snatched up Mick's wrist to look at his watch. "I just went to bed two hours ago. You interrupted some serious REM action. Not to mention a damn nice dream."

"About Mercy, I bet."

"Of course. I am an engaged man, after all."

"Can I come in?"

Sam gazed at him sleepily. "For how long?"

"Thanks," Mick said, using a big arm to nudge his friend out of the way. He strode casually into the cluttered living room and made himself at home in an overstuffed easy chair. "We need to talk."

"About what?" Sam asked as he closed his front door and joined his ex-partner by collapsing onto the sofa. He threw his arm over his eyes and added, "Don't worry, all you have to do is get measured for your tux and show up an hour before the ceremony. The bachelor party should be a piece of cake for you."

"Do you or anyone at the Bureau know anything about the disappearance of a reporter for *The Capitol Standard*?"

Sam lifted his arm and looked at his friend intently. "How do you know about that?"

Mick raised his brows and crossed his legs with feigned nonchalance. "So the Bureau *is* involved."

Sam sat up and rubbed his eyes, trying to shake off the last remnants of sleep. "Look, Mick, I don't know how you found out about this. I don't know much about it myself, it isn't my case, but—"

"What's going on, Sam?" he demanded.

"Who's asking?" the other man shot back.

"The reporter's sister."

"What are you talking about?"

"Remember Emily?" Mick asked.

"The leggy redhead?" Sam grinned, his interest increasing visibly. "The one you're so madly in—"

"The one who lives across the street from my office," Mick intercepted.

"Of course I remember Emily," Sam said. "She's the only woman you've ever fallen in—"

"She came with me on this trip."

"Whoa!" Sam laughed. "She what? Where is she? I want to meet her. Does she know you're in—"

"She hired me to find her brother, a reporter for *The Capitol Standard* who's been missing for three weeks."

Sam's face lost its lighthearted humor at the statement. "That's her brother, huh?"

Mick nodded. "What can you tell me about it?"

"Mick, you know I'm not supposed to reveal the particulars of an ongoing investigation to an outsider."

"An outsider?" Mick gasped in affected horror. *"Moi?"*

"Dante," Sam groaned. "Don't do this to me? Please?"

"I only want to know every little detail you have concerning the case. Is that so much to ask?"

Sam remained silent.

"For Emily," Mick cajoled. Then he added with sudden seriousness, "She has a right to know what's happened to her own brother."

Sam sighed, knowing he was going to eventually give in to his former partner, deciding not to prolong it.

"All right," he muttered. "But like I said, it's not my case, so I don't have all the specifics."

"Just give me something to go on."

Sam ran his hands through his sleep-rumpled hair and took a deep breath before beginning.

"The newspaper called us two weeks ago when their reporter—"

"Mason Thorne," Mick supplied.

"Thank you." Sam continued. "When Mason Thorne failed to make the proper check-in call to his editor. He'd been in Mississippi investigating a smuggling ring he thought The Connery Corporation was running. Evidently the whole company is nothing more than an elaborate crime syndicate. Can you imagine? A business that size—"

"I know about all that," Mick told his friend, adding the details that he and Emily had discovered the night before. "What I want to know is why Emily's being given the runaround in this. Why hasn't she been notified?"

Sam explained. "When Mason failed to check in with the paper as he was scheduled to do, his editor, a guy named Kelly, I think, got worried, tried to reach him at his hotel, asking for him by the name he'd assumed before going undercover. The hotel owner had become suspiciously unnerved and claimed to never have heard of the guy. So then the paper sent another reporter posing as 'just another traveler passing through' to stay at the motel and poke around. He came up with no sign of Mason, but didn't want to raise suspicions further by hanging around. When the paper didn't receive word from Mason for several days, they called the Bureau. I think Clemente and Gambetti are handling the case."

"Oh, swell," Mick moaned. "They should come up with a valid lead sometime before spring."

"They're doing their best, Mick."

"I know," he relented. "I just wish they'd put someone a little more seasoned on the case."

"Like you?" Sam asked pointedly.

"Like you," Mick told him.

Sam thought for a moment. "Look, I can ask around if you want. See what's going on, but I can't promise anything. In turn, I'll want whatever you have on the situation to pass along."

"Fine. But I want to know why Emily's been kept in the dark about this," Mick insisted.

"We're fairly certain that Mason disappeared because his cover was blown. Probably someone in Mississippi caught him snooping in places he shouldn't have been. His contacts and informers at ConCorp have verified that someone made a thorough inquiry to validate his cover, only to find that it wasn't kosher."

"So?" Mick prodded.

"So he was probably kidnapped by someone working for ConCorp, may have even been murdered for all we know. But there's nothing to substantiate that suspicion. The newspaper specifically asked that neither Mason's sister, nor his parents nor anyone else for that matter, be informed about his probable kidnapping for fear that, at best, ConCorp would hear of the allegations and sue the paper for promoting such a rumor, or at worst, do physical harm to Mason or even to members of his family. From what I've heard, they're capable of some pretty abominable things."

"I've heard that, too," Mick said quietly.

"Unfortunately that's just the problem," Sam went on. "There's a lot of hearsay, plenty of suspicions and accusations, but there's no evidence to back them up. And without anything solid, it's impossible to go after ConCorp with a full-scale investigation."

"There is hard evidence that could indict them on a variety of felonies," Mick revealed.

Sam looked at him severely and demanded, "Well, where is it? We can use it to get search and arrest warrants."

Mick shook his head sadly. "All I know is it's in a safe place where ConCorp won't find it. Unfortunately neither will we. Mason's notes in his apartment only state that it exists, not where it can be found."

"Great."

"I've got all the information we found out in the car. I'll leave it with you," Mick offered. "But you've got to promise to keep me posted."

"Deal." Sam chewed his lip nervously for a moment before saying, "One other thing, Mick."

"What's that?"

Sam inspected his fingernails and said, "I think you should stall your own investigation of this case."

"What? Why?"

"Look, the only reason ConCorp has gotten as far as they have with their huge operation is that they've been very, very, *very* careful. They're going to catch on pretty quickly that they're being investigated, and they're going to start covering their tracks and closing doors. The process will just happen faster if they're getting hit on more than one side. Let us handle this, Mick. Please."

Mick gazed blandly at his friend for the period of several moments. He knew Sam had a valid argument. He also knew the FBI had far more advanced technology at their disposal than he had. Even if he did find Mason, he'd be required to inform the FBI anyway. He couldn't exactly take on ConCorp single-handedly. Mason had already tried that, and look what it had gotten him. And then there was the question of the retainer Emily had already paid him. He'd have to figure out some way to repay it without raising her suspicion.

"All right," he agreed reluctantly. "But you'd better tell me every move the Bureau or ConCorp makes."

"I promise. In the meantime, you have to make Emily think that things are going just the way they would if you'd never spoken to me. As far as she's concerned, you're the only one looking for her brother. And you don't know anymore about his situation than she does."

"When can I tell her?" The thought of lying to Emily, of keeping her misinformed, gnawed at Mick's gut like a rusty razor.

"When we find her brother and get him out safely. Not a moment before."

Mick said nothing, lost in thought, uncomfortable with the idea that Emily would be worrying so badly about her brother, and he would be unable to ease her fears by assuring her that the FBI was on the case. He'd never been a very good liar and had hated to do it on the occasions it had been necessary while he was with the Bureau. This time it would be far more troubling. This time he'd be lying to Emily. It made him feel like a worthless creep.

"Mick?" Sam asked uncertainly. "Do we have a deal?"

After a pause, Mick sighed. "We have a deal, Sam," he assured him, thinking then that it felt more like he had just made a deal with the devil.

Chapter Seven

Mick and Emily made the ride back to Cannonfire in relative silence. Mick was brooding over his promise to Sam. He offered Emily little information about his conversation with his ex-partner beyond a vague assertion that Sam was going to look into the matter of her missing brother.

As they drew nearer to Emily's apartment, it occurred to Mick that they could both use an afternoon's diversion. It was a gorgeous Sunday. A steady, gentle wind stirred the trees, and the sun was a bright beacon high in the sky. He hadn't taken *Hestia* out for several weeks. He wondered if Emily enjoyed sailing. He completely ignored the promise he'd made to himself the previous evening after he and Emily had turned in for the second time. The one that said he was going to put a lot more distance between them and keep it there.

"Do you have any plans for this afternoon?" he ventured.

Emily seemed lost in her own thoughts and took a moment to answer. "No. Why?"

"Do you like to sail?"

Her face lit up with a brilliant smile, and her eyes sparkled with pleasure. "I've never been before," she told him, adding with a rush, "I've always thought it would be wonderfully relaxing, though."

Mick's mood lightened considerably when she smiled at him like that. She seemed easy to please, yet at the same time, he worried that he was not in the best of entertaining spirits.

"Want to take the boat out?" he asked her anyway.

Emily's smile broadened. "I'd love it. If you don't mind stopping by my apartment first so I can feed Sophie and change my clothes."

"You got it."

He parked on the street below Emily's apartment, and they climbed the stairs to her front door. When she pushed it open, they saw Sophie perched stolidly on the back of one of Emily's wing chairs, and the cat greeted them with a perturbed meow, indignant that she had been left alone for over twenty-four hours. Emily swept the big orange tabby up in her arms and headed for the kitchen, murmuring profuse apologies and promises to make it up to the animal at a later date.

Mick had to grin at her unabashed devotion to her cat. He'd never had a pet himself beyond the occasional emotionless rodent or reptile, and he frankly had some trouble understanding people who lavished so much attention on the creatures. From Emily, though, the reaction seemed perfectly natural. It struck him again that she was a woman to whom feelings of affection came readily, and he knew, too, that it could only ultimately cause her problems. He knew too well that there wasn't much worth loving in the world. People who loved too easily were simply destined to be hurt badly. It was a cruel fact of life, but one he'd seen illustrated far too many times.

Mick's thoughts were interrupted by the sound of an electric can opener in the kitchen followed by insistent feline demands and Emily's soft assurances that kitty lunch was on the way.

When Emily returned to the living room, Michael was standing where she had left him, once again looking painfully uncomfortable. "Why don't you sit down while I make a quick change?" she suggested.

"I'm fine," he told her.

"You're not going to break anything, Michael. It's a lot sturdier than it looks. I promise."

Mick smiled briefly and forced himself to walk casually to the sofa to sit down. He picked up a small, fragile crystal bowl from the coffee table and cradled it gently in his big hand. He could easily crush it, he realized with dismaying uneasiness. As easily as he could crush her heart if he wasn't careful. He must be out of his mind to have invited her out for a cruise.

"I'll only be a minute," Emily assured him as she ducked quickly into her bedroom.

When she emerged she wore a white, short-sleeved blouse and loose-fitting chambray shorts, and had tied a pale blue scarf in her hair. Mick's insides grew warm and mushy at the memories of the previous night the soft fabric covering her thighs evoked. He wondered if she'd chosen the shorts on purpose. As his gray eyes skimmed up her shapely legs, over her full hips and breasts to finally lock with her glowing green ones, he knew without question that she had. He really was going to have to do something to slow the progress of their attraction to each other, he thought with some annoyance. That's all there was to it. Otherwise, they were both in for a fall. A bad fall.

"You're going to have to change your shoes," was all he said to her in a husky voice.

Her eyes cleared of their passionate heat then grew puzzled. "Why?"

"Because I spent over half the summer refinishing my deck," he told her roughly. "Those things are likely to ruin it again."

Emily's gaze fell to her flat leather sandals. "Oh," she mumbled. "I'm sorry. I didn't know."

"Don't you have anything with rubber soles?" he asked impatiently.

"I have an old pair of Keds that I haven't worn since I played intramural volleyball in college," she snapped.

"Perfect," Mick grated out.

"Fine," Emily grumbled, vexed and wondering what she had done to make him so grumpy. She'd told him she'd never been sailing before. How was she supposed to know what constituted proper footwear? "I'll just go dig them out of the closet, shall I?" she added with more than a little pepper in her voice.

As she spun around and marched back to her bedroom, Mick rested his head on the back of the sofa. What a jerk, he thought. He had all the finesse of a moose in toe shoes. He wouldn't blame her if she backed out on their date. Or threw something at him. Or both.

As it turned out Emily did neither. But her attitude was noticeably cooler when she reappeared, and her offer to make sandwiches to take with them was given with little enthusiasm.

"That's okay," Mick said with what he hoped was a charming smile in an effort to regain some of their earlier camaraderie. "There's plenty of food on the boat."

"Lovely," Emily muttered. "Then I'm ready to go."

He opened his mouth to apologize for being such a bone-head, but stopped at the last minute. Maybe it was better that she was a little angry with him. Perhaps it would be effective in keeping her at a distance. The thought made Mick's stomach churn with fiery discomfort, but it was better for Emily this way, he assured himself. The longer he could keep her at bay, the less involved he became with her, the less painful it would be for her when they finally parted. Mick told himself he was doing it for Emily and ignored that irritating voice within him that told him he was in reality afraid for himself.

Some time later found *Hestia* gliding through the placid blue waters of the Chesapeake toward sea, thoughts of ConCorp and organized crime left stranded ashore in Cannonfire. Michael's sailboat was an older model, lovingly refurbished, made of warm, honey-colored wood instead of stark, white fiberglass. Even the spacious decks and the tall mast were wood, and creaked gently and comfortingly against the strain of a patched sail swollen large in catching the sunny breeze. A beautiful Schumann piano concerto lifted from hidden speakers, and Emily sat silently in the stern of the boat, her face upturned to the sun to drink in its warmth, her lungs filling with the fresh afternoon as she tried to sneak peeks at Michael when she thought he wasn't looking.

Her heart never failed to accelerate when she looked at him. And to behold him as he was now—the pilot of his vessel, a strong and confident captain handling the wheel, a god in skimpy khaki shorts and a tight blue polo, with the sunshine and sea breeze surrounding him—made Emily's blood thicken and her thoughts go wild. She wanted to rise from her perch against the railing to move behind him, encircle his muscular chest with her arms and run her fingers through his dark hair. His neck would be warm and salty from the sun and sea when she placed a kiss there, and he would turn and smile at her and say . . .

"Water looks a little choppy up ahead. You'd better come down from against the rail and sit in the cockpit. It'll be easier than coming about to rescue you when you fall overboard."

With a disgruntled sigh, Emily lowered herself onto a cushion in the designated area, noting once again with dismay that Michael hadn't so much as looked at her since they'd arrived at the marina. First he'd been preoccupied with readying *Hestia* for departure, then he'd had to focus his attention on steering her clear out to open water. Since then he'd been so caught up in the role of captain that he'd barely spoken to her beyond the occasional "Secure that line" or "Watch out for the boom." She was beginning to wonder why he'd bothered to ask her along at all, seeing as he was such an able-bodied seaman in his own right.

"Michael?" Emily ventured after a moment.

"Hmm?" he responded with obvious distraction.

"What are you thinking about?"

Mick's head snapped around to face her, and he was suddenly thankful that he wore sunglasses, knowing they would hide the conflict of emotions he was afraid would be evident in his eyes. He'd been thinking about her, of course, damn him. He couldn't help it. He hadn't been able to keep his eyes or his thoughts from her since they'd left her apartment. Fortunately he'd at least managed to be discreet enough that he didn't think she suspected.

She looked glorious, he thought, sitting against the rail in the sun, her hair a tangled mass of spun copper that seemed to have a life of its own, her eyes bright with the spirit of adventure. But it was more than her physical beauty that appealed to him, much more. Something in her tugged at his very soul, stirred yearnings in him he couldn't understand. She made him want to live it up and settle down at the same time, to go wild and then be tamed.

Those were the thoughts that were clouding his brain when she'd asked him her question, and when he turned to her, confused and morose at the murky jumble of his reflections, he frowned.

"I'm thinking," he replied tartly, "that perhaps we should turn back."

"But we've been out less than an hour," Emily complained. "You haven't even shown me how to drive like you promised."

"You don't 'drive' a boat, Emily," he pointed out impatiently. "You 'pilot' it. And I don't think you're ready for lessons."

"Michael, why are you so mad at me?" she demanded, her voice a hurt accusation, her mouth bowed in an unpracticed pout.

Mick's lips thinned in exasperation, and he inhaled deeply, his chest expanding and hardening impressively with the motion.

"I'm not mad at you," he muttered quietly, sounding not unlike a little boy who's uncertain of the source of his disappointments. "Come here," he added with unconcealed reluctance. "I'll teach you how to pilot the boat."

Emily was angered by his tone, one that implied he was only going to do it because she was forcing him. God forbid he should *want* to share something with her. She certainly didn't want to put him to any trouble if it was such an *enormous* inconvenience.

"Don't bother," she told him sharply, not even trying to cover her injured feelings. "Why should I want to learn about a boat anyway when I'm never going to have any contact with one again? Maybe you're right. Maybe we should turn back.''

She set her jaw with determination and stared out at the peaceful water, but the sight did little to calm the roiling swells in her midsection. If she wasn't in the middle of Chesapeake Bay she'd walk out on Michael Dante without another word. Unfortunately she'd never been much of a swimmer.

Mick watched Emily's withdrawal and hated himself for being the cause of it. She didn't deserve his crummy behavior, and he wasn't normally so ill-mannered. It was just a defense mechanism, he analyzed. But that didn't give him a right to tear into her like it was all her fault when he was perfectly aware that it wasn't.

"I'm sorry," he said suddenly with quiet sincerity. Emily looked at him, suspicion still evident on her face. "I didn't mean to be so contrary," he added.

"You've been contrary all day," she charged.

"I know, and I apologize."

Still, she refused to be humored. She continued to gaze at him evenly, silently telling him his apology wasn't enough.

"Emily, please," he petitioned. "I know there's no excuse for my bad manners and insensitivity today. Put it down to lack of sleep," he threw in meaningfully, and she felt her reserve beginning to crumble. "Let me make it up to you."

"How?" she asked, affecting an unconcerned air.

"I'd really like to show you how to pilot the boat." When she stood her ground and said nothing, he continued. "You'll wish you'd learned next time we go out. Mason will probably be with us then, and you could really show off." He began to grin when he saw the ghost of a smile threaten to mar her reticent expression.

"Come on over here," he wheedled. He pushed himself back to lean against the rail, parting his legs to pat the small opening between them on the cushion for her to sit. "Best seat in the house," he assured her with a playful leer.

Emily's smile rose full power, and she finally succumbed to his cajoling. She rose to take the place indicated at the cradle of his lean thighs muttering, "Sheesh, and they say women suffer from bizarre mood swings."

After she adjusted herself against him, she noted with a pleasant but unsettling observation that he was so close she could feel the heat of his big body against her back, could detect every flexing of his naked, muscular legs against hers. She placed her hands gingerly on the wooden wheel, then Michael covered them securely with his own, and his arms rubbed casually against hers with every slight movement they made. Where before she had sat alone against the rail touched only by the sun and wind, now Michael's body was in contact with hers from nearly head to toe. Every move they made was made together, every touch, every tickle was reciprocated in kind. Inevitably Emily thought of the act of making love.

"Oh, boy," she mumbled thickly under her breath.

"What?" Mick asked, equally distracted by the constant touching of their skin.

"Nothing," she responded somewhat shrilly. "Ahem. Now tell me everything I need to know to be a mariner."

Later Emily would be unable to remember so much as where the compass was. Her mind and all her senses were acutely tuned for certain, but a lesson in nautical proficiency was not what they absorbed. Instead she could only grow warm at the feel of the coarse hair of Michael's legs, could only become weak when his thighs tightened against hers, could only sigh helplessly when his hand left the wheel and slid up her arm to shoo away a fly that had landed there.

And when his lips drew close to her ear to offer quiet instruction, she wanted to crane her neck to face him, to lose herself in his kiss and coax him down to the floor of the cockpit.

"Michael?" she asked somewhat breathlessly at one such point in the lesson.

"Yes?" he murmured, drawing the word out like a languid caress.

"Um, does this boat have an automatic pilot?"

"Weren't you listening to what I told you?" he teased. "Yes, it does. Why?"

"Just curious."

They spent a good deal of time locked together that way behind the wheel. When Mick was confident that Emily knew what she was doing, he dropped his own hands to give her free rein, and settled them comfortably, possessively, around her waist, then rested his chin on the top of her head.

Emily thought it felt wonderful to be held by Michael with such familiarity. It was as if they were a real couple, she realized with a smile. Anyone looking at them now would think they'd known each other for years. And then it struck her again how little she did know about him.

"Michael?"

"Another question?" he muttered with mock exasperation. "Can't we just sit here in peace for a while?"

Emily laughed at his affected tone. "No," she told him with a chuckle. "I want to learn more about you. You know so much about me. It's only fair that you should reciprocate."

She was right, of course, he thought. It was only fair. But that didn't make it any easier to stir up dusty memories that were better off left stagnant and forgotten in the cobwebbed corners of his mind.

"Oh, you don't want to know about me," he tried to dissuade her. "It's all boring and typical and it will only put you to sleep."

"You boring and typical?" she asked doubtfully. "Come on. All I know is that you grew up in Chicago and were with the FBI. Why are you so reluctant to talk about that?"

For no apparent reason, Mick grew restless at her question and brought his hands back up to the wheel to join Emily's. He supposed it was unavoidable. She was going to keep asking him about his past until he surrendered some information. He only hoped he could leave his bitterness in the past where it belonged.

"I was with the FBI for ten years, Emily," he began hesitantly, "and it just wasn't a particularly good time for me."

She turned her head briefly to look at him, but he gazed past her, beyond the bow of the boat, out toward open sea. Emily suspected, though, that he was seeing something other than the beckoning waters of the Chesapeake.

"At the beginning it was all right, I guess," he amended. "I was young and cocky, and I felt like I was really making a difference in the world, making it safe from bad guys, seeing to it that people who committed crimes and brought misery to society were put away where they couldn't hurt anyone. But as the years went by, and I saw no end to it all, I guess I got a little disheartened. For every one person we managed to catch, it seemed like ten more crimes were committed almost as retaliation. I started to get paranoid that people were killing and robbing one another just to make my job more difficult."

"Michael, I'm sorry," Emily said softly when he paused. She supposed asking him about his past hadn't been such a good idea after all. He smiled his acknowledgement of her statement, a sad, detached smile, and continued.

"Worse than the paranoia of conventional investigation, though, was what came with undercover work."

"Why's that?"

"For months at a time I'd have to play a part, *be* a part, of what I was trying so relentlessly to put a stop to. Running around with a bunch of mindless, unemotional creeps who had no regard for anything or anybody, who were just consumed by greed and the drive to accomplish their own twisted goals, no matter what the costs, no matter what they had to do to succeed...." He trailed off, obviously reluctant to go on. "Sometimes I felt myself becoming just like them."

"Michael, you could never be like—"

"Just like them," he repeated as if he didn't hear her objection.

Emily didn't know what to say, so she remained silent. The sail smacked loudly as the wind picked up, and a small spray of cold water stung her skin, causing her to shiver despite the sun's warmth.

When he felt her tremble, Mick replaced his arms around her waist and pulled her closer to him. Having Emily so near seemed to keep his bad memories from getting the better of him as they so frequently did. But now that he had started, he might as well tell her all of it.

"I was shot once, too," he announced blithely, still looking over her shoulder. But when Emily turned to stare at him with a shocked look, his eyes met hers levelly. "And stabbed."

"Shot?" she whispered hoarsely. "Stabbed? Michael, you could have been killed?"

"No, not really. I was shot in the shoulder, and the knife only caught me in the leg. Scared the hell out of me, though."

"I guess so." The thought of something that hideous happening to him made Emily's stomach knot. Thank God it hadn't been worse!

"Actually I got off pretty easy compared to what some of the guys went through. Like what my partner at the time went through."

"What happened to him?" Emily asked, almost afraid to find out.

"We were investigating an especially notorious and vicious Las Vegas gangster who had gone into hiding in Phoenix. Somehow he found out that Sam and I were on the verge of finding him, and he sent out a half dozen of his favorite thugs to intercept us and warn us off. They cornered us in an abandoned warehouse, and we separated in an effort to escape. I made it out all right, but Sam, with the incredible lack of finesse that's made him famous, stumbled right into the middle of them. God, did they work him over good—" His voice broke off, but he immediately took a deep breath and continued. "I saw them dump him in a car and head toward the desert. By the time I got to my car to follow them, they'd gotten enough of a lead to lose me. I looked for him all night, Emily. When I finally found him, I thought he was dead. I wouldn't have been able to recognize him, they'd been so thorough."

"Oh, Michael . . ."

"Anyway," he rushed on before she had a chance to say more, "I got him to a hospital, and eventually he was back to his old, overblown self. But I think that was the last straw for me. Seeing what happened to Sam, knowing it could have been me...and finally realizing just what human beings were capable of doing to one another... It all just left a bad taste in my mouth. I wanted out. People were going to keep being inhuman no matter how hard I tried to stop them. I decided to just find a nice, quiet little corner of the Earth where I could be left alone and let them kill one another off for whatever ridiculous reasons they wanted to."

"So you came to Cannonfire," Emily concluded for him, turning again to meet his eyes.

"So I came to Cannonfire," he agreed, smiling at the picture she made there, her hair tossed around by the wind, her green eyes now cleared of the concern that had darkened them before.

Emily smiled back, and after a moment of thoughtful silence told him, "I'm glad."

Mick gave her waist a gentle squeeze, then he lifted a hand to wind one of her russet curls around his index finger. "So am I, Emily," he said softly. "So am I."

She lifted her lips to his quickly, briefly, in what she intended to be a light kiss between friends, a kiss to thank him for sharing part of his past, part of himself, with her. A kiss to reassure both of them that nothing had changed the closeness they were beginning to feel. With a hasty brush of her lips and a featherlike caress of her tongue, she ended it, and then gazed up at him.

Mick took in her soulful, yearning look. I'll be your friend, that look said to him, if that's all you'll allow, but I can be more, so much more, too, if you'll just let me.

No one had ever looked at Mick that way, as if they needed him. And seeing Emily look at him like that now did strange things to his heart. Before she had a chance to turn away, he tangled his big hand further in her hair until it was splayed across the back of her head. Mick bent to cover her mouth in a hot, hungry kiss. He growled voraciously as the arm around her waist unwound, and his hand journeyed boldly past her belly to rub erotic circles on her thigh as he touched her tongue with his own.

Where had all this passion come from? Emily wondered as she felt her insides turn to swirling hot magma. A moment ago they had felt the need for friendship, yet as quickly as they had recognized their own inner loneliness, they had both seen a way to combat it by reaching out to each other.

As if to illustrate the thought, she let her hands leave the wheel and turned her body fully to weave them into Mick's wind-ruffled hair. Immediately *Hestia* pitched sharply, and Mick nearly dumped Emily to the floor of the cockpit in an effort to steady the boat. His breathing, however, was not so easily steadied, nor was the pounding of Emily's heart.

"Oops," she mumbled, sheepishly pushing herself out of Michael's lap and into a far corner of the cockpit. "Um, sorry about that."

"No problem," Mick said raggedly. "We'll, ah, we'll just finish today's lesson at a later date, what do you say?"

"Fine," Emily tried to say, but it came out as little more than a squeak. She tried again. "That'll be fine," she repeated with a bit more fortitude.

They spent the remainder of the afternoon learning more about each other, everything from favorite childhood school subjects to guilty pleasures in which they secretly indulged. Emily revealed that she had loved art class best, especially on Clay Day, and confessed her unquenchable passion for paperback romances. Of course, the latter was old news to Mick, but the revelation about Clay Day was very enlightening. In turn, he contributed that he had enjoyed geography most and, well, could often be found in front of the television at two o'clock in the morning watching the tireless citizens of Tokyo save their town from yet another angry rubber monster on the rampage.

"I like those movies, too," Emily confided. "Especially the ones with moral and political messages."

"You're talking about *Godzilla Versus the Smog Monster.*"

"Four stars in my book," she assured him.

As the sun turned dark orange and began its slow descent to earth, Mick illustrated for Emily the fine art of "coming about," and they turned *Hestia* back toward Cannonfire. By the time they reached the marina, the town was bathed in splashes of gold, crimson and ocher, with just a trace of purplish-blue twilight smudging the eastern sky. After they tied the boat up in her slip, they walked the short distance to Nickleby's Wharf for dinner.

As she had for most of the day, Emily felt as though she were caught in a dream. Her steps seemed lighter, the town more picturesque, the bay more lovely, and Michael... Well, Michael seemed like a dream come true. Suddenly she felt she was almost too lucky, counted too many blessings, saw a future that was too bright. She had settled into her life very nicely, had grown accustomed to its comfortable predictability. But now love had come along and was turning everything upside down.

Love, she repeated to herself. Could what she felt for Michael really be love? She looked up at the man who walked silently beside her, holding her hand in his as if it was the most natural thing in the world. He looked down and smiled at her. She smiled back. Yes, it could be love that curled her toes and caught her breath. It could be love that was harvesting a garden of delight and joy within her very soul. Maybe it wasn't completely settled in yet, but love had definitely moved into her heart, and from the looks of things, it was already making renovations. Love, it seemed, was planning to stay.

After dinner, Michael drove Emily home and saw her to her front door. When she invited him in, he hesitated a moment before he declined, reminding her that he had a great deal of work to do in the morning. With a flush of guilt, Emily remembered her brother and was ashamed that she'd spent the past several hours completely oblivious to Mason's plight.

"Where will you take the investigation from here?" she asked Mick. She thought for a moment a flash of panic clouded his eyes, but immediately dismissed it as a trick of the moonlight.

"Uh, I'm not sure," he stammered. "I could confront his editor with the notes we discovered and demand a reason for his evasiveness, or I could try to get in touch with his contacts and informers at ConCorp."

At his last statement, Emily became alarmed. "Please be careful, Michael," she urged. "If something happened to you, too, I'd never forgive myself."

"There are other avenues I can explore, too," he told her in an attempt to erase her worried frown. "I won't be in any danger, I promise."

"What kind of avenues?" she insisted.

"Investigative avenues," he said mildly. "Now go inside. I'll call you tomorrow."

"Michael?"

"Yes?"

"I had a good time today. Thank you for taking me sailing."

"You're welcome. I had a good time, too. Thank you for coming with me."

She smiled. "You're welcome."

He placed his hands on her shoulders then let them prowl down her back. After a brief, tender kiss, he pulled her close and held her for long seconds. All the while he reminded himself, I don't love her, I don't love her, I don't love her. She's just a nice kid who's wonderful to be around and who's too trusting for her own good.

A moment later, he set Emily away from him again, and she gazed up at him longingly. She wished he would give more of himself to her, would let her see inside Michael Dante. For now, though, she told herself she was satisfied with their short moments of closeness but would continue to hope that those moments became hours, then days, then months, until nothing was left between them but an endless stretch to infinity.

"Good night, Emily," Mick finally broke the silence that had risen between them.

"Good night, Michael," she replied, watching as he turned to go back down the stairs. As he got into his car and started it, Emily quietly closed and locked her front door.

"We just got word from Nathan, Mr. Destri," Courtney Lofton told the man at the other end of the line from the telephone in Esme Lofton's tiny house in Hack's Crossing.

Steven Destri reeked with contempt for the human race in general and people like the Loftons in particular, and he rarely bothered to conceal his disdain. "Where is he?" he demanded.

"When he went back to Thorne's apartment in Washin'-ton to check it out again, he came across the fellah's sister and follered her back to her place in Maryland. Cannonfire I think he said the town was called."

"So now we know where Mr. Thorne's sister lives, do we?" Destri pondered ominously. "Wonderful. Those little phone games you've been playing to keep tabs on her are becoming rather dull. Tell Nathan to keep an eye on her. Maybe if he gets a chance he can drop in on her place sometime while she's out. If Thorne *has* collected evidence on our little operation, which is likely thanks to the bumbling of those dumb hicks in Mississippi, then it's also likely he would send it to someone. And who could possibly be more trustworthy than his own sister?"

"I cain't thank of nobody, sir. 'Less it'd be a brother, but I ain't for certain he's got one."

"Even if Nathan can't find anything in her apartment," Destri went on as if the other man had never spoken, "tell him to stay in town for a while. He might prove useful in another capacity."

"Yessir."

"I have a feeling this sister of Mason Thorne's may prove to be quite a powerful tool in...swaying him...toward our way of thinking."

"Whatever you say, Mr. Destri."

"And Courtney?"

"Sir?"

"I'll be in Hack's Crossing on Thursday. Try to keep him alive until then, hmm? I have a few little questions for Mr. Thorne myself."

Chapter Eight

It was not quite closing time when Mick met Emily at Paradise Found Books Wednesday evening. Outside the weather had finally caught up with the season. The air was cool and heavy, the sky thick and as gray as slate. A steady rain pattered against the red brick sidewalks of Cleveland Street, dotting store windows with water, sending swirling rivulets of rain down the gutters into ancient sewer grates. Mick lowered his black umbrella and shook it vigorously before entering the bookstore, fingering his damp unruly hair in an attempt to tame the dark locks.

He hadn't seen Emily since that awkward weekend they'd spent together in Washington and on the boat. Despite their daily contact on the phone when he superficially provided her with vague assurances about her brother, Mick's nerves at the moment were far too frayed for his liking. He'd hoped the time he'd forced between them would lessen his desire for Emily. Instead he was trembling with anticipation like a schoolboy at the thought of seeing her again.

A tarnished brass bell above the door tinkled quietly as he pushed it open, and it took a moment for Mick's eyes to adjust to the dimly lit room. All around him, everywhere that he could see, multicolored walls of old books rose to the top of the twenty-foot ceiling. Almost indiscernibly, mellow strains of Mozart lifted from somewhere beyond his vision, and his nostrils filled with the soft, sweet smell of yellowing pages and flaking leather binding. As he tried to keep from dripping on the dark, claret-colored Persian carpet that covered the floor, he finally noticed the tall, slender woman with large hazel eyes looking down at him from atop a library ladder. She ogled him openly and then smiled in a friendly fashion. Instead of feeling insulted, Mick found her assessing look amusing, so frankly was it offered.

"Well, hello there," the woman greeted him with a throaty drawl. "I find it quite amazin' what the rain blows in sometimes, don't you? Can I help you find something?"

Mick lowered the collar of his dark tweed jacket and smiled back. "Yes. I'm looking for Emily Thorne."

The woman's shoulders drooped a little, then she uttered a defeated sigh and replaced the book she had been holding in its proper place on the shelf. "Naturally," she said, carefully picking her way down the ladder as she quietly continued. "How that woman manages to attract all the good ones, I'll nevah know. It's that blasted hair, I just know it. First thing tomorrow mornin', I'm makin' an appointment with Miss Clairol."

"I beg your pardon?"

"Nevah mind. Emily's in the back room. I'll go tell her you're here. By the way, who shall I say is callin'?"

"Mick . . . uh, Michael. Michael Dante."

The woman sighed again, this time somewhat wistfully. "Fine," she said. "If you'll just wait right here?"

"Sure."

While Stella went in search of Emily, Mick browsed through numerous and eclectic titles that comprised the Paradise Found inventory. A literature student could lose his mind in here, he thought, picking up a special edition of James Joyce's *Ulysses*. A very cerebral literature student, he amended.

As he replaced the book, a sound from behind him caught his attention. Emily had emerged from a faded, flowered curtain behind the counter, her eyes shining, her cheeks flushed becomingly, the ghost of a smile playing upon her lips. Her copper tresses tumbled unmanaged around her shoulders, curlier perhaps because of the damp weather, but nevertheless very appealing. As she stepped from behind the counter, Mick took in with male appreciation her shapely legs below the knee-length, black-and-forest-green houndstooth skirt and the curve of her breasts beneath her dark green sweater.

"Hello, Michael," she addressed him somewhat stiffly. He had caught her by surprise, showing up at work that way. She'd rather thought he would call her when she got home, as he had every day since their last questionable date. She'd begun to think he never wanted to see her again, so successful had he been in sidestepping every attempt she'd made to see him. When Stella had come into the back room and announced that there was a "big, gorgeous man with the stormiest eyes I've evah seen drippin' rainwatah on the Oriental," Emily had rushed out to greet him like a nervous adolescent. The rain had left dark patches on his worn jeans, and his damp hair fell forward over eyes the color of the cloudy sky outside.

"Hi," he said roughly, thinking she looked even more beautiful than the last time he'd seen her, alarmed at the degree to which he had missed her. He probably shouldn't have come, but he just couldn't stand it anymore. He'd stayed late at his office for the past two nights watching her after she got home, and he'd be damned if he'd do it again tonight. Things were different now. Now he knew Emily at close range, knew how soft she was, how sweet she smelled, how she sounded when she was overcome with passion. He would never be satisfied to just watch her again.

It was a tormenting dilemma, to want her as badly as he did, knowing that any kind of closeness they might achieve would be short-lived, fruitless and eventually painful. He could either pursue Emily the way his libido told him to, or he could try to keep an eye on her from a distance as his conscience dictated. He knew she was as willing to get physical as he, that their union would be explosive and unforgettable. Unfortunately, it would also be temporary. Mick's intentions toward Emily continued to sway between selfish and noble. They were on a seesaw that could fall either way. And at that moment, seeing her as she was now, excited and flustered at his arrival, selfishness was winning hands down.

"What are you doing here?" she asked him breathlessly.

"I came for you," he told her after a moment, then rushed on. "I was afraid maybe you'd left without an umbrella this morning, since it didn't start raining until this afternoon. I thought maybe we could share this one. Maybe go have some dinner together."

Maybe, maybe, maybe, he berated himself. *Maybe* was a word that had scarcely been present in his vocabulary before he'd met Emily Thorne. Why all the uncertainty? Why couldn't he just make demands the way he normally did with women? Before he hadn't cared what the consequences of his words or actions would be. Suddenly he was in constant fear of saying or doing the wrong thing with her.

Emily smiled at his thoughtfulness. "I *did* leave my umbrella at home this morning," she admitted. "And I'd love to have dinner. Let me make sure that Stella won't mind if I—"

"Go ahead!" Stella called from the back room. "I'm beginnin' to get used to it! But I want an extra weekend off this month!"

Emily's smile became a little sheepish. "Stella's been under a doctor's care recently," she intimated to Mick quietly. "Hasn't been her usual perky self lately."

"That's not true!" Stella's voice was laced with amused warning.

"I'll just get my purse," Emily said quickly.

They huddled closely together under the big umbrella, Mick's arm wound protectively around Emily's waist, his hand virtually covering hers on the handle. As they cautiously avoided puddles and gutter drains, they spoke of the day's events and chose to eat dinner at Modesto's.

It was dark by the time they reached Emily's apartment, and the steady rain had amplified into a threatening storm, complete with sporadic flashes of lightning and low rumblings of thunder. After they rushed up the stairs to her front door, soaking wet and weak from running and laughing, Emily turned her key in her lock, then gasped as the door swung open wildly on a gust of wind. In a quick, shocking realization, she noted the broken pane of glass beside her dead bolt, and a strangled cry escaped her lips when the door slammed against the inner wall, jarring the remainder of the pane into a cascade of twinkling, falling shards.

Nervously, she reached inside to flick the wall switch and was left momentarily speechless by what she beheld. The scene that met her eyes when the overhead light illuminated her living room was devastating. With utter violence and disregard, someone had ransacked her home and left nothing behind but a shambles of shattered possessions.

"Oh, my God," she finally whispered hoarsely, overcome by the sight.

Mick had ascended the stairs behind her, waiting two steps below as she unlocked her door. With her words of shocked horror and the look of alarm on her face, though, he pushed quickly past her, sheltering her with his form. When he understood the situation, his body went rigid with fear and anger.

"Stay here," he instructed her roughly.

"But Michael—"

"Whoever did this could still be here," he told her. "Just wait here until I've had a chance to look around."

Emily began to shiver as Michael entered her apartment. Cold rain pelted down on her so hard she began to think it was hailing. Icy water arrowed down her neck, back and legs and made her sweater cling heavily to her. More than anything, though, her tremors were spawned by fear for Michael, that he might come upon the person who had done this terrible thing, might be harmed because of his involvement with her. Her teeth chattered uncontrollably, and Emily wrapped her arms impotently around herself in a discontented hug.

Mick studied every room of Emily's apartment with the practiced eye of an investigator and knew at once that the perpetrator of the malicious action was long gone. The job was too thorough, too complete for them to have interrupted it. Nearly everything that could be broken was, from her kitchen china to her bedside lamp to the photograph of Emily and Mason that formerly graced her mantel. The arrangement of flowers in the fireplace was strewn across the floor, her marble-topped tables upturned and broken, her pictures of fruit baskets and English gardens now little more than shards of glass and shreds of paper. The upholstery of her couch and chairs was slashed, stuffing pulled from them and tossed around the room. Her bedroom and the spare room, once graced with delicate furnishings and decorations were nothing now but dreary repeats of the debacle he'd discovered in the living room. Whoever had trashed the place had done it with a vengeance, Mick thought, and had enjoyed the destruction the way most people would enjoy a stay at the beach.

"Michael!"

He heard Emily's scream from the living room and nearly broke his leg scrambling over the remains of her bedroom to reach her. She stood amid the wreckage of her furniture with a terror-stricken expression on her face, tears streaming from her fear-ridden eyes.

"What is it?" he gasped out, gripping her shoulders harshly.

"Where's Sophie?" she wailed. "I can't find Sophie! Oh, God, Michael, what if she's... What if they did something to her?"

She began to weep freely then, and Michael pulled her close to him, murmuring quiet reassurances. He draped his arms over her shoulders and lowered them until she was imprisoned in his embrace, then kissed her wet hair and held her tightly. Emily's fists doubled weakly against his chest. All her apprehension and worry about Mason, all her confusion over her feelings for Michael, all her fear and concern for Sophie and her apartment came to a head, and Emily could only cry and cry until she could do nothing more than gasp and hiccup and cling to Michael.

And all the while Mick held her tenderly, stroked her back and hair, and whispered that everything would be all right.

He felt her pain and frustration, her fear and her anger, wishing he could make her feel better, knowing he was powerless to do so. As he held and tried to comfort her, Mick thought again that she needed much more from a man than he could ever give, and the seesaw of his intentions finally dropped. He promised himself to help Emily get out of her predicament. Then he told himself he would get out of her life and leave her alone. He was close to loving Emily, closer than he'd ever been to loving anyone in his life. But he just couldn't take that final step. As much as he wanted her, Emily was a woman that he just couldn't have, a woman who had far more to give him than he could ever offer her. She deserved a Michael he could simply never be. Certainly she was entitled to live a life that was unhampered, unburdened by the likes of Mick Dante.

"I didn't see Sophie anywhere," he told her quietly. "She's probably hiding someplace, too frightened to come out yet. She may have even slipped outside. I'm sure she's fine, Emily. Whoever did this had something other in mind than hurting Sophie."

Emily sniffled and looked up into Michael's gray eyes. Thank God she had him, she thought gratefully. She felt foolish and weak for having broken down in front of him that way, but at the same time relief washed over her that he was able to be strong when she was not. Someday she would return the favor, she decided, and be strong for Michael when he needed her.

She placed her soft palm gently against his rough cheek and smiled shakily. "Thank you, Michael."

"For what?" he asked, confusion mixed with something else in his deep voice.

"For being you," she said simply. "For being here for me. Thank you."

Mick said nothing, but covered her hand with his own and gently removed it from his cheek. He schooled his features to be bland in order to prevent her from detecting the war of emotions that raged in his heart.

Emily sensed his withdrawal but decided it was a result of the break-in, that his mind had shifted into investigator mode. "I guess we should call the police, shouldn't we?" she suggested.

"Yes, we should, but let's not disturb any more here than we already have. We can call them from my office across the street."

She convinced Michael to allow her one last chance to find Sophie and called coaxingly to the cat for some minutes. In her bedroom she was answered by a muffled "meow" and found the object of her search huddled in the corner of her closet beneath a heap of clothing. Emily scooped up the trembling ball of orange fur into her arms, quieting her kittenlike mewling with jumbled words of affection. After wrapping Sophie in a thick bath towel she plucked from the floor of her hall closet, Emily rejoined Michael, and the three of them made the short walk to his office.

The police arrived promptly, but took their time going over the destruction that used to be her home. They found nothing to offer any clues to the burglar's identity, nor did anything appear to be stolen. They assumed the break-in was little more than a vicious act of vandalism, and suggested that Emily was probably just a random target.

"Random target my foot," Emily had muttered at the officer's explanation.

"It's a good thing you went out to eat," the other officer told her as they finished their investigation and made to leave.

"Why?" Emily asked.

"The insurance company downstairs closes at five o'clock. Everyone's probably gone by five-thirty. Since nobody reported hearing anything up here, we figure all this happened between five-thirty and seven. If you got off at six-thirty, you could have walked right in on the whole thing. Could have been dangerous."

Mick's heart pounded at the thought of Emily coming home alone to meet the creep or creeps who had done this to her apartment. He promised himself that if he ever managed to get his hands on the bastards, he'd make them sorry they'd ever come to Cannonfire.

"We'll be in touch," the officer told them as he closed the door behind him and made his way back into the stormy night.

Emily stood silently among the bits of shattered glass and broken furnishings, at a loss as to how or where to even begin the cleanup. Finally she walked into the kitchen to search for some brown paper grocery bags and brought them back into the living room. She stooped and gingerly began to collect the largest shards of porcelain and crystal, making a mental note to rent an industrial strength vacuum in the morning. With any luck at all, perhaps her rug, at least, could be salvaged.

Mick watched her actions with his jaw set grimly and his mind reeling with questions. Somehow he knew this was no random act of an indiscriminate vandal. The whole episode was probably related to Mason's disappearance, but at the moment he was unwilling to consider the particulars of the situation. It was far too late, and they were far too tired. He picked his way through the clutter to where Emily was still stooped to gather up the remains of a rose-colored vase. Wordlessly he reached down and closed his hands over her forearms, pulling her gently up to stand before him.

"Come on," he told her quietly. "Leave all that until morning."

"Michael, I can't sleep in this mess. I have to get it at least a little straightened up before I go to bed."

"Why don't you spend the night with me on the boat?" he suggested, having already decided that's what they should do. "It's perfectly seaworthy, even in this weather, I promise. You can have the forward cabin, and I'll sleep on the settee in the main cabin."

Emily's eyes widened and her heart picked up speed at the invitation. Spend the night? With Michael? On that little boat? No way. It had been disturbing enough to sleep in separate rooms in Mason's apartment. And just being on *Hestia*'s deck with him had led to some pretty unsettling behavior. Closed up with Michael in that tiny cabin where she'd be practically on top of him at any given moment could lead to almost anything. And with the crazy way her heart had been acting lately, she just wasn't sure she could trust her emotions.

"Uh, no, I don't think so, Michael," she said hesitantly. "I don't want to put you out. I'll be fine once I've cleaned up here."

Mick was stung that she'd turned down his offer so quickly, and his words came out sounding more gruff than he intended when he challenged her intentions.

"You can't stay here alone after this, Emily," he insisted. "You'll be much safer on the boat with me." Actually Mick didn't much care for the idea of the two of them in such close quarters for an extended period of time any more than Emily did, especially when part of that time would be spent in the dark, quiet night where any number of intimate things might happen. But what else was he to do? He wasn't about to let her stay here alone, when whoever had ransacked the place could come back at a moment's notice, maybe next time when she was home.

"I just don't think it's such a good idea," she told him.

"Why not?"

"I wouldn't be able to get to work," she finally realized with relief. "The marina's a good three miles away, and I don't have a car."

"I'll drive you in on my way to work," he offered. "And don't try to tell me it's too far out of my way."

"No," she stalled. "I'd be in your way all the time."

"Then I'll stay here with you."

"Michael, you don't have to do that. I'll be okay. I'll have the locks reinforced or something."

"I won't let you stay here alone," he vowed. And that was that.

Emily had seriously mixed feelings about Michael's decision. She was comforted by his presence in one sense, knowing she would be much less frightened of another break-in as long as he was here with her. But she was afraid for different reasons, too. Afraid that a repeat of their brief interlude in Mason's kitchen could be a definite side effect. Emily admitted she wanted to get closer to Michael in just about every sense of the word, but she was still a little concerned about the source and scope of her feelings. She wanted to continue their relationship, of course, but hoped to do so after they found Mason, when she could be more certain of her emotions and his. She wasn't sure she was ready for another heavy breathing session with him just yet.

"I mean it, Emily. I'm staying," Mick repeated, placing his hands on his trim hips, daring her to refute him.

"All right, fine," she conceded, trying to sound flippant but failing dismally. "You can have the spare room that Mason usually uses."

"Is the front door the only way into your apartment?"

"Yes."

"Then I'll sleep on the couch."

"But it's a mess, Michael. Look at it, it's—"

"I'd rather be between the front door and you," he told her brusquely. "You'll be safer that way."

"Oh," she said. Then more softly, so that he almost wasn't sure he heard it, she added, "Thank you."

Together they spent the rest of the evening cleaning up, until most of the debris had been collected and heaped in a massive pile of trash bags. There was enough food in the kitchen to provide a decent breakfast in the morning. Most of Emily's clothes and linens had been spared beyond a malicious heaving to the floor, and she was able to make up a bed for Michael on the couch. Sophie had been banished to the relatively cleaned up spare bedroom as a result of Emily's fear that the cat might step on broken glass or try to eat something she shouldn't. Little by little, Emily managed to put things back into a certain order and regain some semblance of control. It was a small victory by some standards, but it reassured her in a way that allowed her to carry on.

After they had settled in, and as Emily fell into a light sleep late that night, the storm outside began to thrash with renewed rage, hurtling wind and water at her window, bringing violence, persecution and frenzy into what had begun as an innocent, gratifying dream of escape.

In her dream, Emily was a child again, but found herself inexplicably wandering through Washington's National Gallery, an activity she did not enjoy until some years later in her life. The cavernous building was silent, empty and lit with frosty light, its marble walls and floors cool to the touch of her bare fingers and toes. Almost psychically, she absorbed the ethereal pastel gardens of Monet, the yellow sunflowers of Van Gogh and white blossoms of O'Keeffe, and was filled with an overwhelming, all-encompassing serenity. At the end of a long, misty corridor, she saw her brother, Mason, fully grown and vigorously urging her to come to him. His voice and gestures seemed so far away, too far for her to ever reach him, so she smiled and waved, then turned slowly to walk away.

Suddenly, and with stark, horrifying clarity, young Emily heard her brother's bone-chilling scream, and she whipped back around to find the corridor consumed by darkness. Yet still she heard Mason's screams, begging her to help him, help him, help him... She began to run furiously toward his frightened voice, the floor having become bits of broken marble that ate into her tender flesh and inhibited her pursuit, but the farther she ran, the more distant his voice became, until all she could hear were his faded, pain-filled sobs and his weak cries of Emily, Emily, Emily...

"Mason!" she screamed after him with all the terror of a child abandoned to the unknown.

Emily sprang forward convulsively, suddenly alone in her bed, confused and bewildered by her surroundings. A rousing clap of thunder shook the building, and her bedroom door was thrown open with such fury that it slammed against the wall with a menacing crash. In a flash of white lightning, she saw Michael standing in her doorway wearing only his jeans, his bare chest heaving with great gasps of air, his face twisted in an expression of fear Emily had never seen him display.

"Good God, what is it?" he demanded, alarm punctuating his words as he rushed toward her.

Emily realized then that she had screamed Mason's name out loud, that she was crying, and that her heart pounded like a jackhammer. Her struggle for breath was even more frantic than his, and for a moment she found it impossible to speak.

Mick lowered himself to sit on the bed beside her, and reached up to squeeze her shoulders with reflexive intensity. Even though he had been startled awake by her outburst and was concerned for her now, he couldn't avoid noticing the way her hair danced madly around her shoulders and forehead, nor the way her eyes glittered like green fire, nor the ragged rise and fall of her breasts beneath her sleeveless, white batiste nightgown. Crazily he thought that even frightened, Emily was a vision of loveliness.

"What is it?" he repeated roughly. "What's wrong?"

Emily finally found her voice and uttered breathlessly, "Bad dream. Oh, my God, it was awful!" She turned loose the sheet she had wadded violently in both hands and threw her arms around Mick's neck, pulling her body as close to his as she could in an unpracticed, fear-induced embrace.

As his hands left her shoulders to brush across her back, Mick noticed uncomfortably that her normally glowing skin was too cold and she trembled uncontrollably. He also realized that she turned to him not as a result of any physical desires, but in an emotional need to have her fears assuaged by an understanding soul. Yet still he had to bite back the lusty yearning that rose unbidden in his own body. Damn him for thinking about sex when Emily needed so much more from him.

"Oh, Michael," she sobbed, still clinging to him, her face buried in the warm, rough hollow of his throat. "I'm so scared."

"Shh," he murmured. "It was only a dream, Emily. Dreams can't hurt you."

"It was so terrifying! Mason needed me, and I couldn't help him. It was dark.... Someone was hurting him, but I couldn't find him. I was a child, completely helpless..."

"It's all right, Emily," he insisted. "It's all over. There's nothing to be afraid of." He tried to loosen her arms from behind his neck to set her away from him, but she refused to budge. Instead she tightened her grip and pulled herself even closer to his warmth, struggling to ease the tremors still racking her body. Mick sighed in resignation and replaced his own arms around her waist, understanding that she still needed a few moments before she would be reassured.

Gradually her soft skin grew warmer, her shaking lessened, and her sobbing ceased, and Emily was able to ease her death grip on Michael. As her fears had ebbed they began to be replaced by a sweet desire, a desire born of her awareness that she was holding a half-naked Michael to her own scantily clad body, that they were separated only by two thin layers of cotton, and that with two simple gestures, she could be writhing naked beneath him as he caressed and entered her with a passion to match her own. Suddenly her chills were gone, and Emily disengaged herself fully from Mick, her hands falling from his shoulders to rest shyly on his big biceps.

"Uh, sorry about that," she mumbled, unwilling to look him in the eye.

Mick pulled himself back from her a little, but his hands remained settled on her small waist. "Are you all right now?" he asked.

"Yes," she assured him quietly, finally looking up. "I was just a little frightened."

"A little frightened?"

She smiled a shaky smile. "Okay, I was petrified."

"Do you want to tell me about it? Sometimes talking about a nightmare diminishes its power."

Emily shook her head mutely.

He persisted. "Sometimes the scariest aspect of a bad dream is simply the intensity of the emotions we feel in them. Because they're products of the subconscious, dreams tend to magnify the emotions we feel, whether good or bad.

Talking about them brings them into better perspective, lessens the impact of the emotion, that sort of thing."

"You sound like a psychiatrist," she told him half-heartedly.

Mick smiled grimly. "Let's just say I've had more than my fair share of nightmares. Now tell me about yours."

Emily reluctantly recounted the images in her dream, attempting to analyze them as she did so. In a sense, talking about the dream did ease her mind a little, but it also brought back into focus the absolute terror she'd felt upon awakening and gave her second thoughts about going back to sleep. She knew her fears were unfounded, and she couldn't explain her feelings to him. She was, quite simply, just too scared to go back to sleep, and the thought of being left alone filled her with a dread like none she had ever experienced.

"Feel better now?" Mick asked when she finished talking. They sat side by side on the edge of her bed, their feet planted firmly and, Mick thought, symbolically on the floor. A good six inches separated their bodies, but he still felt the pull of desire.

"Not really," she confessed honestly, wrapping her arms around her midsection.

Mick noted the gesture with a frown. "Do you want a glass of brandy or something?" he suggested. "Maybe a cup of tea?"

"No, that's okay. Thanks." Emily smiled weakly at his thoughtfulness and absently rubbed her bare arms in an apprehensive manner. Outside the storm continued to blow ferociously against the building, and her eyes traveled to the window where lightning, thunder and rain took turns exhibiting their menacing power. Fear was beginning to creep into her heart again, and Emily was helpless to stop its approach.

Mick rose abruptly from her bed then, and started to walk slowly toward the door. "I'll go back into the living room, then, and let you get some sleep."

When Emily saw that he meant to leave her alone, she was filled with an unreasonable panic. "No!" she cried urgently, involuntarily.

Mick spun around quickly, startled by the terror filling her eyes. "Emily?" he ventured. "What is it?"

For a moment she couldn't speak, so constricted was her throat, and when she finally found her voice, it was little more than a hoarse whisper. "Please don't leave me alone, Michael," she pleaded, hating herself for being controlled by her irrational fears, but powerless to overcome them.

"I'll just be in the living room," he protested. "You'll only have to call and I'll—"

"I don't want to be alone."

"Emily—"

"I won't be able to sleep in here by myself," she told him.

And *I* won't be able to sleep in here *with* you, he said to himself. His voice came out too gruff as he stated, "It's not a good idea." And with that, he turned around again and made to leave.

"Michael!" she cried as he pulled the door closed behind him, feeling like the terrified child in her dream.

At once he swung the door back open, marveling that she was still so obviously consumed with fear. Once again, she wrung the sheet worriedly in her hands, attempting to stifle involuntary sobs, and tears glistened on her cheeks when lightning filled the room. As if by an invisible thread, he found himself pulled to her side, and he gathered her close to his chest, raining soft, butterfly kisses on the velvet skin of her face and throat.

Somehow Mick prevented himself from lowering Emily to the bed, and somehow he kept his kisses from becoming more than chaste reassurances that he would not leave her alone in the night.

Wordlessly, Emily clung to him, drew on his strength to ease her unreasonable fears, listened to his deep, brandied voice try to steady her nerves, felt his muscular arms tighten around her in an effort to still her body's tremors.

She fell asleep in his arms, and Mick carefully let her fall back onto her pillow. When he tried to remove his arms from around her shoulders, she moaned softly and made a reluctant sound in her throat. Almost as an afterthought, and definitely with reservations, Mick stretched his long body out beside her in the double bed. Immediately Emily snuggled close to him and expelled a contented sigh. He wrapped his arms around her, fully aware that he was behaving selfishly. He was using her fear as an excuse to spend the night holding her, something he'd wanted to do for the past fifteen months, because he knew it would be his first and last chance to do so. Come morning, he decided, there would be some changes made in their relationship. Otherwise, he was headed toward disaster.

As he drifted into a light sleep, Mick felt a good deal of tension ease from his body and mind, and he became more calm, more serene than he had ever been in his life. As he clasped Emily to his heart, breathed in the scent of wildflowers that surrounded her, and let his fingers skim lightly over the downy skin of her arms, shoulders and back, Mick felt utterly at peace. His last conscious thought before sleep claimed him was a feeling that he had finally found his way to a warm, glowing home after years spent wandering in the cold, deadening night.

Chapter Nine

The following morning dawned gray and dreary, with a gentle rain spattering against the bedroom window as if in apology for the storm that had lashed through the previous night. Mick and Emily both still lay dozing in her bed, tangled among the sheets and each other. Emily had casually draped her leg intimately over Mick's thigh, and her fingers twined in the curls scattered across his chest. Mick in turn held Emily protectively, and not a little possessively, to his heart, one muscular arm supporting her neck, his hand pressed lovingly over the small of her back. His other hand had pushed her nightgown well up over the leg that straddled his until he was gently cupping her bare thigh. He was none too quick in waking that morning, and in his state of semiconsciousness, he knew only one thing—he was in bed with Emily, and she was every bit as soft and inviting as he had dreamed she would be.

Still half asleep, he allowed his hands to wander freely over her warm, slumbering form, curious to discover if her skin was that silky all over, delighted by her willingness to be touched by him. When she made a soft, sighing sound in the back of her throat, Mick's brain grew even more muddled. His lips nuzzled her forehead, then found her cheek, and finally hit their mark when she turned her face up to him and pressed her mouth gently against his. He took her lips ardently and groaned with awakening desire. His hand on her thigh came around to splay over her fanny while his other moved around to close gently over her breast. Then slowly he rolled onto his back, bringing Emily to rest on top of him, continuing his relentless foray against her mouth.

Emily was beginning to wake up and gasped at the position in which she found herself. Michael was beneath her, loving her mouth with his, squeezing and caressing her in places few men had ever touched and no man had ever aroused to such a degree as he had. Even more disturbing was the fact that she was letting him do it. More than that, she thought when she realized her own hands were buried in his dark hair and her own lips were returning his kisses with equal fire, she was encouraging him.

But as Michael's hands broadened their exploration, and as his tongue darted out to taste her lips, Emily sighed and decided she didn't mind a bit. Waking up to find herself making love with Michael felt as right and natural as waking up to life itself. As she became more awake, she found herself intensifying her own kisses to match the urgency of his.

Mick responded with a growl, slanting his mouth across Emily's again and again. He held her tightly to him and rolled again until she lay warm and welcoming beneath him. He still wasn't completely aware of his actions, so lost was he in the immediacy of the passion that had risen in him, but when she moaned out loud and murmured his name in the way of a lover, he snapped into consciousness as quickly as if she had thrown cold water on him.

For a moment, he was disoriented and uncertain about how her small body had become so crowded and willing beneath his. Then he looked down and saw that her nightgown was bunched around her waist to reveal long, beautiful legs and lacy cotton panties. His eyes roamed farther up her body, noting the pearly buttons at her throat and breasts that he must have undone, her disheveled hair that streamed across her pillow like dark flames, and finally the naked, unadulterated desire burning in her eyes. All at once, he understood that his dream of making love to Emily hadn't been a dream at all, and now she knew exactly how badly he wanted her.

"Emily, I'm sorry," he muttered gruffly as he began to disengage himself from her. "I was sleeping. And dreaming. I didn't realize I was . . . you were . . ."

"No, Michael, don't," she told him softly, catching his hand to bring it back to settle on her breast. "I don't want you to stop. I knew what I was doing."

"Did you, Emily?" he demanded crossly. He was angry with himself for being caught in a weak moment and angry with her for being so damned desirable. "Did you really know what you were doing?"

Some of the passion left her eyes, replaced by an uncertainty and fear at his rough response. But she nodded slowly, wanting to assure him that she was a woman who wanted a man. What was it about him that made her body respond in a way that she never knew was possible? Why did he reach her in places she'd never felt touched before?

Mick allowed his hand to remain closed gently over her breast, loving its softness, its heaviness. He looked directly into her eyes and gave it a gentle squeeze, and Emily sucked in a quiet breath, the fire in her eyes igniting once again.

"How many times have you made love with a man, Emily?" he asked, even though he was already certain that she had little experience in that department. Her response to him was too spontaneous, too unpracticed for it to be otherwise.

"Michael, I'm twenty-six years old," she said in way of a response, trying unsuccessfully to sound callous and indifferent. He was the last person on earth she wanted to have know of her lack of sexual expertise.

"I know that. But how many times have you made love with a man?" he repeated.

Emily remained silent but looked earnestly into his gray eyes. After a moment she said softly, "I'm not a virgin, Michael. I know what I'm doing."

His smile was predatory, and his eyes flickered with the fire of intent. He caught her erect nipple between his thumb and index finger and gently rolled the tiny bud until her breast felt ready to burst. He slowly pushed aside the soft fabric of her gown and lowered his head until his mouth took the place of his fingers. His lips closed over her, and Emily had never felt anything like the exquisite torture of his tongue as he tasted her. His hand reached lower until it rested at the juncture of her thighs, and he let his fingers go exploring on their own. Emily dug her fingers savagely into Michael's hair and uttered a single, helpless moan, quiet in its volume, but deafening in its significance.

Mick had intended his actions only as a lesson to her that she shouldn't play games. He wanted her to realize that he knew precisely how little experience she had, despite her claims, and that she'd better understand what she was asking him to do. But when he looked up to see Emily's head rolled helplessly back onto her pillow and heard her breathing become ragged and uncontrolled, he realized his lesson had completely backfired. He had wanted his actions to frighten her into a realization that he could offer her nothing more than physical gratification, that his technique, although very satisfying, would ultimately leave her feeling spiritually and emotionally bereft. He had hoped to make her understand that he was only capable of giving to her on a physical level, that he would never be able to provide her with the love and tenderness she deserved and seemed to need.

Instead his actions had apparently only further convinced her that what they could enjoy together would be a deeply satisfying, languid, easy union of both their bodies and their spirits. Despite his effort to show her that he was an emotionless, advantage-taking animal in bed, Emily still wanted him. He would have to take drastic measures, and take them now, if he was going to put an end to this whole sticky mess he'd managed to create. He simply could not, in any way, allow himself to get involved with Emily Thorne. And that was final.

"Emily," he whispered throatily, but she only kept her eyes closed and her hands tangled in his hair, silently begging him not to stop. "Emily, look at me."

Slowly she opened her eyes, now glazed over with longing and fever. The look in those eyes nearly caused Mick to come unglued and forget his good intentions. Good intentions? he scoffed at himself. Good intentions like hell. At this point, he was trying to save his own neck as much as rescue Emily's virtue. If he made love to her now, he would never, ever, be able to come near her again without becoming a miserable mass of raw nerves. Once he had her, he knew he'd never be able to get her out of his system. Yet at the same time, he'd never be able to love her the way she needed and deserved to be loved. He had to put an end to their relationship now, before things went any farther than they had already, before even more damage was done.

"What is it?" Emily asked him raggedly. "Why did you stop?"

"Because I don't think you *do* know what you're doing," he told her angrily in an effort to prove to her once and for all that he wasn't the gentle, tender Michael she thought him to be. It was his only chance if he hoped to keep her safe and himself sane while the search for her brother continued. "I don't care if you're not a virgin," he continued harshly, "I don't think you understand that once you start teasing a man, once you get him going, you can't just ask him to stop at the last minute when you get too scared to go through with it."

Emily's eyes lost their languid passion and narrowed with uncertain anger at Mick's sudden turn in behavior. "I wasn't teasing," she protested. "And I wasn't scared."

"You will be."

Mick's hand brushed slowly back up her body, igniting little fires all along the way, until it rose and cupped her chin roughly. He held her head in place and forced her to meet his eyes, now stormy with an anger she didn't understand. His next words were uttered with steady quiet, and with the conviction and instruction of a determined teacher.

"Because if I don't stop now, if I keep going the way you ask me to, I'm going to do things to you in a way that no man has ever even tried. First I'll remove this chaste little white nightgown," he asserted, bringing his other hand to splay across the soft fabric covering her other breast. "After that, I'll peel your panties down those long legs, kissing every last inch of you as I go." His hand lowered slowly then to grasp her thigh and pull it back roughly up over his denim-clad leg, rubbing his muscular thigh against her with masculine intent. Emily let out a throaty cry that she couldn't control, and her eyes grew wide and dark at the hypnotic quality his voice had adopted.

"I'll kiss you and touch you and taste you in places you've rarely touched yourself, and I'll keep doing it until you cry out at the exquisiteness of it all. Then I'll unbutton my jeans and roll you over onto your back, and I'll bury myself so deep inside you that we'll both go a little crazy."

"Michael..." she moaned softly, both repelled and intrigued by his powerful promises.

"And I mean it, Emily," he continued before she had a chance to say anything. "It will be the first time either one of us has made love with such intensity, and we'll both be a little frightened." He let go of her chin then, and looked toward the ceiling with a hopeless, helpless expression. "There's definitely something burning up the air between us. But I'm not a gentle, tender lover, Emily. I'm not bad, but I'm not one for generosity and self-restraint. I'll wind up hurting you. And you'll wind up hating me for it."

Emily watched him for some moments, trying to understand what really lay behind his outburst. Why was he trying to scare her? Did he really think she believed he was as heartless and calculating as he tried to make her think? If so, he was a little late. She already knew he was a caring, thoughtful person who harbored *some* affection for her, and no amount of affected swaggering would make him seem otherwise. What's more, she knew that she loved him, and nothing, but nothing, would ever change that.

"You could never hurt me, Michael," she told him with quiet conviction after a long moment of silence. "And I could never hate you." She wanted to tell him then that she loved him, but the sudden, pain-filled expression that entered his eyes stopped her. She almost felt like crying. Michael Dante just couldn't accept the fact that he was a decent human being who deserved to be loved. And she didn't know how to show him that he was.

She wanted to say something, anything, to reassure him that they could work out the crazy circumstances of their relationship, but the sudden, harsh buzzing of her alarm clock jarred them both back into bleak awareness of their situation. With the quickness of a predator, Mick rolled back to his side of the bed, and Emily reached up to hit the Snooze button out of habit. Her fingers fumbled as she rearranged and tried to rebutton her gown, but they were uncooperative, and she succeeded only in pulling a small tear in the fabric. She grumbled something unintelligible then pushed her hair back with savage frustration and looked Mick right in the eye.

"I don't know exactly what's happening between us, either, Michael," she snapped at the half-naked man who lay with feigned insouciance on his side next to her. Before he could respond she continued. "Personally, it's like nothing I've ever encountered. It's disturbing, annoying and confusing as hell. But for some *weird* reason, I kind of like it."

"Emily..."

"Don't say a word," she cautioned. "You've said far more than you need to already."

Mick opened his mouth to object again, but she rushed on.

"All I know is that you're right. There *is* something between us. And whether you like it or not, it isn't going to go away just because you don't know how to deal with it. I don't know how to deal with it, either, but at least I'm willing to give it a try."

"Emily..."

"I'm not listening to anything you have to say until you've given some serious thought to things...to us." She stopped for a moment, as her conviction began to deteriorate. "Just don't close the book on us before you've at least turned a couple of pages," she added softly. "Please."

She quickly rose from bed, snapped off the alarm clock before it buzzed again and fled to the bathroom for a shower. Mick watched her jerky movements and contemplated her brisk statements as he continued to lay stretched out on her bed. Damn, he thought. He'd really blown it this time. Emily still seemed to think they had a relationship that was capable of growing into something substantial. She still thought he was that perceptive, considerate Michael she'd assumed him to be on their first meeting, not the rough, indifferent Mick that he knew was a more accurate description.

"Damn," he repeated out loud, reaching unconsciously to where his shirt pocket should be for a cigarette. When he realized he was still lying shirtless in Emily's bed, he got up quickly and returned to her living room to retrieve his clothes. He lit a cigarette while he listened to the shower, and when he heard it cut off, he headed into the kitchen to start a pot of coffee. As the fragrant, brown brew began to drip from the wheezing coffee maker, Mick leaned against the counter and smoked in thoughtful silence.

Emily found him staring at the coffee maker some time later as she exited her bedroom ready for work dressed in baggy, brown tweed trousers with a cream shirt, a matching tweed vest and brown wool necktie. She was fixing a gold hoop in her ear when she looked up to find him eyeing her speculatively, the hand that rested on the counter cradling a cigarette between his fingers, the other wrapped around one of her few surviving earthenware mugs. He was unshaven and still barefooted, and his shirt was unbuttoned to reveal a tantalizing section of his dark chest. The smoke curling up from his cigarette and the steam rising in wisps from his coffee gave Emily the impression that they were results of the heat she knew was so inherent in him and which he could easily spark in her. Inhaling a deep, steadying breath, she reached into the cabinet beside him for another mug, trying to ignore the accelerated pace of her heart.

Mick was amazed that he could be so immediately turned on by a woman wearing men's clothes. If anything, Emily's outfit made her seem even more feminine than her flowered skirts did, because despite this masculine style, she was so very obviously every inch a woman. His fingers itched to remove her clothes and expose those curvaceous inches, and Mick cursed himself colorfully for being so susceptible to her. How could she raise such feelings in him when he had lectured to her less than an hour before that they had to put an end to their growing awareness of each other? Yet as he watched her sip her coffee and stare disconsolately at her violated home and what was left of her belongings, he found himself wishing he could fold her in his arms and kiss away her worries.

"Oh, Michael," she finally said. "Who could have done this? And why did they do it to me?"

"It may be just as the police suggested. Mindless vandals," he proposed.

Emily looked at him skeptically. "This sort of thing just doesn't happen in Cannonfire," she told him. "In the four years I've lived here, I haven't heard of so much as a dognapping, let alone something like this."

"Even small towns have crime rates, Emily," Mick informed her absently.

She looked up when she noted the tone of disbelief that permeated his deep voice. "You don't think it was vandals, either, do you?" she asked him.

Mick took a large swallow of coffee and a deep drag of his cigarette before responding. When he did, he looked meaningfully into her eyes. "No, I don't," he stated simply. "I think it has something to do with Mason's disappearance. I think ConCorp thinks he sent the missing evidence to you, and now they're looking for it."

"But how would they know where I live?"

"You said you left your name and number with the hotel in Roadside, right?"

"And I told them I was Mason's sister," she affirmed.

"It's not that difficult to get an address from a phone number. You just have to know what buttons to push."

Emily was quiet while she absorbed the magnitude of her situation. If ConCorp thought she had Mason's collection of evidence, then she was in as much danger as he. The thought alarmed her greatly until a new realization struck her.

"If that's true, then you're saying you believe ConCorp has Mason."

Mick's silence marked his concurrence. There was no way he could reveal that he'd already known that to be the case after his discussion with Sam, but now Emily was in danger, too, and he wanted to make sure she put herself on the alert.

Emily's concerned expression cleared suddenly and she beamed. "That means Mason's alive!" she said trium phantly. "If they'd already found the evidence they'd have killed him. But since they're apparently still looking for it, then Mason must still be alive. It's like you said, they wouldn't dare risk its making an appearance after his death. They'd make sure they have it safe in their possession before they tried anything."

"Emily, we don't know anything for certain," Mick said, trying to keep her from getting her hopes up too high. "Except that now you might be a target, too, so you'd better be damned careful. All the time."

"What do you mean?"

"I mean if ConCorp is responsible for this mess, then whoever did this to your apartment is probably still in Cannonfire to keep an eye on you."

Emily's eyes widened with fear at his statement. "Someone might be watching me? Without my knowledge? Oh, Michael, that's so creepy. How horrible."

Mick closed his eyes and tried to ignore her comment. He was more than a little frightened himself at the idea of a ConCorp thug following Emily around. He stubbed out his cigarette in a chipped ashtray from the living room and set his coffee mug on the counter. Gently he took her shoulders in his hands and turned her to face him.

"Now listen," he said, fixing her with an intent gaze. "You are not to go *anywhere* by yourself, do you understand?"

"Michael, I don't think—"

"I'll walk you to work in the morning and meet you there when the shop closes. And I'm going to stay here with you at night, too. If you go out to lunch, go with Stella, or call me. Don't even go into the back room at the bookstore alone. And if you see *anyone* who looks unfamiliar or behaves strangely, you call me. Immediately."

"Michael—"

"Promise me, Emily."

She gazed back into his clear gray eyes and sighed in resigned defeat. "All right," she conceded. "I promise."

He continued to hold her shoulders and looked at her face for some minutes. She was so lovely, so trusting, more open and honest than anyone he'd ever known. He wanted to kiss her, then glanced down to see himself in comparison to her. She was fresh and clean from her shower, her hair bright and bouncy from recent brushing. She was well dressed and wonderful smelling. In turn, he was unshaven, unshowered and his own hair was a tangled mass of dark waves. He wore the same clothes he'd slept in and smelled like stale coffee and cigarettes. He dropped his hands quickly lest he contaminate her with some of his sordidness.

"When do you have to be at work?" he asked, unconsciously rubbing his rough morning beard.

Emily was fascinated by the strictly male gesture, but offered no indication of it. Instead she spoke casually. "I have to leave in about fifteen minutes if I walk."

"Do you have a razor?"

"Some disposable ones under the sink. There's an extra toothbrush, too, I think."

"Give me twenty minutes to shower and get ready and I'll drive you," he told her.

"All right. I'll fix us a quick breakfast."

"Nothing for me, thanks," he said brusquely. "I'll just have another cup of coffee while I shave."

"Fine."

Emily watched him retreat to her bathroom and shook her head in puzzlement. He was determined not to let her do anything for him, yet persisted in keeping a vigil on her life. Why couldn't he see himself the way she knew him to be? Why did he insist he was something he was not? Michael Dante was a most curious and complicated man. And she had her work cut out for her in trying to expose him for the decent human being he was.

Late Thursday afternoon marked the arrival of the infamous and illustrious Steven Destri to Hack's Crossing, West Virginia. The small, slim, sallow-complexioned Destri wore a dark, shiny suit and carefully slicked back hair, two features that only served to enhance the inherent oiliness that was such an integral part of his character. His sleek, impeccable dress was in stark contrast to the patched, manure-stained overalls of Courtney and Delbert Lofton, but to Mason Thorne, Destri's fine clothes symbolized all that was really dirty and rotten smelling in the world. In the clouded thinking of a man who has been malnourished and cuffed around for weeks, Mason was quite pleased with his whimsical observation.

"Mr. Thorne," Destri began his first and, he hoped, final session of questioning the prisoner. He really had far better things to be doing with his time. "Why won't you tell the Loftons here what it is they want to know?"

"Well, Stevie," Mason said, smiling inwardly as Destri cringed at the familiar address, "the way I see it, these guys just haven't been real specific about what it is they want to know."

"You have something we want," Destri told him mildly.

"I have a lot of things people want," Mason confessed. "A first-edition Batman comic book, two tickets to the Wynton Marsalis concert next week, which I suppose I'm going to miss now, thanks to your boys here, a 1966 Corvette convertible that runs beautifully, and not too long ago, Diane Merrimac down in the mailroom told me in no uncertain terms that she wanted my—"

"Mr. Thorne, this clever babbling you continue to indulge in is all very entertaining I'm sure to the gang here in Hack's Crossing, but I find it rather predictable. Now if you're not willing to tell us where you've hidden whatever incriminating information you think you have concerning our little operation, then we just may have to resort to something ugly."

"Steve, buddy, no matter how hard you try, I just don't think you can get much uglier than old Delbert here. Unless maybe you prop Courtney up beside him."

Mason's remark elicited a growl and a raised fist from Delbert, but Destri's softly uttered "Delbert, please" immediately returned the man to a restless stance.

"Mr. Thorne," Destri tried a new tack. "I believe you have a sister, have you not? Emily?"

Mason tried to keep his features level and bored, but he couldn't disguise the panic that flashed in his eyes. When he remained silent, Destri smiled and continued.

"A sister who lives at 14½ North Cleveland Street in Cannonfire, Maryland? I'm told she also owns a cat, a large, disagreeable animal, orange in color I believe. I understand someone broke into her apartment last night. Left a terrible mess."

Mason's eyes blazed with genuine rage. "If you've done anything to her, I'll kill you with my bare hands, you son of a bitch."

Destri's smile became evil and victorious. "Temper, temper," he clucked smugly. "Little Emily is just fine. For the moment. But you know how life is sometimes, Mr. Thorne. Here today. . . gone tomorrow."

"If you or any of your goons so much as lay a finger on her—"

"Yes, yes, I know. You'll kill us all with your bare hands. You've said that already. Now tell us something we really want to hear. Tell us where you've hidden the evidence you seem to have gathered on ConCorp's extracurricular activities."

Mason worked frantically at the ropes that bound his hands. He wanted more than anything in the world to wrap his fingers around Destri's throat and squeeze with all his might. Unfortunately his efforts were futile. It was one thing when they had been threatening him. He could take care of himself. But now they were going after Emily, and he had no way to warn her. He was torn by indecision. If he told them what they wanted to know, they'd kill him in a second. If he didn't, they might hurt Emily. He looked up at Steven Destri with renewed hatred. Destri looked back and chuckled at his captive's helpless dilemma.

"Now, Mr. Thorne, I'm going to ask you one more time..."

Mick returned to his office Thursday evening in a foul mood after having chased false leads on another case for the better part of the day. He'd called Emily earlier to tell her he'd be unable to meet her after work, to make certain that Stella accompanied her home. She'd replied that her coworker was taking her to pick up a rental carpet vacuum after work anyway, and that then the two women were planning to go out for a drink. Mick had become inexplicably irritated that she evidently had so little need and no desire to see him, and he had practically hung up on her.

Now as he slumped into his chair and loosened his tie, he realized that he still hadn't had a chance to go by the boat to change his clothes from the day before, and his face still ached from the brutal treatment it had received at the hands of Emily's pink plastic razor. When he telephoned Sam to report the break-in, his friend was distant and patronizing, and the conversation turned Mick's mood wicked mean. He reached for the half-full bottle of whiskey in his desk drawer, not bothering with a glass. Switching off his desk lamp, he raised the bottle to his lips, gritting his teeth as the fiery liquid burned down his throat and ignited in his empty stomach. He opened his office window to allow in a cold, invigorating breeze, and sat back down to watch the bright full moon rise high in the sky over Cleveland Street, all the while wondering when Emily would come home. Wasn't she even going to call?

It was going on one o'clock, and the whiskey bottle was close to empty, when Mick heard a car door slam in the street below his office. He looked out and saw Emily bent to the passenger window of Stella's yellow Volkswagen. With a final laugh, she waved her friend off, and Stella chugged away toward home. The night was so quiet after her departure that Mick could hear Emily's keys jingle in her hand as she began her climb up the stairs to her dark apartment. As she turned her key in her front door and entered, he lifted the bottle of whiskey to his lips and waited for her to turn on a light in the living room. And waited . . . and waited . . . and waited . . .

When no light appeared from her kitchen window, either, Mick grew worried. He slammed the bottle down hard on his desk and with a speed and agility that the whiskey couldn't numb but adrenaline could sharpen, he sprinted out of his office across the street and up the stairs to Emily's apartment. Her front door yawned open ominously, but silence and darkness greeted him.

"Emily?" he called out cautiously. "Are you all right?"

It was the first time since he'd become a private investigator that Mick wished he carried a weapon. Until now it had seemed completely unnecessary, ridiculous even, in a town like Cannonfire. However, this case far superseded anything with which he had come into contact since leaving the FBI. Suddenly he felt as if he was once again on a federal case, one that could put his life, or worse, Emily's, in danger. He remembered Mason's notes, recalled that the people they were dealing with had no qualms about kidnapping and murder, and his blood turned cold at the thought of Emily coming into their line of fire.

"Emily?" he ventured again, feeling blindly for the light switch he knew was on the wall within reach of the front door. When he located it, he flicked it several times to no avail. Someone had either cut the power or unscrewed the bulb in the ceiling fixture. Either action amounted to the same thing. Someone was in there, and they had Emily. And if they'd done anything to hurt her, well, Mick would see to it himself that they were never able to hurt anyone again.

"Emily, it's me, Michael. Are you okay?"

He took one wary step into her dark living room, constantly alert to sounds and shadows. What little light came through the windows from the moon, and a distant street lamp only served to exaggerate the outlines of her furniture and his own imposing form. He took a few more steps toward the couch, in the hopes of locating a brass floor lamp he remembered turning upright and switching on after the previous evening's destruction. But before he had the chance, a small sound to his right caught his attention, and he turned toward it just in time to be smashed in the face by a well-directed left hook.

Before he had a chance to retaliate, a right uppercut followed, and Mick fell backward over Emily's couch. He pulled himself up in time to see the retreating form of a man catapult through the doorway, and he hurled himself over the couch in pursuit. He caught up with the man halfway down the wooden stairs outside and tackled him, sending them both hurtling toward the brick sidewalk.

Mick landed on his back with a painful thud, slamming his head against the bottom step in the process. When the other man came down on top of him elbows first, Mick had the wind knocked out of him, and along with the blow to his head, it was enough to stun him momentarily, a moment which his adversary used to flee into the night.

When he was able to think clearly again, Mick's first thought was for Emily, who he recalled now had never answered his summons. Groggy and hurting, he stumbled back up the stairs and leaned drunkenly in her doorway.

"Emily!" he called breathlessly. "Where are you?"

After receiving no answer, he tripped across the living room to the kitchen and switched on that light. The chalky white fluorescent bulb over the sink shuddered to life, creating shadows more ghostly than those he'd observed in the dark. Still, there was no sign of Emily.

That's when Mick panicked. He flew from room to room, turning on lights, throwing open closets, calling her name until his throat was raw. They couldn't have taken her, he tried to reason calmly. He'd seen her come inside and knew her front door was the only entrance. Yet for a moment, as he'd left his office and come down his own steps to the street, her front door had been out of his vision. Could they have moved her in that moment? No, certainly not. It had been mere seconds, in no way time enough to... and yet... Oh, God, *where was she?*

A low feminine groan caught Mick's attention and sent him flying from the spare bedroom.

"Emily?" he called into the semidarkness that still shrouded her apartment, panic still evident in his voice. He was met by another soft moan.

"Emily," he whispered to himself in relief, trying to restore his breathing to its original level. Her soft moan had come from the direction of the living room. Mick remembered her front closet which at the moment lay in shadow, a condition that had caused him to bypass it in his search of the apartment. He was shocked to discover he was trembling, so overcome had he been with fear for Emily. The relief that washed over him that she hadn't been taken was almost debilitating. Everything would be all right now. Emily was safe.

He rushed to the closet door and opened it to discover an oversize duffel bag that squirmed slightly and groaned again. With deft fingers, he untied the strings, and immediately Emily's copper curls appeared, followed by a hand that rubbed weakly at the base of her skull.

"Are you all right?" he asked her urgently, his fear renewed at the realization that she could have been very seriously hurt.

Emily pushed awkwardly at the hair that had fallen into her eyes and tried to focus on his blurry features. "Wha' happened?" she mumbled thickly, feeling very disoriented. Her eyes widened when she saw the angry scrape that reddened Michael's cheekbone, his swelling eye and the smudge of blood that marred his perfect lips.

"Oh, Michael, you're hurt," she murmured feebly, struggling to raise an undirected hand to his wounds. She tried to concentrate on his fading form, but felt unconsciousness claiming her again. She wanted to stay awake, remembered having asked a question that needed an answer, but couldn't recall what it was. Darkness gradually appeared again before her eyes, splattered with tiny red dots that spun faster and faster, so fast that Emily could actually hear them buzz. She surrendered to the darkness, almost, but not quite, oblivious to the sound of Michael's voice way off in the distance calling her name.

Chapter Ten

Emily came to slowly, her senses gradually absorbing the stimuli offered them. By moderate degrees she became aware that her body was being gently rocked by the slight movement of a boat, and the subtle, steady splashing of water greeted her ears and soothed her mind. The air around her was filled with the warm, luscious aroma of something akin to clam chowder, and her mouth watered with a desire to sample it. The last thing she noticed before trying to open her eyes was that a large, callused hand tenderly enclosed her own.

When she did open her eyes, it was to discover that she was lying in the forward cabin of Michael's sailboat. Her mind registered the hardwood paneling and ceiling, the books held fast in their glass-covered cases, the clothes hung neatly in a tiny open closet, the polished brass fixtures, and finally the big orange tabby sleeping quietly oblivious at the foot of the bunk. Eventually her gaze settled on the man who sat uneasily on a stool beside her, clasping her cool hand securely and warmly in his.

Michael's eyes were filled with worry and something else she was afraid to hope was real. He'd changed into a thick, oatmeal-colored sweater and still wore his uniform faded jeans. He had a full-fledged shiner, the scrape on his cheek was still angry and red, and his beautiful lips were even fuller now from the swelling that accompanied a small cut there. When her eyes met his, and he saw that they no longer carried the vacant, unfocused stare that had met and terrified him at her apartment, he exhaled deeply and lifted her hand to his lips.

"Thank God you're awake," he ground out almost savagely. When she'd lost consciousness that second time at her apartment, he'd been struck with such an enormous blow to his senses that he'd almost passed out himself. He'd realized then and there that if anything ever happened to remove Emily from his life completely, then his life would cease to be worth living. In that bright flash of realization, he suddenly understood that Sam had been right all along, and he'd been too stubborn to recognize it before. He did love Emily. Had probably loved her since the day he'd started following her around Cannonfire like a lovesick puppy.

For fifteen months she'd been an integral part of his life without his even realizing it. He'd looked forward to seeing and hearing her from a distance with far more anticipation and excitement than he'd ever felt toward any woman he'd known before up close. He was drawn to the way Emily looked at life, admired her deep appreciation for it. That was something he'd never been able to cultivate in himself. She was so warm, so caring, intelligent and beautiful. She could laugh at things and find pleasure where he would have overlooked it. *She* was the one who was perceptive and considerate, not he. And if she was able to harbor some affection for him, then maybe, just maybe, there was hope for him after all.

"How long have I been out?" Her softly uttered question brought him back down to earth.

"Almost half an hour," he told her quietly, leaning close to examine her eyes. Her pupils were dilated somewhat, but not alarmingly so. He should probably have taken her to the hospital, but the thought of being parted from her, even temporarily, had filled him with a dread like none he'd ever known. He wanted her where *he* could keep an eye on her. He had retained enough basic first-aid knowledge from his Bureau days to know the danger signs of concussion or shock. Emily had received a bad blow, and she'd probably have a pretty lousy headache for a while, but all in all, the situation could have been much worse. He shuddered to think how much.

"What happened?" she asked.

"You tell me," he said, remembering to be offended by the fact that she'd entered her apartment alone after she'd promised to be more careful. "What were you doing going into your apartment by yourself? Where was Stella? Why didn't you call me?"

Emily shrugged guiltily. "I didn't want to bother you," she muttered quietly.

"Bother me?" he sputtered incredulously. "*Bother* me?"

She hastened to clarify her statement. "Well, this morning you seemed like you were kind of mad at me."

Mick sighed, feeling a little guilty himself. "I wasn't mad at you, Emily," he told her softly. I was mad at myself, he wanted to add but remained silent.

She ventured a small smile at him, then continued. "I left work with Stella, and she was with me all evening. We were having such a good time that it seemed impossible that I could be in any danger. I guess I had a couple of drinks and was feeling a little invincible. I guess I kind of minimized the situation.''

"Why didn't you have Stella come inside with you?'' he insisted.

"She wanted to, was demanding in fact, but I told her not to worry about it, that I'd be fine. I told her I wouldn't go up the stairs until I knew she was on her way home. I'm really sorry, Michael. It was very stupid. But at the time, I honestly thought the whole concept of danger seemed ridiculous.''

"You didn't even call me to tell me when you'd be home. I waited in my office for hours for you to get back. I meant it when I said I was going to stay with you at night.''

"I'm sorry,'' she repeated, but her heart became lighter at the sound of utter disappointment in his voice. He *did* care for her.

"You scared the hell out of me,'' he stated baldly, his eyes growing bright with emotion. He caught her other hand in his and added, "Don't ever do that again.''

"I won't,'' she promised.

He quickly gathered himself together, unused to letting his emotions come so easily to the surface. "Now,'' he said after clearing his throat, "what happened after you went into your apartment?''

"After I unlocked the door, I reached for the light switch, but nothing happened. I figured the bulb had gone out. I left the front door open to allow in the light from the street lamp and started toward the kitchen to switch on the light over the sink. Before I could get to it, I heard someone else in the apartment with me. Just when I was getting ready to scream, whoever it was hit me with something, and that's all I remember.''

"Do you remember coming to for a few seconds in your front closet?''

"No," she told him, slowly turning her head from side to side on the pillow and wincing when she realized how painful the slight movement was. Mick's hands tightened on hers at the movement. "I was in the closet?"

He nodded.

"What did I say?"

"You were concerned about my face."

She smiled at his wording. "I've been concerned about your face from the first moment I laid eyes on it. It's quite a nice face. Usually. How did it come to be so banged up?"

"When I saw Stella drop you off, I watched you go up to your apartment. I should have left my office the minute I saw you down in the street, but I was...well...in something of a bad mood. Anyway, when I didn't see a light come on, I got a little concerned and came over to see what was going on. I guess I interrupted the party, because whoever floored you laid into me, too. I went after him. We both fell down the stairs, and well, the rest is pretty evident. Needless to say, he got away."

Emily was shocked that her thoughtless, overconfident behavior could have had far more serious results. She freed one of her hands from his and lifted it to gingerly brush her fingers over his scraped cheek. "I am so sorry, Michael," she told him. "Are you okay?"

"Just a little stiff. It'll work itself out. *You're* the one I'm concerned about. Are *you* all right? How's your head?"

"It hurts. But not as badly as it probably could. Do you have a couple of aspirin?"

Mick smiled. "Extra-strength. If you're hungry, I'm heating up some seafood stew. It's my one and only claim to culinary ability. It wouldn't hurt to put something in your stomach."

Emily inhaled appreciatively. "It smells wonderful. And I am a little hungry."

"Can you sit up?" he asked her, rising from the stool to help her.

"I think so," she told him. "I just have to go very slowly."

Together they got her into a sitting position on the double bunk. Mick plumped up the pillows behind her back and found an extra one to place gently behind her head. He'd removed her necktie and vest before he'd moved her to the boat, and now he pulled the aged, faded blanket that covered her legs up to her neck to keep her warm. Emily laughed out loud at his mothering, and Mick looked at her, clearly puzzled.

"What's so funny?" he asked.

"I was just thinking that since I've met you, you've taken better care of me than my own mother. More than Mason has, even."

He fixed her with a heated gaze that set her heart back to that erratic, accelerated pace she'd come to know very well since meeting him. "I don't want to be your mother, Emily," he stated levelly. "And I don't want to be your brother."

"What do you want, Michael?" she demanded softly, her voice a throaty whisper.

In response he let his eyes rove openly and hungrily over the curves of her body outlined by the blanket, lingering on all the soft places he'd touched and tasted that morning before they came back to fix feverishly on hers. "First I want to get you feeling better," he said roughly. "After that, well, I promise you'll be the first to know."

He turned then and headed out to the main cabin of the boat, toward the tiny galley, but not before Emily had seen something else mixed with the desire in his smoky eyes. A small explosion warmed her stomach and rose to encircle her heart. She smiled at the broad back retreating from her and sighed. Despite everything that had happened in the past week, maybe things were going to work out after all. It had taken some rather extreme conditions to do it, but they were conditions that had somehow acted to break down the wall Michael had built up around himself. With a little luck, maybe she could clear away the rest of the rubble by herself.

The late night had become early morning by the time Emily's head stopped hurting and she felt wound down enough to sleep. Mick offered her the use of one of his T-shirts and his own toothbrush, apologizing for not having the foresight to keep a spare around as she did herself. Emily grinned and graciously accepted both, thinking it silly that he would consider her put off by the thought of sharing a toothbrush with him after some of the kisses they'd exchanged.

She washed her face, brushed her teeth and slipped Mick's T-shirt over her head. It was loose fitting and amply covered her thighs, but it had a V-neck that displayed a little more of her tender flesh than she would have liked. Oh, well, she reasoned with some dissatisfaction, Michael was certain to sleep in the main cabin as he'd said the other night, so what difference did it make? Still, they'd have to go by her apartment before she went to work tomorrow so she could change.

As she settled under the covers in the forward bunk, Emily listened to the sounds of Sophie's contented purring, of the water lapping tiredly at the bow of the boat and the clattering of Michael as he cleaned up in the kitchen and then prepared for bed in the bathroom. Emily found that she liked the feeling of hominess it gave her to listen to such things late in the dark night as she lay quietly in bed.

When the water in the bathroom shut off, Emily closed her eyes, expecting to hear Mick retire into his own bed on the settee in the main cabin. Therefore, it came as quite a surprise to her when the side of her bed nearest the door sagged under his weight as he climbed in beside her. Her eyes snapped open, and in the vague light offered by the open hatch above them she could see that he was nearly naked. For her sake, she assumed, he had left on a pair of navy gym shorts.

"Michael, what are you doing?" she asked with obvious apprehension and confusion.

"I'm going to bed," he replied simply. "I'm very tired. It's been a long day." He pulled back the sheet and blanket that covered her and pushed his body in next to hers. "Good night," he added as he closed his eyes and settled his arm lightly across her waist.

"You're going to sleep here?" she persisted.

"Mmm-hmm," he muttered sleepily, his eyes still closed. "What's wrong? Last night you wanted me to sleep with you."

Emily's eyes widened at his phrasing. "But last night was different. There was the break-in, and the storm and my nightmare. I was scared. I didn't want to be alone."

Mick opened his eyes and lifted himself up onto one elbow to gaze down at her. Emily felt the heat of that gaze as if he'd struck a match to her heart. Unconsciously she pulled the blanket higher to cover her exposed flesh. Mick smiled with genuine warmth at the action, but wound his arm even more securely around her waist.

"Tonight, Emily, there was a far worse break-in. Someone tried to take you from me. That's *my* nightmare. Tonight *I'm* scared. Tonight *I* don't want to be alone."

He lowered his head and rubbed his lips softly against hers in a light kiss that spoke volumes. When he looked into her eyes again, his pupils were large with fear and wanting. The hand on her waist rose to cup her cheek. "You're stuck with me now, Emily," he told her evenly. "I won't let anything ever come between us again."

She dared not let her heart take flight the way it longed to, but she couldn't keep herself from voicing the question that followed. "Michael," she whispered to him in the darkness, "what are you saying?"

It was only three words, he told himself. Only three tiny words. *I love you.* Say it. Tell her. But he had never uttered those words to anyone, not even his parents. It was still too new. He hadn't even gotten used to *feeling* the words, let alone speaking them. He loved Emily, yes, without question. But something inside, some unexplainable fear, still prohibited him from vocalizing his feelings.

"Go to sleep, Emily," was all he said to her. "I'll be here when you wake up. I'll be here whenever you want me." His smile became a little sad as he added, "And even when you don't." With one last kiss, he snuggled up beside her and pulled her close. Within moments he slept, a deep, untroubled sleep, the sleep of a man who has opened a window and allowed fresh air and sunshine into a room that has been left stale and musty for too many years.

Emily, too, eventually fell asleep, deeply puzzled, but feeling safe and loved ensconced in Mick's embrace. Loved, she thought just before sleep claimed her. Was she really loved by him? Was that what his cryptic words had meant? Dare she hope that Michael Dante might at last have allowed himself to recognize his humanity, might finally let himself enjoy the most basic human joy of all—the ability to love and be loved? She sighed and nestled her body into his, wondering if it was Sophie or herself who was purring so contentedly after all.

When she awoke the next morning, Mick was, as he'd promised, still lying next to her, holding her even more intimately than before. Emily stretched languidly and glanced at the brass clock bolted on the wall opposite the bed. She had to squint to see it in the dim light of the cabin, but it looked like it said . . . ten-thirty?

"Omigosh," she gasped, throwing back the covers and struggling to free herself from Mick's insistent embrace. The gesture startled Sophie, who meowed with indignation before making a hasty departure from the foot of the bunk.

"What's going on?" Mick asked groggily as her frantic actions woke him up as well. "What's the matter?"

"I'm incredibly late for work," she wailed as she tried to crawl over the top of him, annoyed that he seemed to be purposely hindering her escape. "Stella's going to kill me!"

"No, she's not," Mick told her, placing his hands firmly on her small waist to hold her still as she straddled him. "Trust me. Stella won't mind a bit."

"How do you know?" Emily ceased her struggling and eyed him skeptically, suspicious of his genuinely happy smile. It was the first time she'd seen him smile because he was actually happy. She really hadn't thought anything could improve his good looks, but that big, silly grin that went from ear to ear and eye to eye, made him . . . well, hunky came to mind. Along with scrumptious and adorable and lots of other dumb words that Emily had never used in relation to men before.

Mick thought Emily looked lovely with her curls falling all over the place and her face flushed and soft from the morning, her dark green eyes still a little drowsy. Best of all, she hadn't realized yet that the T-shirt she wore was bunched up around her waist, and the plunging V-neck revealed a lot more skin than she'd probably choose to display. He decided it would be ungentlemanly to point out such obvious breaches of etiquette and instead just enjoyed the view.

"I just, uh, know for a fact that Stella would understand if you didn't come in to work today," he assured her.

"Are you crazy?" Emily barked. "All week long I've been missing work, leaving early, coming in late, taking long lunch breaks. Stella's a very nice person, but I wouldn't blame her if she never spoke to me again after this week."

Mick's smile broadened. "Stella's a wonderful person. And she's your friend. I called her last night before I came to bed and—"

"You woke her up in the middle of the night?" Emily squeaked. "Now I know she'll kill me."

"—and I explained the situation to her. I told her you wouldn't be in to work again until Monday, that you needed a few days off to recover. She was very sympathetic."

Emily's expression softened. "Yeah, I guess she would be. You're right, she is a wonderful person and a good friend."

"And she said to tell you it was very nice of you to insist that she take the weekend off, too. I think she said something about meeting her sister in Ocean City."

"What?"

"Now, I'm playing hooky from work, too, so we have three whole days off ahead of us. How would you like to spend them?"

"Michael, what did you do?" Emily demanded, unconsciously gripping his broad shoulders with untamed fury.

"I told her you said it was only fair that she take the weekend off, too. Especially after all the allowances she'd made for you all week. I mean, after all, you've been coming in late, leaving early, missing days altogether, taking long lunch breaks . . ."

"But, Michael, that means no one will be there to open the store! What if Mr. Lindsey finds out? He'll fire me!"

"I'm sure Mr. Lindsey is a reasonable man. If he knew the circumstances, he'd understand."

Emily did some quick calculating. "This might be the weekend he's going to visit Claudia in Newport."

"Claudia?"

"His daughter. My old dorm mate."

"Oh."

"Or was that last weekend?"

"Emily, will you quit worrying? He won't fire you for this."

She looked at him doubtfully. Mr Lindsey was by no means an unreasonable or ill-tempered man. In fact, he was probably the most easygoing person she knew. Given the circumstances, she was certain he'd understand the situation. Especially after he met the indomitable Michael Dante.

"Okay, I'll stop worrying," she agreed reluctantly. "But if he does fire me, then you'll have to support me for the rest of my life."

The smile on his lips faded, but the happiness in his eyes sparked even brighter. "Gladly," he vowed. "I can think of no greater pleasure in life than to be connected to you forever—in any way that you'll let me. As long as I can be with you every day, I can die a happy man."

"Michael, you confuse me when you say things like that," Emily told him softly. "Especially after all the things you said yesterday morning."

"Yesterday morning I hadn't considered the prospect of having you removed from my life forever. So I guess today I'll have to do something to unconfuse you, won't I? Something that will show you unequivocally how I feel."

His eyes grew dark with passionate fire, and Emily realized too late the vulnerable position she was in, straddled across his muscular body, half naked and giddy with desire for him. The hands on her waist rose to close over her breasts briefly, then went to her shoulders where they pushed the V-neck of the shirt down over her shoulders. The movement stretched the soft fabric taut across her breasts, clearly revealing her dark aureoles, straining against her tight nipples. Mick groaned when he saw what his gesture had provoked. He raised his head to cover the peak of her breast with his mouth, and the cotton shirt became wet with the workings of his lips and tongue.

"Oh, Michael," Emily whispered as she tangled her fingers in his hair and pressed him closer to her. For several minutes he continued his assault, then he turned his attention to her other breast. A cool breeze blew down through the open hatch, chilling her damp flesh until Mick covered it with his hand and began a gentle massage.

When he thought he would go crazy with wanting her, Mick grasped the hem of the T-shirt and hastily drew it over Emily's head. She still sat atop him, her face flushed, her lips parted and her eyes sparkling with passionate longing. Mick had never seen her look more beautiful. He groaned out loud as his hands sought her breasts again, and when Emily lowered her head to kiss him deeply, the soft, sensitive globes rubbed against the coarse hair of his chest. Mick slanted his mouth ravenously over hers, hungrily devouring her lips. As his curious tongue probed deeply into dark recesses, his hands found her soft derriere, and with one quick, sure motion, he rolled their bodies over until Emily lay writhing beneath him.

As Mick's knowing mouth and wandering fingers stirred parts of her she'd never thought could be excited, Emily did a little exploring on her own. Her silky legs tangled with his brawny ones, and her feverish brain lovingly registered every solid, straining muscle that her fingertips encountered. His back was a veritable symphony of strength, his arms long, lean collections of tendons and sinew. He was every inch a man, more man than she'd ever seen or touched. Her man, she thought, her pleasure becoming enhanced tenfold.

Emily cried out as one of Mick's hands stroked the inside of her thigh and pushed her legs apart to discover the most intimate, most sensitive part of her. His fingers began a gentle massage that his tongue repeated at her breast. Emily's nails scraped lightly up his back and shoulders to dig into his big biceps, and his satisfied groans nearly drowned out her own strangled gasps for breath.

With another swift movement, Emily found herself once again on top of Mick, but this time when he looked up at her, his chest was rising and falling in rapid, ragged breaths, and his eyes were worried questions.

"I want to make love to you more than I've ever wanted anything in my life," he told her roughly. "But if you want me to stop, I will." I think, he added silently to himself.

Emily rubbed her body languidly against his and could feel his pounding heart and heated skin, knew his blood was racing in his veins as quickly as hers. Beneath her flat belly, she could feel the hardness of his body, the rigid stiffness below his waist that reminded her he was so much a man. She cupped her hand softly over him there, and Mick closed his eyes, moaning low with ecstasy. As she continued to caress him, she lowered her lips to his and kissed him deeply. Mick growled low and wrapped his arms securely around her waist, rolling once again until she was pinned beneath him.

"That better mean you want me, sweetheart," he announced breathlessly. "Otherwise, you're in serious trouble."

"Haven't you realized yet?" she asked, her voice gritty and low from desire. "I've wanted you from that first day in your office. Even then there was something between us.

Since then, it's grown into so much more. Frankly I think we've created a monster."

His eyes softened a little at her comment, and he lifted a hand to tangle in her hair. "Sometimes I feel like a monster next to you," he said quietly. "Beauty and the Beast you might say."

"Oh, Michael, how can you think that?" she whispered, her own fingers smoothing back the dark locks that had tumbled onto his forehead. "There's never been anyone more perfect for me than you. You're what I've looked for all my life without even realizing it. You *are* gentle and tender, no matter how often you deny it, and just because you have a big body doesn't mean you're a beast."

His gaze fell playfully to indicate their position in bed, she lying vulnerable beneath him, he towering above her like a predator who's caught his prey.

Emily giggled a little breathlessly. "Okay, so maybe you're just a little beastly. It's something we can work on. A lot. But not too much, because I kind of like the animal in you." Her smile warmed and her eyes filled with love as she added, "And the reason you were endowed with such a big body is that they needed to make room for that oversize heart of yours, that's all."

Mick's own eyes fixed hungrily on hers. "I love you, Emily," he said suddenly, and Emily thought her heart would burst. "I want you to know that before we go any farther. I've never loved anyone in my life, but I do love you."

"Oh, Michael," she whispered, "I love you, too."

She brought her arms around his neck and pulled his head down to hers for a blazing kiss. Immediately the fires of passion and desire burned fierce again, growing hotter and brighter until they threatened to consume them both. Emily's hands pushed down Mick's back with thorough slowness until they reached the waistband of his shorts. She made a sound of annoyance at the barrier that met her fingers, and Mick, understanding her meaning, deftly removed them. Her hands closed over his taut buttocks then and pushed him intimately against the cradle of her thighs, gasping at the stabbing pleasure that shot through her like a missile.

Mick made his own sound of annoyance, then, one that Emily understood, and she quickly slipped out of her panties. His hand closed over her wrist then, and guided it back to where it had formerly wreaked such havoc in him. As their tongues tangled in an erotic dance, Emily led him to her, and Mick entered her slowly and deeply, allowing her a moment to get used to his invasion. She sighed and moaned with such contentment that he nearly lost control, but he held back for her, beginning with an easy, languid rhythm that grew more insistent and went deeper with every stroke.

Together they climbed to heights neither had ever neared, and together they transcended those heights to see and feel things few mortals ever knew. There was sweet, silent music and soft swirling colors, then a prism of light exploded and fell to the earth in a starry cascade. As Mick and Emily followed those stars back down, they both felt more alive than ever before. When their heart rates slowed and their breathing steadied, they looked at each other with a newly awakened knowledge, smiling conspiratorially because they had discovered something unspeakably wonderful together.

"I love you," Mick vowed solemnly again. How could he have found those words so difficult before? Loving Emily was the easiest thing in the world.

"And I love you." Emily sighed and smiled dreamily, wanting to laugh with joy at all the emotion that crowded into his gray eyes.

Mick turned over to lay flat on his back in the bed, with Emily on her stomach beside him, resting her chin on the arm she settled on his chest. Her fingers wound delicately in the dark hair she found there, and he bunched a handful of russet curls tightly in his fist. Had it been only a week ago that he had fantasized about such a moment? How could he have become one of the lucky few whose dreams became reality? He really didn't deserve it, he told himself. But he'd be damned if he would give it up now.

"What would you like to do today?" he asked her suddenly. "It's supposed to be nice. We could take the boat out if you want. Or we could go to the beach. It's too cold to swim, but it might be nice to just—"

"Michael?" Emily interrupted, the happiness that had filled her eyes now replaced by a vague uneasiness.

"Yes?"

"Uh, what about Mason?" She felt guilty again that in her preoccupation with Michael, she had once more neglected her duty to her missing brother.

Mick became more than uneasy at her question. "What do you mean?"

"I mean shouldn't we do something to keep the investigation going?"

"Like what?"

At his apparent stalling and lack of concern for her brother, Emily became a little indignant. "Well, I don't know, that's *your* job. That's why I hired you after all, you know. To find Mason. I'm not paying you to take joyrides around Chesapeake Bay."

"And I'm not charging you for them," he retorted sharply. "What's gotten into you anyway? We were enjoying quite a nice little moment there. How come you want to destroy it?"

Emily's shoulders slumped sadly and her eyes became vacant. "I'm sorry," she said. "I didn't mean to get so angry. But I just don't feel like we're doing very much to help Mason, and you don't seem very anxious to get on with the search."

She was right, of course, Mick realized. But ever since his conversation with Sam last weekend, he hadn't felt as though the case was his to pursue. And it wasn't. He'd let the FBI take over, knowing they'd be able to go about it with far greater manpower and technology than he possessed. However, Emily had no way of knowing that, and he had no way of telling her. Naturally she would think he was falling down on the job, because he was. But only because he knew he'd just be a hindrance to the investigation if he'd kept at it.

"Listen," he began slowly, trying to restore their conversation to its original serenity. "I made some calls yesterday concerning your brother." Well, one call anyway, he amended to himself, and it was last night, not yesterday. Silently he begged Emily to forgive him for bending the truth.

"What did you find out?" she asked immediately. "And why didn't you tell me?"

Mick fumbled for acceptable excuses that would allow him a way out without having to lie to her. Unfortunately when he saw the honest concern and blatant anxiety that filled her green eyes, he panicked. Unable to come up with a sufficient stall tactic, he was forced to resort to deception.

"Well, there was everything that happened last night, and not that much to tell, and I didn't want to get your hopes up unnecessarily," he dodged her questions.

"Michael, tell me what you found out," she demanded.

"Look, it was just kind of a lead from someone at the newspaper." He felt the razor gnawing inside him as he fabricated the lie. But what else could he do? If he told Emily the truth now, she'd know he'd been withholding it from her all week, and she'd hate him for it. He couldn't risk that now, not when what they had discovered together was still so new, so fragile. He wanted the fires they had started in each other to keep burning with fierce, bright heat, and he ignored what might happen when Mason was found and she discovered the true extent to which he had deceived her. If misleading her now meant they had a few more precious moments together, then he saw no choice. He had to buy time, to show her how much he loved her, how important she was to him. Later, when she was certain of his feelings, knew how deeply his love for her went, and was as hopelessly in love with him as he was with her, *then* he could tell her the truth. By then their love would be strong enough to overcome her anger and disappointment. Right now, things were still too shaky, too uncertain.

"What kind of lead?" Emily insisted, reminding Mick he had left his statement unclear.

"A tip, you might say," he told her evasively.

"What kind of tip?"

"Emily," he said with obvious exaggeration. "It's something I can't follow up on until Monday. I'll have to go back to D.C. then." There, that should buy him time enough to prove his love and show her he would never do anything to hurt her, that his actions had been for her own protection. That should give him time enough to try to secure her love for him. If not, it also gave him time to come up with a better stall.

"Monday?" she cried, lifting herself on her hands to lean over him. The action allowed her breasts to swing freely above his chest, and despite their belligerent confrontation, Mick felt desire rise within him once again.

"Yes, Monday." He tried to speak evenly, but the subtle sway of her heavy breasts fairly hypnotized him.

"But anything could happen between now and Monday," she protested, her words becoming a little less vehement when she saw where he was looking and watched the flame jump and kindle in his eyes. Her lips suddenly became dry, and she allowed her tongue to travel slowly over them, leaving a moist trail in its wake.

The gesture caught Mick's attention, and his next words were hoarse with wanting when he uttered them. "I'm sorry, but there's nothing I can do until then. Not for Mason anyway."

His hands rose and clasped her breasts tightly, pushing them back toward her body before relaxing and letting them fall again. With aching, deliberate slowness, he thumbed the rosy peaks to ripeness and guided first one, then the other, to his hungry mouth. As his lips took up the motion his fingers had abandoned, his hands traveled leisurely down Emily's body to caress her soft hips and derriére.

Emily brought one leg over him until she straddled him again, weaving her fingers wildly in the hair on his chest, shocked that she could want him again so soon after their recent journey into delirium. With a cry of mad delight, she filled herself with all of him. This time their union was even more scintillating than before, bringing them even greater joy, blinding them with even more brilliant colors.

And as the stars they'd created began to darken one by one, the lovers lay contentedly together, cuddling close. Emily thought vaguely before sleep claimed her that the gods must be smiling at her now, having finally seen fit to grant her the passionate love she had sought for so many years.

Chapter Eleven

Mick and Emily spent the greater part of the weekend doing the things that lovers do. They took *Hestia* out far into the sparkling blue waters of Chesapeake, even ventured once to make love on her warm, sun-kissed deck, beneath the cloudless sky, cooled by the autumn breeze, reveling in their nakedness, feeling at one with nature. At night they journeyed hand in hand down Cannonfire's sand-and-pebble beach, collecting broken seashells and watching the bright silver moon tossing down glittering coins onto the dark water. At one point they stumbled onto a clambake, and at the participants' insistent invitations joined the festivities, savoring every succulent clam they could dig from the pit, sipping warm cider and wine, bathed in the amber light of a bonfire as they listened to colorful stories of Cannonfire that the old-timers told.

Emily had never been more happy in her life. Those days with Michael were filled with more joy, more appreciation, more love than she'd ever known she was capable of feeling. Her moments with him made the rest of her existence seem a pale and artificial charade, a series of faded, photographic images that held none of the activity, none of the sheer *life* that consumed her when she was with him. Michael gave her mundane life new meaning, made it special, showed her that there was so much more she could accomplish, could enjoy, when she had someone to share in her day-to-day existence. Michael made things romantic. And she'd never loved life more than when they were together. She hoped nothing ever changed what they had discovered together, and prayed that it would continue on forever.

Late Saturday evening, following an afternoon spent investigating the tiny antique and curio shops that dotted Cannonfire's waterfront, Mick and Emily shared quiet moments and a bottle of burgundy in the cockpit of his sailboat. She had stayed with him there since Thursday evening after a brief trip back to her apartment for clothes and toiletries. The evening was cool, with a steady breeze coming in off the bay that pushed little lapping waves against the boat and promised the Indian summer they had enjoyed for so long had finally come to an end. It kissed Emily's face and lifted a few copper curls from the windswept mass gathered at her nape with a pale gold ribbon. She pulled down the sleeves of her matching sweater and wrapped her arms around her jean-clad legs, looking out toward the water as if expecting something to appear there.

Mick noted her posture with curiosity but said nothing, taking another sip of his wine. He didn't know how it was possible, but Emily became more beautiful with each passing day. Tonight she looked like something Mother Nature had created from pieces of the sun and bits of autumn to illustrate what honest beauty was meant to be.

Since Thursday night, his life had taken a one-hundred-and-eighty-degree turn, and his brain was still spinning from it. All of a sudden, his life was full and happy, satisfying to the point of disbelief. Mick had never known a time when there wasn't something to prevent him from feeling utterly at peace. Even in the two years since he'd left the Bureau, when he'd told himself he was perfectly content, he'd been aware of an absence in his life that he'd tried to ignore, a yearning vacancy he'd been unable to name.

Emily had filled and warmed that void completely, spilling out over it to contribute to every aspect of his existence. He loved her. It startled him still to realize it. Yet every beat of his heart made the feeling grow larger and warmer, until he almost feared it would overcome him. He'd never felt so strongly toward another human being. If anything ever happened to remove her from his life, it would take his heart, indeed his very soul, too, and he would cease to live.

He wished fervently that the FBI would hurry up and find Mason so his reluctant masquerade could come to an end. With any luck at all, Emily would never discover that he had known of their investigation, and had ceased his own because of it. Hopefully, when her brother was found by the feds, he could act just as surprised as she, then they could share in their relief that the tension was over. If everything could work out right for him, just this once, he would never have to deceive her again, and they could finally be happy together.

Happiness. It was something he had sought unconsciously for years and found accidentally with Emily. But he could wind up losing everything if she discovered the truth. Mick gazed at her openly in the soft darkness that descended upon them and prayed silently that everything would work out all right.

Emily looked over at him then, and was puzzled by the look of desperation that clouded his eyes. He looked like a man tottering on the edge of a precipice, not certain whether he should try to save himself or throw himself over the side. Suddenly his features cleared, and the image faded. She pushed back a stray curl and looked at him tentatively.

"What are you thinking about?" she asked him, speaking quietly in deference to the serenity of the night.

"Nothing important," he sidestepped her inquiry. "How about you? You're staring pretty pensively out to sea."

She took a sip of her wine and smiled a satisfied smile. "I was just thinking that except for the situation with Mason, my life would be close to perfect right now." After a moment, she added parenthetically, "Of course, I suppose the situation with Mason is what started all this in the first place."

"A perfect life is quite an accomplishment," he told her.

"Yes, I suppose it is," she agreed. "But I don't honestly think you can get much better than this."

"What do you mean?" he asked, encouraging her to continue because he loved the lilting, peaceful quality her voice had adopted.

She shrugged a little airily before she explained. "I live in a wonderful little town to which I feel a deep kinship. I have a job I enjoy surrounded by the world's most classic and inspiring literature. I have lots of friends who care for me and a brother with whom I've cherished a very special closeness all my life." Her eyes became saddened by that statement, but she quickly pressed on. "And now, I've reached the pinnacle, Michael. I've found the most important thing of all—someone to love who loves me back, who sees life the way I see it, and who finds pleasures in the things that I enjoy. All in all, I'd say I'm one of the luckiest people alive."

Mick's heart raced and his blood warmed at her statement, and little fires shot through him at the look of love in her eyes. "I'm glad you feel that way, Emily," he told her roughly. "I want you to realize how very important you've become to me, too." He wanted to tell her she'd become important to him fifteen months ago, the first time he'd seen her on that bright summer day, looking to him like a golden promise of good things to come. Then he remembered how she'd reacted to the thought of someone from Con-Corp watching her and decided some things were best left secret. "And I want you to know that I feel every bit as fortunate and as happy as you," he added.

Emily's smile became warmer as she said, "I guess that means we're going to be hanging around together a lot, huh? Even after we find Mason."

"I hope so," he muttered softly as he raised his glass to his lips. God, he hoped so.

When they went to bed that night, they turned to each other with loving passion and tender yearning, still not quite believing the extent to which they had come to need each other. Mick caressed Emily's breasts almost reverently, stroking the rest of her body with an aching gentleness born of quiet uncertainty and the fear of what might come in the future. When he rolled her onto her back and parted her legs, he entered her with an exquisite slowness and depth, waiting many moments before he began a gentle rhythm that carried them both to ecstasy.

In the morning, he awoke first in the gray light of dawn and watched her as she slept. Her thick, dark amber lashes lay against her ivory cheeks like late autumn leaves on an early snowfall. Her rosy lips were parted only slightly, the hand near them on her pillow softly clasping an errant curl that fluttered gently with her quiet respiration. She looked almost like a child, Mick thought fondly. And with her, he sometimes felt childlike, himself. His eyes traveled down her bare body to absorb her creamy shoulders and the long indentation of her spine exposed above the softly draped curves of her fanny. Then he recalled their enjoyable activities of the night before and decided they could in no way be compared to children.

He bent and placed a light kiss on her forehead, holding his breath and remaining motionless as she made a contented sound and turned her face away from him. With a satisfied smile, Mick rose from bed and padded to the galley to start a pot of coffee brewing.

It was only seven o'clock, so he decided to let Emily sleep. When he returned from the marina's office with a Sunday newspaper, she showed no sign of stirring, her deep steady breathing an indication that she was nowhere near wakefulness. Mick poured himself a cup of black coffee and found his way to the boat's tiny head for a shower.

Emily didn't hear the phone at first. She was too busy dreaming. Sweet, sensuous dreams of a dark-haired man with stormy eyes who touched her with languid thoroughness and sent her body into an uncontrolled writhing. Way off in the distance, a most annoying sound made him stop his persistent, pleasure-giving exploration, and in her semiconscious irritation, Emily vaguely understood that a telephone was making the awful sound, and that if she wanted the sexy man to come back into her dream, she would have to put an end to its ceaseless ringing by answering the silly thing.

Still half dreaming, and with the throatiness of a woman preoccupied with thoughts of passion, Emily answered Michael's cordless telephone with a deep and masculine-sounding "Hmpf?"

"Mick!" a man's voice at the other end of the line shouted loudly, waking Emily to the point that she realized she was holding a telephone in her hand. The man rushed on before she had a chance to correct his assumption. "It's Sam. Thank God you're home. Sorry to wake you, but have I got news for you! We found Emily's brother! In West Virginia, just like you thought. After weeks, a *month* even, of investigation, we finally get a substantial lead on the Thorne kidnapping."

Sam's announcement fell on Emily's ears like a ton of wet cement. Mason found? Just like that? By someone other than Michael who had been investigating his disappearance for weeks, a month even? Suddenly Emily remembered the friend that he had gone to see in Washington, and confusion muddled her brain, preventing her from saying a word. Relief washed over her that Mason was alive and someone was going to help him. But Michael had evidently known something more about his disappearance than he had told her. Why hadn't he said anything about another investigation? Why had he deceived her? With quickly spoken words, the man continued his rapid-fire report, and Emily gripped the phone with white knuckles, trying to understand.

"Everything's gonna be fine, pal. We got a call this morning from a woman in West Virginia who told us where to find Mason Thorne. He's *way* out in the boonies somewhere. I don't know any more about it than that, Mick, but I thought I should call you right away. Figured you might want to start thinking about what you're going to tell Emily when she finds out. Kind of a delicate situation, that. How are things between the two of you anyway? You guys done the dirty deed yet or what? Or are you still stringing her along with that strong, silent type bit you've used with such huge success on so many other women?"

Emily's worry became horror at the other man's statements. Just what had Michael told his friend about her? What was going on? How did Sam know about a previous investigation for her brother, how did he know for sure Mason had been kidnapped, and why hadn't Michael filled her in on it all? Most of all, what had Michael told Sam about their relationship, and why did the other man make it sound so tawdry? Was Michael, in fact, just playing a part with her as he had with other women, just to lure her into his bed?

She heard the shower then and realized Michael had no way of knowing that her world was falling into a miserable heap at her feet. She didn't know what to do. She was lying naked in a man's bed after having spent several nights making love with an intensity she hadn't known she possessed, and now it occurred to her with frightening clarity just how short a time she'd known him. Maybe Michael Dante wasn't who she'd thought him to be after all.

At the other end of the line, Sam sounded a little anxious. "Mick? You there, buddy? I know it's early, and I know how you cherish your Sundays, but hey, I thought this was *good* news!"

"It is good news," Emily spoke levelly, but her voice was edged with a raggedness she felt all the way to the pit of her stomach.

Silence met her ears first, followed by a slowly uttered, "Who is this?"

"This is Emily," she stated evenly, proud that her voice displayed none of the quivering despair she was beginning to feel.

"Oops."

"Who is *this*?" she demanded, ignoring the man's comment.

"Is Mick there?" Sam stalled.

"He's in the shower. Answer the question, please."

"Uh, my name is Sam Jackson. I'm a friend of Mick's."

"You want to tell me what's going on here? How do you know so much about me and a month-long investigation into my brother's disappearance?"

"Listen, Emily," Sam began. "Maybe Mick ought to explain all this to you."

"Oh, he'll explain all right. But I want *your* version, too."

A masculine sigh met her ears. "I just don't think I should—"

"What did you mean when you used the phrase, 'delicate situation'?" she commanded. "And why would Michael have to *think about* what he was going to say to me when I found out about Mason? And how long have you known about Mason in the first place?"

"You call him Michael?" Sam almost chuckled. "That's a new one."

"Mr. Jackson, you'd better start talking, and I'd better like what you have to say," Emily instructed, growing more angry and hurt by the minute.

"You're not going to," he warned her halfheartedly.

"Try me."

She heard another long, hopeless sigh, then Sam Jackson began to explain himself. Emily listened to what he had to say with growing alarm.

"I'm a federal agent," Sam said. "Mick was my partner before he resigned and went into private practice. We've been friends for about eight years."

"Go on," Emily told him.

Sam reluctantly continued. "After you hired him to find your brother, he came to me to see if I'd heard anything about a missing newspaper reporter. I had. We exchanged information."

"That I figured," she responded caustically. "Do you know anything about a lead he was going to follow up on Monday?"

"Lead?" Sam's voice was puzzled. "What lead? He promised me he was going to knock off his investigation until..." he trailed off, apparently realizing that he had just turned an already terrible situation into a nearly hopeless one. "I mean—"

"Michael told you he was going to stop looking for my brother?" Emily asked quietly, unable to disguise the anguish she felt. "When was this?"

"Did I say knock off his investigation?" Sam stammered. "I meant *speed up* his investigation. Yeah, that's it. He said he was going to try even harder to—"

"When was it?"

"Last weekend," Sam told her miserably. "But only because I made him promise," he hastened to add. "The federal investigation could have been shot to hell if..."

But Emily had ceased to listen. Michael had lied to her. Had been lying to her practically since they'd met. All week he'd known that her brother had been kidnapped and was being held by ConCorp, and he'd known the FBI was looking for him. Yet he'd told her nothing. He hadn't even been looking for Mason himself the way he'd led her to believe. Monday's lead had probably been just one more in a string of deceptions.

What else had he lied about? she wondered. As far as she knew, every word that had left his mouth could have been fabricated. Did he really have a father in Chicago? Had his ex-partner really been left near death in the desert? Was he actually single, or did he have a wife and family stashed somewhere? Did he truly love her? Or had the whole week been part of some elaborate plan to get her into his bed and keep her preoccupied while the guys at the FBI went about their search? All at once, another of Sam's statements came back to haunt her.

"Mr. Jackson," she interrupted his defenses of Mick's actions. "What were you referring to when you mentioned 'the dirty deed'?"

"Oh, no," Sam groaned at the other end of the line. "God, did I say that? I think you must have misunderstood."

"No, I heard you quite clearly. You distinctly said 'the dirty deed.'" She enunciated each word slowly and clearly.

"Oh, damn, damn, damn!"

"Were you referring to sex, Mr. Jackson?" she asked him angrily. "Has all this been some sort of bizarre, cruel joke? Or was it just an elaborate scheme planned with malice aforethought? That is the correct phrase, is it not? Malice aforethought?"

"Bloody hell," Sam muttered. "How did I get myself into this? Yes, that's the correct phrase, but you've got this all wrong."

"How so?"

"Is Mick out of the shower yet? I really think he should be present when I totally wreck his life. He might have something to say about it."

"Water's still running," Emily told him emotionlessly. "Him and his long showers."

"You were saying, Mr. Jackson?"

"Emily, *please* don't make me say anymore," Sam pleaded. "I really have done more than enough damage, and knowing what I do about myself, I'll only manage to make things worse."

"Please continue, Mr. Jackson," she said.

Sam uttered a quiet oath, but went on as she'd told him to. "You don't know it, but this all actually started more than a year ago."

A year ago? she wondered. "I beg your pardon?"

"Mick's fascination with you," Sam clarified. "It started over a year ago. Not long after he moved to Cannonfire."

"Mr. Jackson, what are you talking about?" Now she was really confused.

"Well, his office is right across the street from your apartment," Sam informed her unnecessarily. His voice rose with his growing irritation at the situation. "And the way you come home at night and switch on all the lights and parade around in your damned nightgown, what did you expect? The man's not *blind*, for God's sake!"

Emily's face went white. Her self-righteous anger became stark and utter embarrassment. Michael had been *watching* her from his office? For over a *year*? Her flesh crawled with the knowledge. All this time he'd been sitting over there in the darkness, watching her when she came home and went about her life, blindly secure in the knowledge that she was safe in her apartment. And worse, apparently he'd invited his friend to come over and enjoy the show. Emily's stomach churned with nausea. She felt... violated. Used. Oh, God, she felt as if she was going to be sick.

It had been horrible to know Michael had lied to her about Mason, but the idea that he had been spying on her for over a year, had made a habit of peeping in her windows while she was doing who knows what... Her eyes widened with shock. It was simply unforgivable.

Sam babbled on at the other end of the line, but to Emily it sounded like annoying radio static. She dropped the telephone blindly back into its cradle, her mind cloudy and confused from all that she had learned in the past several minutes. Emotions swirled and ricocheted in her heart. She was relieved and curious about Mason, hurt and disillusioned about Michael's deception, angry and fearful that he had been spying on her for over a year. Silently she pulled the bed sheet more tightly around her. During her conversation with Sam, she had unwittingly wrapped it about her like a cocoon, and now she looked down at the tangled folds and wondered what she should do.

When she heard the water shut off in the bathroom, she lifted her head slowly, and her eyes rested on her clothes that mingled harmoniously with Mick's in the closet. With all the speed she could muster, she began to dress in her discarded clothes of the previous evening, pausing only momentarily when Mick's big body filled the portal. Emily faltered a little at the sight of him, damp and naked to the waist where a dark blue towel was knotted precariously. His hair was wet and disheveled, and tiny droplets of water clung like little crystals to the wiry hair sprinkled across his muscular chest. He was so very handsome. And he had lied to her.

Mick had sensed something wrong the moment he'd opened the door to the head. The air fairly crackled with tension, and Emily's eyes were filled with painful emotion. He continued to watch her wordlessly as she hastily finished dressing and began to fill her small canvas bag with her clothes. He waited patiently for an explanation of her behavior while his gut knotted in a nervous twist. When she offered him nothing, only looked upon him with anger and disappointment darkening her emerald eyes, he prepared himself for battle. He didn't know what was going on, but, by God, he intended to put an end to it.

Planting his feet firmly in the passageway, he lifted his corded arms to the frame of the door, effectively blocking her way should she try to leave him. "Emily," he began, remembering to keep his voice calm. "Would you like to tell me what's going on here?"

She jerked her head up to look at him, throwing back her unruly curls with the gesture. Her traitorous heart turned over at the sight of him looking naked and vulnerable, genuine fear and uncertainty evident in his eyes. God help her, she still loved him. But she couldn't trust him, not ever again. Uncontrollable tears began forming in her own eyes, but she willed them not to fall.

"Your friend Sam, called," she said softly, unable to manage the vehemence she'd hoped to feel when she delivered her explanation.

Mick's whole body went rigid at her announcement. "Sam?"

She nodded mutely.

"What did he have to say?" he went on cautiously, knowing full well that his ex-partner ran on at the mouth worse than anyone in the animal kingdom. On more than one occasion the big boys had threatened to pull him from the field if he didn't curb his wagging tongue.

"Oh, not much," Emily told him with uneasy sarcasm. Her voice was beginning to tremble, and for the life of her, she didn't know how to make it stop. "Just that they knew where Mason is in West Virginia and are on their way to get him. He said everything's going to be fine."

Mick's heart hammered hard in his chest. He'd faced men with guns and knives, been shot and stabbed and beaten within an inch of his life, but he'd never been as terrified as he was now.

"That's great news, Emily," he said evenly, not knowing how to begin the explanation she no doubt expected him to offer. Instead an ominous silence loomed between them.

"You knew all along, didn't you?" she accused him quietly. She wished she could be angrier with him, but disappointment more than anything else crowded into her heart, and now she just felt defeated and tired. "You knew he'd been kidnapped, that the FBI was looking for him. Why didn't you tell me? Why did you lie to me, Michael? Why?"

Mick took a deep breath and looked helplessly toward the ceiling. He couldn't stand the look on her face, the forlorn bitterness that made her eyes seem even larger. He despised himself for making her so sad. Why hadn't he just left her alone in the beginning like he'd known he should? He had seen this coming, and known he would hurt her, yet he'd still acted selfishly in deceiving her, and worse, in making love to her.

"Emily, I swear I never meant to hurt you," he told her. His eyes came back to meet hers, now every bit as pain filled as the ones that met his gaze. "It hurt like hell to have to lie to you, but it was for your own good."

"My own good?" she sputtered. "What's *that* supposed to mean?"

"Just that there was a good reason for hiding the truth from you."

She emitted a humorless chuckle and raised her hand to her forehead in an effort to hide the newly forming moisture in her eyes. "Yeah, right," she mumbled, biting her lip to keep it from trembling, then lowering her head to look at the floor when she knew her tears were inevitable.

Mick wanted to reach out to her, to take her in his arms and hold her until she believed him. But he feared she would push him away, both physically and emotionally, and the thought of her rejection drove rusty nails into his heart.

"I promised Sam," he began hopelessly. "The FBI was worried that if Mason's family found out, then news of his kidnapping might leak to the press and put him in even greater danger. There was also a fear that it might endanger his family." He paused for a moment, then added meaningfully, "Which as we both know was a substantiated fear, wasn't it?"

Emily finally looked up at him, her eyes bright pools of fathomless green, her lips turned down in defeat. Her silence hurt Mick as much as anything. If she would at least yell at him, argue with him, he'd know there was still a chance to make her understand, to make things right. But her subdued, spiritless surrender told him he had little chance of winning her back. She had already decided the outcome. She wasn't even willing to fight to the end.

"Emily, please try to understand," he pleaded. "I'm sorry I lied to you. I've never been sorrier for anything in my life. If I could take it all back I would, but the damage has been done. All I can do now is try to prove to you how much I love you."

His words brought more tears to her eyes, and this time they were angry ones. "Don't say those words!" she hurled at him with such unrestrained rage that he took an involuntary step backward. "Don't ever say that to me again," she sobbed. "You *lied* to me, Michael. I can never trust you again."

Emily cried freely then, no longer able to contain the fury that clenched her heart and shook her very soul. She wrapped her arms tightly around her waist as if holding herself up, and fat tears tumbled in steady streams down her cheeks as her body was racked by ragged sobs.

Mick had known she would be angry about his deception, but this...this intense reaction was totally unexpected. Cautiously he entered the cabin and reached tentatively out to Emily. He placed a warm hand over her shoulder, and she feebly shrugged it off. When he tried again, she spun away from him, backing against the wall of the cabin until she could put no more distance between them. Mick noted her retreat with a frown, at once angry and full of despair that she could react to him with such repulsion. Suddenly a new fear gripped him. Sam had an incredibly big mouth. He'd probably said something else he shouldn't have, and Mick wanted to know what it was.

"There's something else that's bothering you, isn't there?" he asked. "What else did Sam say to you?"

"Nothing," she mumbled, trying to collect herself, staring desolately at the floor again. She just wanted to forget this week had ever happened. She wanted to forget the big gorgeous man who had come into her life long enough to show her how wonderful it could be before he ripped it to shreds. She wanted to go to a hotel with Sophie and look through the real-estate section of the Sunday paper until she found a new apartment. Then she wanted to be left alone to pick up the shattered pieces of her life that had been broken up and trampled on like everything else she possessed.

"What did he tell you that he shouldn't have, Emily?" Mick demanded, closing the distance between them in two long strides. He placed one hand on her shoulder, tightening his grip when she tried to shrug him off once more, and cupped her chin with the other to force her to face his angry expression.

Her eyes glittered at the challenge he proposed. Her next words were slow and sharp, delivered with all the vehemence she had wanted to feel earlier, and then some. "He told me how much fun you guys have had sitting over in your office watching the free show I offered for your enjoyment every evening after dark."

"He *what?*" Mick roared.

"Yeah, gee, I hope it was worth your time," she continued coldly. "I mean, I hope you weren't disappointed. I'm not really into props or anything, and Sophie's not much of an exotic animal. And I guess black leather and tassels might have been a bigger turn-on than white cotton and terry cloth, but all in all—"

"Emily, stop it," Mick cut her off. "It wasn't like that at all."

"Then you admit you've been watching me," she charged, all of the possibility of error gone with his statement.

Mick looked at her levelly, wanting to strangle Sam, knowing it was useless to deny her allegation. "Yeah, I've been watching you," he admitted. "But not in the way you seem to think."

"Oh, Michael," she muttered miserably, "how could you?"

"How could I?" he counterdemanded. "How could I not? You're the most beautiful woman I've ever seen, Emily. From the first day I saw you walking down Cleveland Street, I wanted you. There was something about you, even then, that spoke to something deep inside of me that no one else had ever reached. Even then, I think I loved you."

"Stop it!" she shouted at his words, clapping her hands viciously over her ears. Gradually her anger receded, only to be replaced by sadness, and she slowly lowered her hands. "Just . . . just stop." She slipped from his grasp and walked disspiritedly to the portal behind him. "If you wouldn't mind getting dressed, I need to get my things together and call a cab."

"A cab?" he asked sourly. "What for?"

"Because I need to go back to my apartment and collect some things before I catch the train to Washington."

"Whoa, Emily, I don't think—"

"No, you don't think, Michael," she told him calmly. "This is none of your business. *I'm* none of your business. The FBI has found my brother, and they are going after him. I plan to be in D.C. this afternoon to meet him when he gets there. I can't think of any way you could possibly fit into this scenario, unless you want to call your friend Sam, and tell him to let the FBI know I'll be waiting at Mason's apartment. On second thought, don't bother. I'll call them myself." After a moment she added, "And by the way, I want my retainer back."

"Emily—"

But it was too late. She closed the cabin door with an ominous click of the latch, and Mick heard her pick up the phone in the galley to call for a cab.

"Dammit," he snarled as he whipped the towel from around his waist and threw it on the floor with unbridled fury. He was going to kill Sam, that's all there was to it. His partner had caused trouble for the last time. As Mick pulled on fresh jeans and a faded gray Northwestern University sweatshirt, he realized he had made a grave mistake three years ago when he had gone into the Arizona desert to look for his friend. He should have just left the little windbag there for the vultures.

Chapter Twelve

Y̶ou realize of course, Mick," Sam said as he strained the perfectly chilled gin into crystal martini glasses and added a single olive to each drink, "that this whole thing could have been avoided if you'd just listened to me a year ago and gone into the bookstore where she works to introduce yourself. You might even have beaten *me* to the altar."

Sam came around the sofa to sit beside a slouching, brooding Mick, who stared vacantly into his friend's apartment. Unlike his former partner, whose crumpled jeans and baggy, tattered sweatshirt genuinely reflected the raggedness of his mood, Sam wore tailored trousers and a monogrammed, designer sweater that had cost him a fortune to make him look relaxed and easygoing. Currently, though, the sweater was stretched completely out of shape, and the shirt beneath it spilled from the waistband of his wrinkled trousers. He also sported an impressive black eye that put the fading purple and blue smudges that still darkened Mick's eye to shame.

He had opened his front door fully aware of what awaited him. It wasn't the first time he and Mick had duked it out over a difference of opinion, especially one involving a woman, though they both hoped this time would be the last. In many ways, the two men were the childhood friends neither had found as youngsters. Unfortunately, when it came to roughhousing now, they were both entirely too well equipped to manage it, but no longer resilient in springing back once it was over.

Mick took the delicate martini glass Sam offered him and stared at it disconsolately before downing the contents, olive and all, in one hefty swig. It was the only solid food he'd had all day. When he'd finished dressing that morning, Emily had made good on her promise. She'd wordlessly collected all her things along with Sophie's, ignoring every word he'd uttered in his defense. The only time she'd reacted had been when he'd told her he loved her, and then she had snapped her head around to gaze at him with such pain-filled eyes that he hadn't been able to say anything more. The taxi had come to take her away, and he'd tried calling her at home, then at Mason's, but to no avail.

"I hate you," Mick mumbled at Sam.

"I know it," Sam assured him as he refilled the empty glass that Mick still clutched to his stomach. This time he added an extra olive.

"What am I going to do, Sam?" he demanded. "She won't listen to me, she doesn't trust me. Even Sophie looked at me like she wanted to scratch my eyes out."

"Sophie?"

"Her cat."

"That is serious."

Mick nodded dumbly and swallowed his drink. Sam, ever the good host, amply refilled his guest's glass one more time.

"And thanks to you she thinks I'm some twisted, perverted Peeping Tom who's been getting his jollies for the past year staring into her window." He gulped back his drink for a third time.

"Well, now, Mick, that isn't entirely off base, you know," Sam told his friend after taking a sip of his own martini, and smacking his lips.

"Whose side are you on?" Mick insisted crossly, looking at his friend for the first time since they'd become too exhausted to finish their fight. He grimaced at the bruise rising angrily above Sam's patrician cheekbone. "Sorry about the eye," he added sheepishly.

"No problem," Sam told him, emptying the remains of the cocktail shaker into his ex-partner's glass. "And I'm on *your* side, though God knows why I bother sometimes."

Mick responded with a muffled oath, then asked, "What am I drinking?"

"Gin."

"I hate gin. It gives me incapacitating hangovers."

"I know."

Mick gritted his teeth at Sam, then set his glass down on the coffee table and rose to pace like a nervous animal. "There's got to be something I can say to make her change her mind," he muttered.

"There's nothing you can say to make her change her mind," Sam told him. "You're going to have to resort to action."

Mick stopped pacing and looked at his friend. "What do you mean?"

"You said it yourself, Mick. She won't listen to what you have to say, and she doesn't trust you. She thinks you lied to her. Well, of course you *did* lie to her, but that's beside the point." He looked at Mick, who was snarling and ready to pounce. "*Anyway,* you know what they say: actions speak louder than words."

"Sam, what are you talking about?"

"I have a plan," the other man announced.

"Your last plan landed us in the cargo hold of a freighter taking the slow route to Abu Dhabi," Mick reminded him.

"This one's even better," Sam said with a smile.

"Oh, gee, well in *that* case . . ."

"Trust me, Mick," Sam cooed. "Just this once. Trust me."

At George Washington University Hospital, Emily, too, paced like a nervous animal while she waited to see her brother. The federal agent who had picked her up at Mason's apartment had filled her in on all that had transpired in the past twenty-four hours. Evidently Lou Lofton had finally found an excuse to visit relatives in Tooley and had placed a call to the FBI to alert them to the state of affairs. Numerous federal agents had then swooped down on Hack's Crossing, West Virginia, without so much as a snapping twig announcing their arrival. They'd rudely interrupted the Lofton Clan's Sunday supper at Fairmont Lofton's modest home, clapping handcuffs on everyone present, including one Mr. Steven Destri, their guest of honor, with little more than a howdy-do.

After that they had proceeded on to the rail yards where they had discovered a large shipment of contraband that had arrived in town only the day before. And in one lone freight car that sat off by itself, they discovered a bound-and-banged-up Mason Thorne, who had quickly taken them to task for taking their sweet time in finding him.

Now it looked like the end for the Connery Corporation and for Everett Connery himself, thanks to what the FBI found at the scene, along with testimony from honest family members like Lou. Not to mention the missing evidence, which Mason had revealed he'd sent to his downstairs neighbor Cinnabar Gamboge for safekeeping, and which Cinnabar had already turned over to the authorities encased in a plaster-of-paris buffalo.

Emily's pacing increased as she waited while the doctors finished looking Mason over and the federal agents finished questioning him. She'd heard one of the nurses say he'd demanded access to a word processor before he'd asked for anything else, and she'd known then that her brother was going to be fine. With her worries about Mason fading, thoughts of Michael began to take their place.

She hadn't allowed herself to think about him since she'd climbed into the taxi that had taken her back to her apartment. She'd telephoned Stella at home and given her a tearful, abbreviated version of the weekend, then said she was going to spend a few days with her brother to help him convalesce. Stella had assured her that no apology was necessary, that she understood completely and that not only would she pass the word along to Mr. Lindsey, but also she would be more than happy to keep Sophie for a few days. Emily had decided that Stella was the most tolerant person on the face of the earth and had come up with numerous ideas about how to overcompensate for her own lax behavior in the coming weeks.

After that, her thoughts had turned to Mason and stayed there until a little while ago when a young intern had informed her that her brother was suffering from malnutrition, exhaustion and some lacerations and contusions. He also had two cracked ribs that they had taped up and which were already beginning to heal, but all in all, he would be just fine, had in fact already made dates with several of the nurses and the orthopedic surgeon.

Emily had breathed a deep sigh of relief then, but now that she knew Mason was going to be all right, images of Michael sprang unbidden to the forefront of her mind: Michael behind the wheel of his sailboat, confident and at peace; Michael at the clambake, listening with eager interest as an old sea captain described his experiences during the hurricane that had rocked Cannonfire in '33; Michael trying to make friends with Sophie, daring to scratch her behind her flattened ears while the animal growled low in her throat. The cat had ended up curling into quiet slumber in his lap later that night, she recalled. She also remembered Michael helping her pick up her ruined belongings after the first break-in, and waking up to find him holding her hand after the second.

In her mind she also saw him as he was that first night they had gone out—had it really been only a little over a week ago? He'd tried to be so distant and cold, had attempted to put her off, but she had sensed something in him, even then, that had reached out for her blindly.

He'd told her that he loved her. That he only deceived her for fear of her safety. That he had watched her at night because he had loved her even then. He'd promised that nothing would ever keep him from her. Emily stopped her restless pacing, listening absently to hospital sounds— chimes paging nurses, a metal gurney rattling along with a reluctant wheel. Gradually she began to wonder if perhaps she had reacted somewhat hastily to Sam's badly offered information. Why had she listened to a total stranger in the first place? She'd given Sam a better chance to foul things up than she'd given Michael to explain them. Maybe she'd been in too much of a hurry to believe the worst of Michael. Maybe in her fear of the intensity and quickness of her love for him, she had been too eager to think their relationship was too good to be true. Maybe...

"Miss Thorne?" It was the physician handling Mason's case, Dr. Harrison, she remembered he'd said when he'd introduced himself.

"Can I see Mason now?" she asked him anxiously.

"He's been demanding to talk to you," Dr. Harrison told her with a smile. He looked to be only in his forties, but had already lost the vast majority of his hair. He peered at her warmly over his glasses, tucking Mason's chart under his arm.

Emily followed him down a long corridor until they came to a room guarded by two men in suits. Inside, her brother was wide awake and chatting amiably with a beautiful, dark-haired woman who wore a white coat over her tailored skirt and blouse, whose only jewelry was a stethoscope that hung unfettered around her neck.

"Mason?" Emily's voice sounded distant to her own ears, but Mason turned immediately to smile at her. He had lost so much weight! He was pale and weak looking, with bruises on his face and white bandages around the wrists that lay still against his sheet. His once thick mane of golden-blond hair now lay in dingy, lifeless strands around his head. But his eyes, his big, expressive blue eyes sparkled with animation and joy. His eyes let her know he was still the same old Mason.

"You look awful," she told him with a shaky smile.

"Hey, blame my travel agent," he quipped. "And if she tries to sell you this great package deal to Hack's Crossing, West Virginia, tell her you want to take a Caribbean cruise instead."

Emily looked at her brother and shook her head, wondering how she'd made it through the past four weeks not knowing where he was. She almost hadn't, she reminded herself. Until she'd met Michael Dante.

"I was worried about you," she told him, moving quickly to the side of his bed, where she looked questioningly at the woman on the other side.

"Oh, Em, this is Dr. Petra Ivanovich," Mason introduced the other woman. "Petra, this is my sister, Emily."

"How do you do?" Petra said in a lightly accented voice and extended her hand gracefully to Emily across Mason's bed.

Emily smiled and shook it. "Dr. Ivanovich. Nice to meet you."

Petra returned her smile, then said to Mason, "I have to make my rounds now, Mason, but I'll come back before I go home tonight."

"Great," Mason replied. "We can talk about next weekend."

"You're going to be here until next weekend?" Emily asked him, puzzled.

"No, I'll be out on Tuesday," Mason said, watching the other woman's elegant movements as she made her way to the door.

Emily's confusion grew, then she narrowed her eyes suspiciously. "I thought Dr. Harrison was your doctor."

"He is," Mason told her, his eyes finally returning to meet hers when the door to his room swung closed with Petra's departure.

"Then who…" Eventually she began to understand, and she gave her brother a disapproving frown. "Mason," she scolded. "Don't you think next weekend is just a tad bit early?"

"Em, the doctor told me I had to rebuild my strength."

"Mason!"

"Come on," he prodded her with that disarming Mason smile that had been many a woman's downfall. "Tell me everything that's happened to you in the past month."

Emily smiled back cheerlessly and said, "Oh, not much. Hired a private investigator to find you, a big, good-looking son of a gun whom I promptly fell in love with. We lived in sin on his boat for a while after some thug trashed my apartment and tried to kidnap me, then I found out he was a liar and a Peeping Tom, and I left him. But other than that, things have been about the same."

"No, *really*, Em. What have you been doing to keep occupied?"

"I just told you," she said, trying to remain glib, trying unsuccessfully to keep her pain and confusion buried deep within her.

But Mason knew his sister too well. He recognized the sadness that clouded her normally happy eyes, and saw the dark shadows that had settled in below them. "What happened, Em?" he asked her quietly, raising his pale hand to cover hers on the bed rail.

At his soft urging, she couldn't stop the tears that had been threatening her since she'd left the boat that morning. "I don't know, Mason," she said honestly. "Everything went so fast."

She took her time telling her brother about the events of the previous four weeks. After giving all the details of the break-in and kidnapping, she went on to describe how things had escalated between her and Michael while she'd stayed with him on the boat. Then she told him abut her flight from him after her ensuing discovery of his deception and nightly viewing habits.

"I just don't know what to do," she concluded finally. "I feel like I can't trust him, like he betrayed me. But at the same time, I can't stop thinking about how loving he always was." She took a deep breath and looked to her brother for help. "Oh, Mason, he just seemed so...so wonderful...so decent." Her eyes fell to the small hands she had nervously tangled with her brother's larger ones.

Mason gazed steadily at his sister. He'd never seen her features come alive the way they did when she talked about her Michael Dante. If there was one person in the world he could read and understand, that person was his sister. Emily loved this guy with all her heart. And she wasn't going to be whole again until she patched things up with him.

"He was right in not telling you about my kidnapping," Mason stated honestly, and Emily's attention returned to her brother, her expression telling him she thought he was a traitor, too. "It's true, Em," he insisted. "The newspaper swore the FBI to secrecy, knowing what kind of people they were dealing with, realizing the danger I could have been in, and *you* could have been in," he added meaningfully, "if my investigation of ConCorp and my kidnapping had been made public. You say this guy was a federal agent before, right?"

Emily nodded sadly.

"Then when he found out the truth from his ex-partner, he had no choice but to keep it from you. Not only would it have been unethical, it would have been dangerous."

Emily said nothing.

"But I think you're beginning to realize that, aren't you?" Mason asked her tentatively.

Emily looked back down at her hands and nodded reluctantly.

"Which means," her brother continued, "that the really serious charge against our Mr. Dante is that one about his nocturnal activities, right?"

"How could he do that to me, Mason?" she demanded softly, still twisting her fingers nervously in his. "It's so... so... unnatural."

"Unnatural," Mason repeated, a wide, nostalgic smile that Emily couldn't see brightening his features. "You know, Em, I seem to recall that spring of my senior year at Notre Dame when you took to following around one Lionel Dunstan, the chemistry professor's son, remember that?"

Emily looked up at her brother through narrowed eyes and opened her mouth to protest. Unfortunately for her, Mason plodded on before she had a chance.

"Yeah, all semester long you dogged that poor guy's steps, trying to pretend you weren't interested."

"Mason, that's altogether a different situation," Emily said, but her brother went on, oblivious to her protest.

"And old Lionel did pretty well ignoring you until that one Saturday night just before classes got out."

"Mason—"

"If only you'd been born with better balance," he told her, his smile growing even larger at the color creeping into her cheeks. "I remember you could hear your scream all the way to the library when you fell out of that sycamore tree behind the Dunstan house. You remember, Em? That big, gnarled one about ten feet in front of Lionel's bedroom window? Good thing the binoculars got caught on a branch. Dad would have tanned your butt if you'd broken them."

"Mason, that was a long time ago," Emily mumbled sheepishly. "I was practically a child."

"Seems to me it was right before your sixteenth birthday," Mason recalled. "And Lionel was what, about twenty?"

"Twenty-two," Emily muttered.

"That's right," Mason said, still grinning. "It was his last year as running back, wasn't it?"

Emily tried to look angry with her brother, but at his self-satisfied smile she had to laugh. "All right, you've made your point," she told him. "There are exceptions to every rule, even where Peeping Toms are concerned."

"From the way you describe this guy, he doesn't seem the type to go around spying on women because he's a pervert. He just knows a good thing when he sees it, that's all. I'm sure if given the opportunity to explain he could give you a sufficient reason for how this all came about."

"You're right, of course," she told him after a moment. "As usual."

"What can I say?" Mason leaned back in his bed, tucking his hands confidently behind his head.

Emily smiled at her brother and said, "I've really missed talking to you. I don't know what I would have done if anything had happened to you. Won't you *please* get into some safer aspect of journalism? Household hints or the society page or something?"

"Not a chance."

Emily lifted her hand and ruffled her brother's hair affectionately. Suddenly the door to his room swung open and a small, lithe young woman entered nervously.

"Mason?"

Emily noticed that Mason's eyes warmed considerably at the sound of the voice.

"Lou!" he greeted her excitedly. "Where you been, kid?"

Lou wore an oversize, federal-issue, navy-blue wind-breaker over her loose, faded red dress. She came slowly to the other side of Mason's bed, her dark eyes flitting nervously between him and Emily. "I been talkin' to the feds," she said quietly. "They want me to testify for 'em. You a friend of Mason's?" she asked Emily pointedly.

Mason raised one hand to cover both of Lou's that rested on the bed rail and grinned at her with unabashed affection. Emily beamed at her brother, but he didn't notice it.

"Lou, this is my sister, Emily. Emily, this is Miss Halouise Lofton, my salvation."

Lou relaxed visibly at the introduction, but still looked at Emily with an uncertain expression. "Hey," she said in way of a greeting. "Mason's told me a whole lot about you."

"I hate to think what," Emily said, staring at Mason with new interest. Was it possible that he had actually made *friends* with a woman? She'd never known him to be capable of such a thing. Maybe there was hope for him yet.

Lou mistook Emily's sisterly teasing as a serious statement. "Oh, only good thangs," she assured her. "He really loves you a lot."

Emily tried to hide her smile. "I know he does," she said quietly.

Mason's gaze had gone from one woman to the other during their exchange, but now he turned his attention to Lou. "Are you all right?" he asked her.

Lou smiled at Mason and nodded quickly. "They said between what they found durin' the raid, the stuff you got on 'em in Roadside and everywhere else, and some other people who knowed thangs and was willin' to talk, that ConCorp oughta just be a bad memory afore long. They's gonna put everybody away for a good, long time."

"Well, I got my story filed anyway," Mason said smugly. "Scooped 'em all this time, that's for sure."

"You're far too preoccupied with getting your story, Mason," Emily warned him. "There are a lot of more important things in life, you know?"

"She's right, Mason," Lou agreed with a vigorous nod.

Mason looked at both women suspiciously. "Yeah, well, maybe," he said slowly. "Speaking of which, Em, don't you have some straightening up to do in your own life? Don't feel like you have to stay here nagging me about the dangers of my job all night. Lou, here, can do that just fine by herself."

"I don't feel right leaving you here like this," Emily protested. "Besides, it's too late to go back to Cannonfire tonight. The last train goes at eight-thirty. I'd never make it."

"Then go back to my place and get some sleep so you can get up and catch the early one in the morning."

"Mason..."

"Visiting hours end soon anyway," he reminded her. "Lou can keep me company until then."

"If there's some place you gotta be, Emily," Lou said earnestly, "then you best get there. I'll keep an eye on Mason so he don't go creepin' off again."

Emily smiled at Lou. "If anyone can manage that colossal feat," she said, "I think you might be just the one to do it, Lou."

Lou returned her smile, and Mason looked confused. Emily laughed at her brother's expression, then she leaned down to kiss him lightly on the cheek.

"I really do hate to leave you, Mason," she told him. "But I think I need to talk to Michael as soon as possible."

"Didn't I just say that?"

"Anyway, it's not like you never took off and left me hanging, is it?"

"Will you get out of here?" he insisted.

Emily rumpled her brother's hair one final time then turned to Lou. "It was very enlightening meeting you, Lou," she told her.

Lou looked somewhat puzzled at Emily's choice of words but nodded her acknowledgement. "Nice meetin' you, too," she said.

"And *you*," she said ominously to Mason.

"Yes?"

"Behave yourself." And with that command, Emily turned to leave.

"Call me!" Mason yelled after her as the door swung closed on her departure. "I want everything to work out for you, little sister," he added quietly. "More than anyone else, you deserve it."

Emily took a taxi back to Mason's apartment, unwilling to take any of the agents who offered her a ride away from their duties. She was immensely relieved, not only that Mason had been returned safely to her, but also that his kidnapping hadn't been for naught. From what she understood, the entire corporation, from Everett Connery on down, had already begun to crumble, thanks to the quickness with which the federal authorities had been able to act once they'd gotten their hands on the evidence Mason had collected.

As Emily climbed the stairs to Mason's apartment, she passed Cinnabar's front door and paused. Imagine, she thought as she shook her head slightly. All along, the elderly artist had had a package full of incriminating photos and documents sealed inside that tacky buffalo. One of the agents had even revealed that Cinnabar had gone on to paint the silly thing chartreuse, as if it were just another one of her regular sculptures. Cinnabar and Mason in cahoots all that time, and no one would have ever suspected. Emily silently sent up thanks that everything had worked out all right before she continued her ascent.

She was searching in her purse for her keys when her foot hit the third floor. Mick gazed at her hungrily from his post at Mason's door. He took in the tumble of autumn-colored curls, the red wool scarf looped around her neck, the oversize white sweater that lovingly curved her jean-clad thighs and he uttered her name on a soft sigh.

"Emily."

She heard his deep, smooth voice at the same time her fingers closed over her keys. Slowly she lifted her head to meet his gaze, stunned by the genuine fear and sadness that met her eyes. He still wore the clothes of that morning, but now they seemed even more rumpled than before. His hair was a mess, as if he'd been constantly and viciously weaving his fingers through it, and her first instinct was to go to him and bury her own hands in his hair, to straighten the unruly mass herself. She barely managed to keep herself still as she continued to stare at him.

"How did you get into the building?" she asked him quietly. "The front door is always locked."

Mick tried to read her expression, to fathom just what she was feeling, but found her emotions impossible to gauge. "I buzzed Cinnabar and talked her into letting me in this far. But she warned me she'd be listening for any signs of foul play."

"Why did you come?" she continued, taking a few wary steps toward him as if pulled by some intangible force.

So she was still angry with him, Mick thought sadly. She still didn't understand why he had acted the way he had. Well, tough. She was going to listen to his explanations if he had to gag her and tie her up in a chair. He loved her, dammit. Wanted to spend the rest of his life with her. And if she couldn't see the reality of that, then he would just have to be a little more persuasive.

"I had to get over here before Sam did," he told her. "He had a plan."

Emily looked at him, obviously puzzled, and said, "A plan for what?"

"It's a long story. Something about gypsy violinists and mariachi bands and Rod McKuen poems. It got pretty bizarre after that, and I stopped listening." He shook his head in thought and mumbled, "I really have to wonder if Mercy Malone knows what she's getting herself into."

Emily watched him for a moment longer, not certain how to act. She'd planned to come back to the apartment and have a cup of tea while she thought about what she wanted to say to Michael. Instead she'd been denied that luxury and would have to face up to the situation right now. She juggled her keys absently and contemplated Michael's expression. He looked beat, as if he'd been wrung through the wringer and left in a heap. He looked like a man who'd been hurt very badly. With a stunning realization and no small amount of guilt, Emily understood she was the reason for his pain and knew that he probably harbored fears and emotions similar to the ones she had suffered all day.

"Oh, Michael," she said in a broken voice as she suddenly closed the remaining distance between them and wrapped her arms around his waist. "I missed you." She laid her cheek against his solid chest, closing her eyes at the relief and contentment that came over her as she did so.

Mick couldn't believe his incredible good luck. She didn't hate him. She didn't even seem to be mad at him anymore. Eagerly, and with a great easing of tension, he wound his arms tightly around her, too, tangling one hand in the curls at the base of her neck, pressing his lips into her hair. "God, Emily," he growled hoarsely, inhaling great gulps of the flowery fragrance that surrounded her. "I missed you, too. Don't ever leave me like that again."

She smiled and lifted her shining eyes to his. "You still want me, then?" she asked with a slightly teasing tone in her voice.

"*Want* is a pretty tame word for how I feel about you," he told her with an affectionate squeeze. "*Need* you may be closer on the mark. *Hunger for* you could also be appropriate. But most specifically, I *love* you. I guess that sort of encompasses all the rest."

"I love you, too," she told him quietly.

"Emily, what—"

"Michael, I—"

They spoke as one, each lost in the deep emotion reflected in the other's eyes. When they both stopped abruptly, Emily suggested they take their conversation into Mason's apartment where they had a little more privacy. They made small talk while Emily started a pot of coffee, knowing, hoping, it would be a long night. When they were settled in on the sofa, Emily took a sip from her mug while Mick sat in thoughtful silence. Finally he voiced the question that had been rattling around in his brain since she'd come to him in the hall.

"Emily, what happened? Don't take this the wrong way, but why aren't you still mad at me? I came over here ready to camp out on the front stoop if that was what it took to see you. Maybe I'm pushing my luck here, but you don't seem like you're angry with me anymore. Dare I hope that's the truth?"

She grinned inwardly at the uncertainty reflected in his voice. Michael Dante probably hadn't been uncertain of very many things in his life, she speculated. But now he was cautious and solicitous in his fear of losing her. It reassured her that he seemed to feel exactly the same way she did.

"No, I'm not mad at you anymore, Michael," she confessed. "I think more than anything else, my reaction this morning was sprung from shock. Since then I've had time to think about things." She paused until his silent gaze told her to go on. "I'm not much for self-analysis, but looking back on the way my life has been heaved upside down and inside out in the past couple of weeks, I think maybe everything just boiled over this morning and I finally reacted to it all. It finally sunk in just what was happening to me, and ... it scared me. A lot."

"What do you mean?"

She shrugged and took another sip of her coffee. "Just that, until Mason's kidnapping and my meeting you, my life for twenty-six years had been one long string of quiet experiences and tepid relationships. My emotions have never been very strong ones, except for Mason. I'd never been particularly happy or sad. I'd never been overly excited or especially angry. I'd never been really scared before. And I'd never been so much in love. So maybe this morning, after Sam's call, my brain finally said, 'Enough.' Maybe I had to remove myself for a little while from what had caused all those feelings to readjust myself. Maybe I just needed a little time to realign my perspective."

Mick thought about what she said and understood completely. In so many ways, what she described was exactly what he'd gone through in the past weeks, himself. "So how's your perspective now?" he asked her.

Her eyes filled with warmth as they met his. "Thanks to Mason, it's back on track."

Mick lifted his brows at her admission. "Oh? I guess I owe the man a great deal, then, don't I? How did he manage to nudge you back on my side?"

Emily grinned at Mason's reminder of Lionel Dunstan. Maybe someday she would tell Michael about her experience with the running back and the sycamore tree. Maybe. Someday. "Let's just say Mason is real good at presenting two sides to every situation," she told him vaguely.

His face remained a question mark, but Emily just laughed. She scooted across the couch to cuddle up next to him, sighing with contentment at how good it felt to be so close to Michael again, both physically and spiritually. Silently he wrapped his arms around her and pulled her into his lap, curling his hand under her chin to lift her face up to his. He searched her eyes for something he couldn't name, and his heart began to drum feverishly as he became lost in their green depths.

"So what happens now?" he asked her quietly, his voice a husky caress.

Wordlessly, Emily raised a hand to switch off the light beside them and plunged the room into soft darkness. Her hand came back to gently cup his rough cheek, and she raised her lips to brush them with aching tenderness over his own. Mick groaned quietly as he tightened his hold on her.

"Well," she whispered as her lips left his mouth to travel across his whiskery cheek. "I thought we might try getting a little sleep." She trailed kisses down his neck and over his throat, then embellished them with light, playful strokes of her tongue. Mick groaned again and let his hand leave her waist to close gently over her breast. Her next words came out a little breathless. "After all, it has been a long day. What do you say? Are you sleepy? Want me to fix your bed up here on the couch?"

Mick's chuckle was low and lascivious. "Oh, we can use the couch for a bed all right," he told her as his hand began a slow massage that his tongue and lips mimicked against her throat. "But sleep wasn't exactly what I had in mind."

With one quick, capable movement, he maneuvered Emily's soft body beneath his own as they stretched out on the sofa. He slanted his mouth across hers in a hungry kiss that she met eagerly and countered with one of her own. As his hands fumbled with her sweater, hers tangled at the hem of his sweatshirt. She found the satiny skin of his back at the same moment his fingers closed over the agitated peak of her breast. They both sighed and moaned in unison. After more moments spent absorbed in the thorough exploration of each other, Mick raised his head to look searchingly at Emily's expression.

"I love you," he said suddenly, fiercely, his hand moving to stroke the soft skin of her cheek. His eyes pleaded with her to love him, too, to promise she would never turn her back on him again.

She, too, lifted a hand to his face and gazed at him solemnly as she whispered, "And I love you."

"Forever?" he asked her quietly.

She nodded, her eyes shining with her love for him. "Forever," she promised.

With that gentle reassurance they went on to illustrate the absolute depth of their feelings for each other. Their journey that night may have begun in Mason's plain, sparsely furnished apartment, but by morning they had traveled to the most spectacular places either had ever known. And when the morning sun crept silently into the bedroom, it was to warm two people who slept soundly and utterly at peace in each other's arms.

This time Emily was the first to awaken and watch soundlessly as the man she loved continued to dream. However, this time there was no alarming phone call, no heart-wrenching news to throw up a wall between them.

When Mick opened his eyes to behold a beaming, grinning Emily, a warmth closed over his heart, while love and relief turned his hard bones to liquid fire. Last night hadn't been a dream after all, he realized as he gazed longingly at the woman beside him.

He looped a muscular arm around her neck and pulled her down to receive his good-morning kiss, then smiled when she snuggled her lush body close to his. It was the fourth morning in a row that he'd awakened beside her, and he knew with unquestionable certainty that he would never be able to face another day of waking up alone.

"You know, a man could get used to this," he spoke his thoughts out loud.

"To what?" Emily purred from her position beside him.

"To waking up to find you beside him looking gorgeous and desirable every morning."

She smiled and placed a quick kiss on the warm skin over his heart. "Not just any man, I hope."

"Well, no," he admitted. "I did have one in particular in mind."

"And who, pray tell, might that be?" she ventured playfully as she ran her fingers up and down his rib cage.

"Stop that," he said, gently trapping her fingers in his.

"Why?"

"Because it tickles."

Emily raised herself on one elbow to peer intently into his eyes. "I didn't know you were ticklish," she said.

"Look, do you want to know who I have in mind for the job of waking up beside you every morning or not?" he demanded gruffly.

Her eyes told him she already knew, but was going to indulge him anyway. "All right. Who?"

"Me."

She took a deep breath and let her gaze wander toward the bedroom door. "You, huh?" she said with affected indifference. "Why would I want to wake up next to you every morning?"

Mick waited a moment before offering his suggestion, a tiny part of him still unsure of how she felt about him. He looked down at the small fingers tangled with his and spoke slowly and very quietly.

"I, um...I thought maybe you might...we could...that is—"

Emily smiled when she returned her gaze to find him staring at her fingers and stumbling over his words. "Michael," she began, trying to sound flippant, "call me old-fashioned, but I don't think I could wake up next to a man every morning unless I was married to him."

"Yes!" His eyes were filled with excitement when his head snapped up to meet her expression.

"Yes, what?" Her smile became broader when she saw the relief that slashed through his eyes at her statement.

"Yes, I'll marry you," he told her animatedly. He pulled her back down to the bed and rolled over on top of her, ready to seal the agreement with a kiss.

Emily couldn't help laughing as she said, "Michael, I don't recall asking you to marry me."

He stopped himself before his lips met hers, realizing she spoke the truth. She hadn't actually phrased a question, had she? "Oh," he mumbled thoughtfully. "Then will *you* marry *me*?"

Emily's arms wrapped snugly around his neck and she continued to smile as she responded. "Gee, I don't know. I've only known you a little over a week. Things have happened so fast."

"But you yourself said that you've experienced more emotion since you met me than ever before," he reminded her. "You said you'll love me forever. And we have been living together, after all," he threw in meaningfully. "You have your reputation to think about. I mean, think about it for a minute, Emily."

She did. Then after a minute she said, "Okay. I'll marry you. But it's only because I love you and can't live without you. You'll be wise to remember that."

"Yes, ma'am."

"And I'll need Sophie's approval, of course."

"Piece o' cake," Mick assured her, knowing all the tuna fish—albacore at that—that he'd slipped to the animal during her stay on the boat had won him the cat's approval long ago.

"And Michael?"

"Yes?"

"Thanks."

"What for this time?"

Emily shrugged. "For improving the quality of my life."

He smiled and buried both hands in her russet curls. "Believe me, it was strictly a selfish gesture on my part. I'm just thankful you're happy about it, too."

"Happier than I've ever been."

Mick smiled and coiled her unruly curls around his fingers. "Emily?"

"Yes?"

"Promise me you'll never cut your hair short again."

"How did you know it used to be . . ."

Her voice became indignant, but he laughed happily and headed off her anger with a kiss that went straight to their souls. And as the sun rose higher in the sky and shone brightly down into the room to douse them with warmth, Michael and Emily created some incandescence and heat of their own that drove the sun back into darkness.

Epilogue

All right, everybody, settle down. It's almost midnight."
Mick Dante hushed the crowd seated at one of the larger
booths near the stage at Havern's Tavern. Willie and the
Wailers had just finished their last set, and Willie and
Gizelle now joined Mick and Emily, Mason and Lou and
Sam and Mercy at their table. Tonight everyone wore hats,
brightly colored ones with feathers and glitter and shiny
paper foil. "Willie," Mick continued, "You got the good
stuff ready?"

"You know it, baby," Willie told his new friend. "Rose!"
he called to the server who had waited on Emily and Mick
three months before. "Bring out the bubbly!"

Rose nodded and within minutes returned with an oversize, freestanding wine cooler housing three magnums of
champagne, already glistening with condensation in the dim

light. Mick plucked one of the bottles from the ice and deftly removed the foil and wire cap covering the cork.

"Everybody ready?" he asked.

Everyone nodded and murmured that not only were they ready, but they were also thirsty, and midnight was only scant seconds away. As the band onstage began the ten-second countdown, Mick popped the cork on the bottle and filled eight crystal champagne flutes with the effervescent wine. He had just topped off his own when festive choruses of "Happy New Year!" went up around him, and he lifted his glass with the others.

While the band struck up a bluesy rendition of "Auld Lang Syne," Emily sang out happily with everyone else at the table. When they finished, they each took turns making toasts. As her turn came around, Emily raised her glass high, thankful and hopeful for so many reasons, not certain where to begin.

"There's so much," she said voicing her thoughts. "Here's to my new husband, of course." She turned to smile lovingly at Michael, who smiled back and raised his own glass to his new wife. "And here's to our new house in Cannonfire that we'd like you all to come see just as soon as we've finished painting and wallpapering."

"And fixing stairs," Mick added. "And putting on a new roof, and refinishing floors, and getting new screens and storm windows, and—"

"And here's to my brother, Mason," Emily quickly interrupted her husband's complaints, "who's off to God knows where next week to investigate who knows what story."

"It's a secret," Mason announced in a loud stage whisper.

"And here's to Lou," she added, indicating the young woman who had unwittingly been responsible for so many changes in so many lives. "Good luck at American University this spring. Have you decided what you're going to major in yet?"

Lou shrugged, obviously uncomfortable at being the center of attention. "I don't know yet. Maybe I'll go to law school eventually."

"Law school?" Mason sputtered, almost choking on his champagne. "I thought you wanted to become a journalist. Like me."

"Well, that was before the ConCorp trial. I thought all that litigatin' was kinda interestin'."

"Boy, and after all the favors I called in to get you enrolled after the deadline," Mason mumbled. "That's gratitude."

Lou laid a small hand over Mason's. "I appreciate all your help, Mason," she said quietly. "What with gettin' me admitted and findin' me a place to live and all. I'm just not sure yet what I want to do with my life, that's all."

"Yeah, well, just don't go running off somewhere without telling me."

"I promise I'd never do that," Lou said with a grin.

Emily smiled at the pair. She'd never seen her brother so dedicated to another person besides herself. She turned her attention to and toasted Sam and Mercy. "May your life together be long and happy, and may you find the utter joy that Michael and I have found together."

"I still can't believe you beat me to the altar, Mick," Sam muttered, shaking his head.

"Me, neither," Mercy agreed. The tall brunette entwined her fingers with her fiancé's. "From the things Sammy said, I was afraid you'd try to talk him out of it."

"Sammy?" Mick asked his friend, trying unsuccessfully to suppress a laugh. "She calls you *Sammy*?"

Sam colored as he took a quick, deep sip of his champagne. "Yes, she does, *Michael*. What of it?"

The two men gazed at each other in good humor before they simultaneously lifted their glasses in a silent, private toast.

Emily's eyes sparkled at the gesture before she turned to Willie and Gizelle.

"Don't say a word, baby," Willie said, holding up his hand before she could speak. "Gizelle's got ideas enough in her head now, and she'll be impossible to live with after tonight."

"Willie!" The dark, extremely well-dressed woman punched him playfully in the arm. "I only asked you to think about it."

Emily laughed. "I was going to say congratulations on the recording contract."

"Oh. That," Willie murmured sheepishly. "Thanks."

Emily nodded and looked again at her husband. Her *husband*, she repeated to herself, the word still sounding strange in her mind. The feelings, however, had become very familiar and were growing more and more every day. One feeling in particular was especially strong at the moment, and her hand beneath the table closed suggestively over the upper portion of Mick's thigh. She took a deep swallow of her champagne and watched his expression from the corner of her eye.

When he felt Emily's fingers begin stroking his inner thigh, Mick clamped his teeth down so hard on his glass, he thought he would shatter it. He glanced over at her quickly, but she was pretending to engage Gizelle in a conversation about jazz music. Well, two could play that game. As he turned his attention to Sam, Mick let his own fingers glide up beneath Emily's skirt to pause at the heated juncture of her thighs. He heard her voice break on the words, "Baritone sex, I mean sax," then he felt her hand close possessively over the hard ridge that had formed in his jeans. He then made a decision, which although independent of his wife's consent, he was certain she'd find agreeable.

"We hate to call it a night so early," he told everyone, "but Emily and I really must be leaving."

Everyone tried to dissuade him except Emily, who gazed with languid eyes at her husband, eyes filled with intimate promises.

"No, really, we have to get back to our hotel," Mick insisted.

"Hotel?" Mason asked, somewhat surprised. "I thought you'd be staying with me."

Emily and Mick looked at each other, then at Mason, and spoke as one when they said, "Nah."

"But . . ."

"We'll see you all at brunch tomorrow," Emily added as she scooted out of her seat behind Mick. "Right? Eleven-thirty at the Four Seasons? Mason's treating, you know," she added.

"Now wait just a minute," Mason began in indignant denial.

"We'll be there," Sam said.

"Us, too," Willie assured them.

"And me," Lou put in, then turned to Mason and asked, "Do they serve lobster there? I understand that's s'posed to be very delicious, and I've never tried it before."

"Hey, hold on," Mason tried again, and amid the ensuing turmoil Mick and Emily slipped away.

"That was a dirty trick you played back there on your brother," Mick chided her lightly when they were safely on their way back to the hotel.

"Well, he deserved it," Emily said. "Taking off again after all that worry he caused everyone. Talk about dirty tricks."

"Yes, let's do," Mick said in a thick voice. "I have one or two in mind we can play together."

Emily smiled broadly. "Why, husband, whatever could you be thinking?"

"Oh, I don't know, maybe something different," he suggested with a voice full of promise. "Something we'll have to do at a close range. A *very* close range."

"I see. Well, we may have to do it more than once before we're satisfied," she warned him. "That seems to be the way with us, you know."

"That's okay," he told her. "We have all the time we'll need."

"A lifetime," Emily agreed with a vigorous nod.

"A lifetime," Mick repeated, closing his hand over his wife's.

And for the first time, Emily and Mick were looking forward to living life to its fullest.

* * * * *

Silhouette Special Edition

COMING NEXT MONTH

#595 TEA AND DESTINY—Sherryl Woods
Ann Davies had always taken in strays—but never one as wild as playboy Hank Riley! She usually offered tea and sympathy, but handsome Hank seemed to expect a whole lot more....

#596 DEAR DIARY—Natalie Bishop
Adam Shard was falling hard for his childhood pal. But beneath the straightforward, sardonic woman Adam knew so well lay a Kerry Camden yearning for love...and only her diary knew!

#597 IT HAPPENED ONE NIGHT—Marie Ferrarella
When their fathers' comedy act broke up, impulsive Paula and straitlaced Alex grudgingly joined forces to reunite the pair. But after much muddled meddling by everyone concerned, it was hard to say exactly *who* was matchmaking whom...

#598 TREASURE DEEP—Bevlyn Marshall
A sunken galleon, a tropical isle and dashing plunderer Gregory Chase... Could these fanciful fixings finally topple Nicole Webster's decidedly *un*romantic theory on basic biological urges?

#599 STRICTLY FOR HIRE—Maggi Charles
An accident brought unwanted luxury to take-charge Christopher Kendall's fast-paced life—a lady with a limo! And soon bubbly, rambunctious, adorable Tory Morgan was driving him to utter amorous distraction!

#600 SOMETHING SPECIAL—Victoria Pade
With her pink hearse, her elderly companion and her dubious past, there was something mighty suspicious about Patrick Drake's new neighbor, beautiful Mitch Cuddy. Something suspicious, something sexy...something pretty damn special !

AVAILABLE THIS MONTH:

#589 INTIMATE CIRCLE
Curtiss Ann Matlock

#590 CLOSE RANGE
Elizabeth Bevarly

#591 PLACES IN THE HEART
Andrea Edwards

#592 YOUNG AT HEART
Elaine Lakso

#593 KINDRED SPIRITS
Sarah Temple

#594 SUDDENLY, PARADISE
Jennifer West

Silhouette Romances®

DIAMOND JUBILEE
CELEBRATION!

It's Silhouette Books' tenth anniversary, and what better way to celebrate than to toast *you*, our readers, for making it all possible. Each month in 1990, we'll present you with a DIAMOND JUBILEE Silhouette Romance written by an all-time favorite author!

Welcome the new year with *Ethan*—a LONG, TALL TEXANS book by Diana Palmer. February brings Brittany Young's *The Ambassador's Daughter*. Look for *Never on Sundae* by Rita Rainville in March, and in April you'll find *Harvey's Missing* by Peggy Webb. Victoria Glenn, Lucy Gordon, Annette Broadrick, Dixie Browning and many more have special gifts of love waiting for you with their DIAMOND JUBILEE Romances.

Be sure to look for the distinctive DIAMOND JUBILEE emblem, and share in Silhouette's celebration. Saying thanks has never been so romantic....

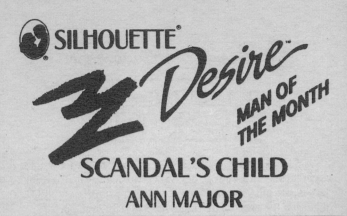